THE GERMAN DRESSMAKER

A WWII Historical Novel

SUSAN SHALEV

Producer & International Distributor
eBookPro Publishing
www.ebook-pro.com

THE GERMAN DRESSMAKER
Susan Shalev

Copyright © 2023 Susan Shalev

All rights reserved; No parts of this book may be reproduced or transmitted in any form or by any means, electronic or mechanical, including photocopying, recording, taping, or by any information retrieval system, without the permission, in writing, of the author.

ISBN 9798389851719

Chapter Twenty-five...163
Chapter Twenty-six..171
Chapter Twenty-seven...175
Chapter Twenty-eight..181
Chapter Twenty-nine...189
Chapter Thirty..197
Chapter Thirty-one...203
Chapter Thirty-two...207
Chapter Thirty-three..213
Chapter Thirty-four..219
Chapter Thirty-five...223
Chapter Thirty-six..231
Chapter Thirty-seven...237
Chapter Thirty-eight...241
Chapter Thirty-nine..247
Chapter Forty...253
Chapter Forty-one..259
Chapter Forty-two..263
Chapter Forty-three..271
Chapter Forty-four...275
Chapter Forty-five..279
Chapter Forty-six...283
Chapter Forty-seven..289
Chapter Forty-eight..299

*Dedicated to my wonderful family
and friends for their unwavering love
and encouragement*

CONTENTS

Prologue 7
Chapter One 9
Chapter Two 13
Chapter Three... 19
Chapter Four 25
Chapter Five 31
Chapter Six 37
Chapter Seven 43
Chapter Eight 47
Chapter Nine 53
Chapter Ten 63
Chapter Eleven 69
Chapter Twelve 77
Chapter Thirteen 83
Chapter Fourteen 91
Chapter Fifteen 95
Chapter Sixteen 101
Chapter Seventeen 109
Chapter Eighteen 117
Chapter Nineteen 125
Chapter Twenty 131
Chapter Twenty-one 137
Chapter Twenty-two 145
Chapter Twenty-three 151
Chapter Twenty-four 157

PROLOGUE

Theirs was a chance encounter – an alignment of the stars that would alter the course of their lives in unimaginable ways. If he had refused the invitation of his comrades to join them for a drink, as he had done so often in the past, he would never have met her. If her circumstances had been more fortunate, their paths would never have crossed and their histories would have been very different. But such is chance, or fate, perhaps. It was meant to be.

He should have nipped their relationship in the bud. She was lost, innocent, vulnerable. He, many years her senior, should have been the responsible adult – lent his help, walked away, and left her to make her own future. Once she was settled, he should have bowed out. She was beautiful and intelligent and could have had her pick of more suitable suitors. But she had unknowingly cast a spell over him, making it impossible for him to resist the temptation of seeing her again. And she had fallen in love with him. He had put them both at risk by continuing their forbidden romance in the climate of the times, but he couldn't help himself. And because of his stupidity and weakness, she lost her life.

Her lovely face was a snapshot imprinted in his memory, which aroused him in his dreams and haunted him in his nightmares. The image was still sharp. His time had come and soon he would be reunited with her, in death if not in life.

As he neared his end, Heinrich vividly recalled the moment he had first laid eyes on her, and a wistful smile accompanied him into oblivion.

CHAPTER ONE

Breslau, Germany. 1937
Heinrich stood at the side of the smoke-filled noisy room, nursing his beer and wondering how soon he could take his leave without offending anyone. He was regretting having accepted his comrades' invitation to the beer tavern to celebrate his recent promotion to Major. The regiment had been away from the city for several weeks and Heinrich knew the men were thirsting for alcohol and women. He usually declined such invitations, but, conscious of the jealousy, hidden and overt, of some of his fellow officers caused by his meteoric rise in the ranks, he felt it would be prudent to be outwardly sociable with both friends and foe. He looked across towards the bar, where he saw that the usual girls were out in force, laying on the charm, having been deprived of their livelihood while the officers were out of town. They wouldn't have to work too hard this evening to lure their customers, Heinrich thought.

And then he saw her.

She wasn't one of the regulars. Her demure manner set her apart from the more experienced girls lounging at the bar. They modelled themselves on Marlene Dietrich, trying to recreate her sultry look with pouting red lips, thinly penciled eyebrows, platinum blonde hair, and tight-fitting silky dresses in bright reds and greens. Her angelic face, its perfect porcelain complexion devoid of excessive make-up, was framed by luxurious titian curls which tumbled carelessly over her shoulders, and her dress was simple, almost austere, without a hint of invitation to ogle the wares underneath. Her natural beauty left him momentarily breathless.

What was a girl like her doing in a tavern full of hot-blooded army officers? She must be new to the game, he thought – but if she was serious, why did her appearance say otherwise? There must be a story here. He wasn't in the habit of rescuing damsels in distress, and yet, much to his own surprise, he discovered that his personal code of honour would not permit him to stand idly by while this vulnerable creature fell into the hands of some boorish, lecherous brute.

As Heinrich studied her more closely, he was shocked to see that she was trembling with fear and her resolve seemed to be dissipating as she registered the greedy looks of his fellow officers, always on the prowl for fresh meat. They were almost salivating as they took in her hair and voluptuous figure. He watched her visibly flinch in revulsion as the first drunken lout approached her, standing too close for comfort and exhaling liquor-laced breath in her face.

Pulling rank, Heinrich intervened. "I believe this one's mine, Lieutenant Bauer," and he steered her away from the bar to a quieter corner. "I haven't seen you here before," Heinrich said to her, with a query in his voice.

"A friend brought me along. She assured me I'd have no difficulty in attracting admirers." She dropped her gaze to the floor and her blush spoke volumes, revealing that this was her first foray into uncharted territory.

"How about we get out of here?" he offered. "Don't worry, I'm not like the rest of these animals. You have my word as an officer that I will behave like a true gentleman as befits my rank."

The other men watched him with ill-disguised envy as he draped her coat around her shoulders and, holding her gently by the elbow, led her outside.

"Lucky bastard," one of them shouted after him. "Give her one for me, Major," added another with a lascivious laugh.

"Please tell me about yourself," said Heinrich, when they had swapped the foggy atmosphere of the tavern for the clear cool evening air in the street. She told him her name was Lily. Her father had died after the Great War, leaving her mother to raise her alone. Having suddenly lost a lucrative job, which plunged the family into financial hardship, her mother had worked all hours to put food on the table, but this past winter she had succumbed to influenza; hunger and work had taken their toll, and her mother had not been physically strong enough to withstand the virus. Left alone, Lily had taken whatever work she could find, but had not managed to secure a permanent position. Her situation had made her desperate and, deciding she had no other option for survival, she had agreed to accompany the girls to the bar. "This is my last resort," she said, tears welling up in her eyes.

"There must be an alternative," Heinrich insisted. "I will make some inquiries. Perhaps some of the wealthier people I know have a vacancy for a cleaner or kitchen maid. Promise me you won't go back there."

He escorted her home and, making sure she was safe, he retraced his steps back across town. "What was I thinking?" he asked himself, wondering what had possessed him to make such an offer. How exactly could he help? Whom could he ask? He was estranged from his last remaining brother, and most of his friends were in the military. His wealthier acquaintances were not the sort of people he could ask for help. After a great deal of thought he uncomfortably concluded that he had only one option.

The following day was the Jewish Sabbath. He made his way to the synagogue, a place he had not frequented for many years. Like many well-to-do German Jews, most of his extended family members had assimilated, having little interest in their religion and heritage and rarely attending services, save perhaps on the High Holydays of the New Year and Yom Kippur, the Day of Atonement.

As he entered, several boyhood friends with whom he had remained in loose contact after he had enlisted in the army looked up in surprise.

"What's up, Heinrich? Someone died?" joked Isaac, giving him a friendly punch on the shoulder.

"Hey, don't make me feel even more out of place than I already do," he said.

"I am trying to help a girl find employment. Does anyone know of a family needing a maid or cleaner?"

"I knew there would have to be a woman involved," said Isaac with a wink. "There are plenty of Jewish households short of domestic help, but unless your girl is Jewish or over forty-five, she can't be employed by any of them under the Nuremberg Laws. You'd have better luck approaching your swanky *goyische* friends."

When services ended, Heinrich stayed around to chat a while. As he made to leave, Isaac pulled him aside. "Don't be a stranger my friend. And don't rely on your status as an officer in the German army to protect you from the Nazis. Your heritage will catch up with you in the end. No one is safe."

Many months later, when his world was turned upside down, Heinrich would chastise himself for not having taken his friend's words seriously. Had he really been that blind to the fomenting situation in Germany? Had he really believed that he was immune? That his friend's prediction was without foundation?

CHAPTER TWO

Grateful to be back in her own apartment, Lily closed the door, leaned her back against it, and tried to make sense of what had transpired as she relived the evening. It certainly hadn't turned out the way she had expected. She had dreaded accompanying her friends to the bar. They weren't exactly friends, in fact – just a couple of girls she had met while doing some temporary waitressing. She was so alone and desperate that she was actually grateful they had offered to include her in their evening outing. They were rather brash and obviously what her mother would have called "loose women", but Lily didn't know what else to do. The rent money was due and her landlord was merciless.

As she undressed for bed, she looked wistfully around the apartment. She wondered how much longer she would be able to stay before he evicted her. Her eyes roamed the room and, settling on her mother's sewing knick-knacks, they filled with tears. Lily missed her so terribly. She was mortified to think what Mama would have thought of this evening's outing and her intentions. Desperate circumstances, desperate measures? No, Mama would never have condoned it.

She couldn't believe how lucky she was that Heinrich had come to her rescue. Her pulse quickened as she recalled the faint touch of his hand on her arm as he'd led her out of the tavern. As promised, he had behaved like the perfect gentleman he had professed to be. He had saved her from demeaning herself at the bar and doubtless from losing her virginity. Why had such man taken an interest in her? He had made no advances or demands, when he could easily have done so, and seemed genuinely concerned for her well-being. Even though he was a stranger, she had felt inexplicably safe and calm as he had escorted her home. Lily had been so ashamed and humiliated by the circumstances of their meeting, she had felt unable to look him too directly in the face or study him closely. For most of the walk home she had kept her eyes downcast. Nevertheless, she saw he was a very attractive man, quite a few years her senior. He was well-spoken, and his soft but confident voice had given her encouragement that all was not lost. It had been a long time since she'd felt that way.

Lily picked up a photograph of her father, himself a soldier, and wondered what he would have made of Heinrich. Sadly, she barely remembered him.

Lily was born at the end of the Great War, the only child of Helmut, a mechanic and Greta, a seamstress. At the start of the war, her father had managed to evade the trenches, since his expertise was needed behind the lines. But as Germany's situation had become dire, he had been catapulted into the thick of the fighting. After several terrifying months, he had been hospitalised with multiple shrapnel wounds and shell shock. He'd never fully recovered. At first, when he had returned home to the comfort of his devoted wife, things had seemed to improve. But he couldn't manage to hold on to a steady job and the stress of additional responsibility with the arrival of baby Lily had aggravated his already fragile mental state. Lily's only memories of her father were his vacant staring eyes and his spine-chilling screams in the night. When she was five years old, he had committed suicide.

Her mother, Greta, had been a skilled seamstress. She worked for the highly regarded Schwartz Couture-Haus und Kurzwaren on Breslau's major fashion thoroughfare, and was considered one of their most talented dressmakers. On the ground floor of the three-story fashion house, Herr Schwartz oversaw the extensive range of haberdashery goods: box upon box of buttons in every shape and hue, meter upon meter of lace, ribbon, fringes and piping, all kinds of trimmings and notions, and every sewing necessity. In the first-floor salon, Frau Schwartz's clientele chose the designs for their day and evening wear inspired by the latest fashions from Paris and London. The impressive salon was decorated in muted tones of creams and browns and tastefully furnished with silk-upholstered armchairs and chaises longue, and sumptuous Aubusson rugs. The walls were decorated with framed copies of signature fashion magazine covers, while the latest editions were spread out on highly polished mahogany occasional tables, for customers to browse while they waited for a consultation or fitting. Frau Schwartz made sure they were treated to a fine selection of teas and coffees accompanied by a choice of expensive patisserie and pralines. Her attention to detail was legendary. Lily brushed her hair and sighed. Schwartz's was an enchanted wonderland compared to the austerity of her meagre lodgings.

As a child, Lily had adored her visits to Schwartz's. Greta's employers had great regard for her talent and, rather than have her miss a day's work, they'd allowed her to bring Lily with her when she was off school due to illness or vacation. Lily would spend hours in the sewing room on the third floor above the salon, enchanted by the fabrics and trimmings and mesmerized by the adept and nimble fingers of her mother and the other seamstresses, watching with fascination as they sewed beads, sequins, and crystals onto silk, chiffon and organza, creating the most stunning evening gowns.

Greta would give her daughter remnants of fabric, ribbons, and lace with which to decorate her dolls, and when Lily was old enough, Greta began to teach her rudimentary stitch craft. Lily had inherited her mother's skillful fingers and was a fast learner. She devoured the out-of-date fashion magazines her mother brought home from time to time – *Vogue, Harper's Bazaar, Elegant Welt*. Her idols were Chanel and Schiaparelli and Hollywood's femmes fatales. At school, Lily's teachers had been impressed by the effort she had made to master English and French, unaware that she had been motivated purely by her desire to keep up with the latest European fashion news and trends.

For the widowed Greta, work had been plentiful and she

had been able to support herself and Lily while managing to put aside some savings. Even when the economy was bad, well-to-do Germans spared no expense in replenishing their wardrobes with both day and evening wear. The run-up to Christmas and the New Year were especially busy times, with last-minute commissions for soirees and events of the festive season. Herr Schwartz had often called on Lily to help out on the ground floor or in the upstairs sewing room, doing odd jobs and errands for which she would earn some pocket money. It had been her dream to join her mother at Schwartz Couture-Haus as an apprentice seamstress. But dreams have a way of dissipating into thin air.

One afternoon, Greta had come home early from work unexpectedly. She was red-faced and flustered and in a terrible state, almost collapsing under the weight of several bulky packages.

"Mama, what's wrong?" asked Lily as she relieved Greta of the parcels and helped her to a chair.

"Two Nazi hoodlums came to Schwartz's waving a document. Under Hitler's Nuremberg Laws, Jews are no longer allowed to own businesses. They barged their way inside and have seized the property. All the employees have been sacked. They physically threw poor Herr and Frau Schwartz out into the street. When they told us to pack up and leave, I managed to gather together a few bits and pieces: the dresses I'm working on, a few patterns, my notebook with clients' details and measurements, my thimble, pincushion, tape measure – whatever I could lay my hands on – and I stuffed them into these bags."

Lily sat in stunned silence and then asked her mother, "What are we going to do?"

"First thing tomorrow, I will go to the Schwartz's home and see what I can do to help them. And then I will have to look for another job. I have a good reputation and many satisfied clients, so I don't think it will be a problem."

Day after day, Greta had gone in search of a new position. When she was turned down by fashion houses, she tried the department stores. It didn't take her long to realise that, because she had worked for Jews, no one was willing to give her a job. She had been blacklisted by the Nazis.

"I will just have to set up my own workshop at home," she told Lily. "A sizeable number of Frau Schwartz's customers are the wives of Breslau's Jewish industrialists, doctors, and bankers, and she has promised to direct them to me."

Even some of her old Aryan clients continued to use her services surreptitiously for a while. But even with a little help from Lily, she only had one pair of hands and her clients did not have the patience to wait for the completion of their orders.

Then one evening, Herr and Frau Schwartz came to see her.

"We have come to say goodbye, Greta," said Frau Schwartz sadly. "The situation has become unbearable for us here in Breslau. We are leaving tomorrow, and many of the Jewish clients we sent your way are also making arrangements to leave. We wish you and Lily all the best, and we thank you for your years of devoted service."

Gradually, the work dried up and Greta was reduced to doing small repairs and taking in laundry. Lily had a part-time job at a small restaurant and received meals as part of her wages, for which Greta was very grateful. There was little money left for heating and food once the rent had been paid. Greta's savings were diminishing quickly. Exhaustion and deprivation had turned her into a mere shadow of her former self, with dark circles under her eyes and sunken cheekbones. And so, when she became ill with the flu, she had no reserves with which to fight it.

Lily had buried her mother three months before she met Heinrich. She no longer had the job at the restaurant and Greta's savings had finally run out. And so she had hardened her resolve and gone to the tavern as her last resort for survival. As she made ready for bed, Lily wondered what would happen to her now ... Could she really put her faith in Heinrich? She knew nothing about him. Did he really mean to help her to find her employment as he had promised? Or was he just like all the other officers in the bar, merely nurturing her trust only to betray it in the future?

CHAPTER THREE

After rescuing Lily from the officers in the bar, Heinrich was determined to keep his word, if only to have an excuse to see her again. Finally, his efforts to secure her employment bore fruit. He returned to Lily's apartment a week later with a prospective offer.

He had chanced to overhear a conversation in Neuman Cigarren, his preferred tobacconist on the corner of *Grosse Feldstrasse*.

"I'm very sorry to keep you waiting," the proprietor was *apologising* to a customer who kept looking irritably at his watch. "I'm short-staffed," he explained, "because I had to let my assistant go. His being Jewish, I had no choice, despite the fact that he was a loyal employee for many years."

"Be that as it may, my man, it's not really an excuse for keeping me waiting so long," replied the customer. "My wife is searching frantically for a live-in general help for the same reason, and yet she manages to keep to schedule."

"Pardon me, but I couldn't help overhearing," Heinrich said to the customer. "Perhaps I can be of assistance, Sir. Permit me to introduce myself. My name is Major Heinrich Graber."

"Erhard Müller," said the customer, accepting Heinrich's handshake.

"I know of a very reliable young Gentile woman who is currently unemployed and who would be suitable for the position your wife is seeking to fill, if your terms are acceptable."

"Well, this is a happy coincidence. My wife would be terribly grateful if your young lady meets with her approval and can start at once."

Now, Heinrich related the encounter to Lily. "I know the salary won't be much," he apologised, "but it seems your duties will not be too burdensome, and the position offers you a roof over your head and three meals a day." Heinrich surveyed Lily's dingy apartment.

Although her beauty, which was as stunning as he remembered, lit up the room, the lodgings were in dire need of repair and a fresh coat of paint. Surely whatever accommodation the Müllers provided would be an improvement.

Lily needed no persuading. At this point she would have taken anything respectable. How had her rescuer managed to find a position so quickly? She had hardly allowed herself to believe that he would make good on his promise, and certainly not within so short a time. And the job sounded more than she could have hoped for. She prayed that the prospective employers would like her and that they were good people. What more could she ask?

Her interview with Frau Müller went without a hitch. The two women took to each other immediately, and although Lily understood that she was a servant, she nevertheless felt part of the family from the start.

The Müllers' apartment was very spacious, occupying a complete floor of an impressive building in a desirable part of the city. Tastefully decorated and furnished with understated elegance, it was divided into two distinct domains. One area was home to the bedrooms and washrooms. The master bedroom with dressing room and private bathroom was at the far end of a long corridor, separating it from the children's quarters and giving the parents privacy and quiet. A second bedroom was shared by two girls, while the youngest child, a boy, slept in the nursery, which was also the children's playroom. A second bathroom was positioned between them. Lily was shown to a small room adjacent to the nursery. She was immediately enchanted, never before having had the luxury of a girly bedroom of her own. The wallpaper was patterned with two-tone white and deep pink roses on a paler pink background interspersed with sprigs of baby's breath and delicate butterflies. In addition to the bed, which was covered in a bedspread embroidered with roses to match the walls, there was a small bureau, a chair, a single wardrobe, and a corner unit housing a sink.

The other part of the apartment served as the living area, including a kitchen and pantry at one end, a sitting room, the salon for entertaining guests, and a large dining room. A discreet alcove housed a cloakroom and guest washroom.

The Müllers were well-to-do, and employed a cook and a daily domestic help for heavy housework.

"Your duties include light cleaning to maintain an air of tidiness at all times, particular in the children's rooms," Frau Müller instructed her. The three children, Sofia aged ten, Johanna, seven, and three-year-old Armin were also her responsibility. "You will get them ready for school and kindergarten in the morning when Herr Müller and I prefer not to be disturbed. You will supervise them in the afternoons, help the girls with their homework, and have them bathed and in their night clothes ready for a story from me and a goodnight kiss from their father."

Lily was shocked at first by how little time the family spent in one another's company. Herr Müller generally ate breakfast alone, as he rose earlier than his wife and left the house before she was up. They took their evening meal together alone in the dining room or quite often at one of the city's many fine restaurants. They entertained frequently and received many reciprocal invitations. During the week, Lily and the children ate their meals together in the kitchen.

She was pleased to discover, however, that the weekends were family time, when Herr and Frau Müller devoted attention to the children. On Lily's first Sunday in her new job, the Müller family outing took them to the *Liebichshöhe* pleasure gardens. Sofia and Johanna chased each other along the semicircular colonnade of the magnificent Belvedere, much to the chagrin of the more sedate walkers out for a leisurely promenade, and while Herr Müller took them up to the top of the observation tower for a magnificent view over the city, Lily kept a close eye on Armin, who was fascinated by the dancing fountain in the middle of the expansive circular terrace.

She had to pull him back several times to stop him getting wet from the spray and to thwart his attempts to jump in. After a couple of hours of simple fun, Herr and Frau Müller treated the children and Lily to ice cream while they savoured freshly ground coffee at the garden café. The late spring weather was balmy and she felt relaxed and hopeful for the first time in two years.

Frau Müller informed Lily that every second Sunday she was free to spend the day as she wished. On her first Sunday off, Heinrich came to call, but only to tell her that his unit was being sent on maneuvers.

"I have no idea how long I will be away, but I will be in touch as soon as I can," he promised. Lily was sure she would never see her knight-in-shining-armour again. Why would he be interested in her when he could have his pick of gorgeous women? Surely, he would have other conquests waiting for him to return to Breslau, women more in his league. And while she had no idea what maneuvers entailed, she feared he would be stationed in another city where romantic opportunities could present themselves. Or, now that he had made good on his promise and found her employment, would he merely have forgotten about her by the time he returned?

Several weeks passed. Lily was content in her work, adored by the children, and appreciated by her employers. On sunny afternoons, she took the children to a nearby park and began to make friends with other nannies and child-minders. Now and then she bought little treats for the children, but otherwise spent very little money. She was determined to save most of her pay for her future. In her dreams she still fantasized about finding an apprenticeship in a prominent fashion house. And these fantasies had been joined by dreams of a future with Heinrich. Two fantasies which, if she was truthful with herself, had little to no chance of fulfillment.

One Saturday afternoon, she was getting the girls ready for a birthday party at the home of one of their cousins. A spoilt Sofia was fussing that she had nothing to wear, testily discarding one dress after another. Coming into the nursery to see if her daughters were ready, Frau Müller noted the pile of dresses on the floor and, feigning an air of exasperation, declared, "What am I going to do with you, Sofia? You grow out of your new dresses almost as soon as I hang them in your wardrobe. Johanna, I must insist that you eat all your vegetables so that you grow into these lovely hand-me-downs as quickly as possible," she added with a laugh.

Summoning up her courage, Lily addressed her employer. "I am quite handy with a needle and thread, Frau Müller. With your permission, I can alter some of the clothes that no longer suit Sofia so that they fit Johanna. It would be a shame for such lovely things to gather dust and moths until Johanna can wear them, by which time they might be ruined." She waited for Frau Müller's reply, her hands trembling and pulse racing. What if she had overstepped her place?

Frau Müller didn't hide her surprise. "Why, thank you, Lily. That is a very good idea. I look forward to seeing an example of your work."

Lily was delighted to have something to occupy her on her next day off. She had not heard from Heinrich. She had no idea whether he was still away or had just forgotten her. Her free time dragged on miserably, overshadowed by her distress at the thought of never seeing him again. Rummaging among her things, she retrieved her only inheritance – a thimble inscribed with her mother's initials, a tape measure with *Greta* printed in indelible ink at one end, and a purple pin cushion decorated with the daintiest embroidery. Choosing two dresses which Sofia had outgrown, Lily set to work. Rather than just shortening and tucking, she remodeled them completely, so that Johanna would feel that she had something new and different to wear rather than just cast-offs from her older sister.

Having been educated by her mother never to waste what could be saved, Lily used the surplus pieces of fabric to make outfits for the girls' dolls.

Frau Müller was delighted with Lily's handiwork. She was visibly astonished when she examined the stitching. "Wherever did you learn to sew so beautifully? This looks almost like professional dressmaking."

Lily hesitated. When she'd first met Frau Müller for her interview, she'd thought her potential employer seemed familiar. As their conversation had progressed, Lily had realised that she had been a client at Schwartz's prior to her mother's dismissal. When asked for details of her education and previous positions, Lily had decided to tread cautiously, and had made no mention of her vacation work in the sewing room of the salon. Perhaps the Müllers would refuse to employ her if they knew who her blacklisted mother had been, Lily had thought.

Now, too, she refrained from going into detail. "My mother taught me a few basics and I loved sewing so much that I practiced at every opportunity, making my own dolls' clothes, and later following patterns to make clothes for myself which we could not afford to buy."

"Well, I am certainly grateful for your talent, Lily," said Frau Müller, looking at the happy faces of her daughters, who were delighted with the dolls' clothes, and at Johanna admiring herself in her mirror wearing one of her new outfits.

"I would be happy if you could do additional alterations when you have the time, and I will remunerate you for this extra work."

Lily was ecstatic. Frau Müller was impressed by her work and was even willing to pay her for it. Could this be the first small step on the way to realizing her dream?

CHAPTER FOUR

Lily had almost given up hope of ever seeing Heinrich again when he finally came to call and invited her to join him on her next free Sunday.

"If you're not too busy, that is. I'm sorry I have been away such a long time and I won't be surprised if you already have other arrangements."

"Nothing special …" Lily tried to sound nonchalant. "I would be delighted to meet you."

They arranged to rendezvous at the *Hauptbahnhoff*, Breslau's main railway station, well away from the prying eyes of the Müllers.

The days rolled by far too slowly; Sunday couldn't arrive quickly enough for Lily. Now that the day was finally here, she was barely able to control her excitement. She took special care with her appearance, willing her trembling fingers to stop shaking as she buttoned her blouse. If only she had something new and chic to wear. She prayed Heinrich would not be put off by her simple outfit and that it would be suitable for wherever he intended to take her.

Not wishing to appear overly keen, she arrived at the forecourt of the *Hauptbahnhoff* a couple of minutes late. Even on a Sunday, trams and cars competed for space in front of the train station, and all of Breslau seemed to be out on the streets enjoying the glorious late spring day. She took a deep breath to calm her nerves.

Heinrich had arrived early and was waiting for her. He was surprised by how much he had missed Lily while he was away. In fact, he had thought of little else. Now that he was back in the city, he was longing to spend more time with her. As she walked towards him, he was bowled over yet again by her beauty. They greeted each other awkwardly, unsure whether a handshake or an embrace was appropriate. Lily blushed and kept her hands clasped while

Heinrich busied himself with the picnic basket he was carrying, so they just smiled and said hello.

"I hope you like surprises," he said when Lily ventured to ask where they were going.

She was no wiser as he helped her up onto a tram, but after it crossed the Kaiser Bridge and turned into *Tiergarten* Strasse, she guessed where he was taking her. By the time they reached the entrance to the Zoological Gardens, Lily was as excited as a small child.

"Oh, Heinrich, this is a wonderful surprise." She explained that this was her first-ever visit. "I was a baby when the zoo closed down and the animals were relocated to other zoos across Germany. When it reopened, my mother promised to take me, but by then my father had passed away and she was working all hours. Somehow we never managed to find the time to visit."

"My parents took us a number of times as small children before the war, but this is also my first visit since it reopened," said Heinrich as he tentatively took Lily's arm.

They strolled around the various enclosures. Lily stopped to read the signage in front of every cage.

"This hippopotamus is called Anton," she informed him. "This is a sea cow named Muschi, apparently the only manatee in captivity in Europe," she enthused.

As they walked, Heinrich stole furtive glances at her. He knew he had been right in choosing this venue for their first real date. He was enchanted by her patent youthful enjoyment, the blush on her cheeks and the sparkle in her eyes. In fact, he was captivated by her. Although his army career kept him busy, he had had his fair share of women, mostly uncommitted relationships which had lasted no more than a few dates. Lily was a good deal younger than his past conquests, but she displayed a maturity and composure hardly seen in women twice her age.

When he sensed that she was beginning to tire, Heinrich

suggested they find a quiet corner to eat their lunch. They settled under a tree in a spot which gave them a clear view of the impressive circular *Jahrhunderthalle*, Centennial Hall, the pride of the city, whose magnificent concrete and steel-domed structure dominated the surrounding area.

While Heinrich set out the contents of the picnic basket, Lily allowed herself to quietly scrutinize him. The uniform certainly did not make the man, she decided. He was just as handsome in regular clothes, and she somehow felt more at ease with the informality. He was of medium height and his athletic build suggested physical strength. As required by his profession, his brown hair was cut very short, but here and there Lily glimpsed strands of auburn glinting in the sun's rays. Above all, she was mesmerized by his beautiful eyes; they were of indeterminate colour, framed by lashes which would make most women green with envy. The irises were extraordinary. She could only describe them as two tiny kaleidoscopes, flecked with changing hues of green, hazel, and grey. Years later, when it became difficult to summon up his fading image, she would easily recall his magnetic eyes. She was momentarily overcome by her intense attraction to everything about this striking man, and she looked away from him towards the Centennial in the hope that he wouldn't notice the colour that flooded her cheeks.

"A glass of wine, Lily?" Heinrich proffered as he drew her attention back to their lunch.

He had laid out plates of creamy potato salad, bratwurst, and sauerkraut, a selection of cheeses and fresh rolls, and apple strudel. "Please help yourself. I hope you will find something you like."

They ate in silence for a while. The wine, good food, and warm sunshine relaxed Lily and made her comfortable enough to ask Heinrich about himself.

"You know everything about me," she ventured, "but I know next to nothing about you. Have you always lived in Breslau? What was your childhood like? What made you decide to become a professional soldier?" She hoped she wasn't being too forward, and was relieved to be met by Heinrich's smile, which surely reflected the pleasure he felt that Lily was at ease in his company.

"I was born and raised here in Breslau, the youngest of four brothers. My father ran a thriving import-export business and we lived very well. But he had to travel a lot on business, and when I was ten years old he was killed in a train crash on his way home from Berlin. My mother was devastated and never really recovered." Lily registered the fleeting look of sadness which passed across his face. "My eldest brother, Martin, who had dreams of an academic career, shelved his scholarly plans and reluctantly took over the business. He was surprisingly successful at it. On one of his business trips, he was introduced to the daughter of a prosperous wine producer whose vineyard served Czechoslovakian royalty, and he made an advantageous marriage. Our two middle brothers, Erich and Josef, were conscripted into the army just before the outbreak of the Great War and soon became officers. They both died defending the Fatherland, and posthumously were decorated with the Iron Cross in recognition of their illustrious service. Lured by their stories, their heroics, the uniform's shiny buttons," Heinrich smiled and winked as he said this, "I decided to enlist after the war was over."

"But weren't you afraid, after what happened to your brothers?"

"The Great War was the war to end all wars, they say, and I believe that Europe has learned its lesson. That doesn't mean that Germany need not be prepared. I am an officer with a handsome salary and privileges, and while I choose to believe that I won't be called upon to defend my country, I will be ready to do just that if necessary."

Lily wanted to ask Heinrich what he thought about Herr Hitler, his racial laws and his belligerent manner, but thought better of it. Why ruin a perfectly lovely afternoon with politics, and risk offending this man whom she hoped to see again, and again? So instead, she asked, "How did your mother and brother react to your decision?"

"My mother succumbed to the 1918 flu epidemic before I joined up. Unfortunately, my brother Martin and I hold different opinions on a number of issues. My decision to enlist was the final nail in the coffin and he cut all ties with me. We have not spoken for years."

Seeing her distressed expression, he quickly changed the subject, lightening the conversation with anecdotes from his recent training course. Lily responded with stories about the Müller children and her attempts to invent interesting ways to occupy them, before shyly telling him about her dressmaking activities.

All too soon, it was time to leave. They walked hand-in-hand towards the tram which would take Lily back from this dreamy day to reality. At the train station, Heinrich took her hand and kissed the back of it in formal fashion.

"I would be honoured if you would permit me to see you again, Lily."

"I would like that very much." She smiled demurely, barely able to contain her excitement, but not wishing to display unseemly enthusiasm. Surely he could see her heart beating wildly under her blouse or feel her pulse racing under his touch.

"Thank you for a wonderful day, Lily, which I hope we will be able to repeat very soon."

Lily relived the day in her head as she made her way back to the Müller home. It had been perfect – the zoo, the picnic, the conversation. The spell was broken as soon she opened the door and Sofia and Johanna pounced on her, demanding to know where she had been. Lily began to describe her visit to the zoo, but the girls soon lost interest.

"We've been there loads of times, Lily. It's not that special and the animals are smelly," said Sofia, and Johanna pinched her nose and made a face of disgust in agreement with her older sister.

CHAPTER FIVE

Lily's daily routine was disrupted by the summer break from school. Now that the children were at home all day, in addition to her usual duties she had to find ways to amuse them and keep them out of mischief. They were easily bored, and because of the age difference, it was a challenge to find activities that would appeal to everyone and occupy them together.

"How would you like to create a puppet theatre?" she asked the children one morning. "Sofia, see if you can find some pieces of card or wood among our handicraft materials. Armin, you have a look through this bag of fabric scraps and pick out the ones you like the best."

"What can I do?" said Johanna.

"Go and ask Cook if she has an empty box we can use."

Soon they were all busy cutting and colouring and gluing, and together they made the puppets and accessories.

"That's enough for today, children. I want you to think of ideas for a play we can produce to show to your parents."

A few days later, after quite a lot of arguing between the girls over the storyline of the play and the allocation of the puppets, they had practiced enough to put on a presentation to their surprised and delighted parents.

When they had tired of the theatre, Lily took them on hunting expeditions in the park to collect wild flowers, pine cones, and interesting leaves. These were followed by visits to the library to consult reference books in order to identify their specimens and learn more about them. She taught Sofia and Johanna how to press the flowers, and how to rub a pencil on a piece of paper placed on top of the leaves to produce a sketch. The girls were enthusiastic participants, but while little Armin enjoyed rummaging around in the dirt looking for things to collect, he quickly became bored afterwards, and Lily had to win his cooperation with the promise of ice cream and other bribes.

One evening, after the children were in bed, Lily came downstairs to make herself a cup of coffee to drink with the delicate lemon and poppy seed biscuits Heinrich had recently brought her from Conditorai W. Brandt, one of Breslau's most fashionable patisseries. He never arrived empty-handed when he came to take her out. He liked to spoil her with small treats, and his thoughtful generosity made her blush, deepening the strong affection she already felt for him.

As she passed the sitting room on her way to the kitchen, Lily couldn't help overhearing raised voices through the slightly open door.

"I don't approve, Erhard. I don't wish to encourage the messages, or should I say the *indoctrination*, disseminated by the movement."

"I understand your position, my dear, but Sofia does not wish to be alienated by her friends. They are all joining, and when she returns to school in September, it will look very odd – if not dangerous – if she is the only one not to conform."

Frau Müller sighed. "I won't argue any more, Erhard. But I refuse to have a part in it. I will send Lily with her to the enrolment station."

"Very well, my dear. As you wish."

Lily hurried on to the kitchen before she was caught eavesdropping. She couldn't be certain, but she had a fair idea of what the argument was about. For several weeks, Sofia had been asking if she could join the *Bund Deutscher Mädel* – The League of German Girls – the female section of the Hitler Youth, whose aim was to develop girls into women dedicated to the ideals of Nazism.

Lily abhorred the ideas which Sofia would have to accept and abide by. She wondered whether one day Frau Müller, who openly articulated her reluctance to let Sofia enroll, might be informed upon by her own daughter. Lily knew such things were encouraged and rewarded within the movement. Lily's own mother had categorically forbidden her to join up when she was fifteen years old. As she drank her beverage and savoured her biscuits she recalled her mother's words.

"*Lily,*" she'd explained, *"I know the movement's activities seem fun and worthwhile, but understand that they have not been randomly chosen. Sports options such as athletics and gymnastics brainwash young girls into accepting harsh discipline and being competitive. And singing in choral groups is a mask for promoting a sense of unity, encouraging obedience and teamwork. It's bad enough that your school curriculum has become strongly influenced by Nazi doctrine. You have to attend school and get an education, but I will not allow you to be further indoctrinated in your spare time."*

That conversation had taken place four years earlier, when enrolment had been voluntary and up to the individual. While it was still not compulsory, peer pressure had become fierce and opting out hardly acceptable. Lily knew that if she were asked to take Sofia to the enrolment station, she would have to hold her tongue, keep her anti-Nazi sentiments to herself, and do as requested.

Sure enough, the following morning while Lily was eating breakfast with the children, Frau Müller came into the kitchen.

"Lily, I have a special assignment for you today. You are to take Sofia to the League of German Girls enrolment centre and sign her up. I have prepared an authorization signed by her father, in case it should be required. When the arrangements have been completed please take Sofia to the store to buy her uniform. The staff at the enrolment centre will tell you where to go."

Sofia jumped up in excitement and flung her arms around her mother.

"Thank you, dearest Mama."

Lily was relieved that Sofia could not see the troubled look on her mother's face.

Lily and Sofia took the tram to the enrolment station which was located in Market Square. As always, the large paved plaza was a hive of activity. Several stall holders had set up their stands and were hawking a variety of wares, trying to entice the passers-by to part with their money. Lily's favourite, the flower stall vibrant with a profusion of colourful blooms, diffused a heady cocktail of sweet fragrances into the air. Children queued for ice cream from a popular street vendor. One side of the medieval square, or The Ring, as it was known to locals, was flanked by a row of charming colourful townhouses, each façade a different shade, occupied by retailers and offices. Majestically overseeing the square was its most impressive building, the Old Town Hall, a gothic structure of steeples, spikes, and spires, endowed with an ornately decorated exterior and several large clocks.

Lily's gaze wandered from this breathtaking piece of architecture to the adjacent New Town Hall, the *Rathaus*, and her mood darkened. Red banners and flags decorated with black swastikas adorned the building and she found the sight of them repulsive and intimidating. They had been hanging there for some time now but she had refused to accept their presence. In her mind they were the precursor of a virus which threatened to spread, infect, and destroy all that was familiar to her. She had witnessed firsthand what had happened to her mother's employers, the Schwartzes, and others like them, and this blatant representation of Nazism aroused in her a shuddering sense of foreboding.

Sofia had run ahead and was waiting for her outside the building which housed the enrolment office.

When they went inside the enrolment officer greeted them. "We are delighted to welcome you into our ranks, Sofia. I am sure you will be an excellent addition to the League and a worthy member." Turning to Lily, she asked, "Are you a member, Fraulein?"

"I'm afraid not," Lily replied diplomatically. "I am nineteen years old, above the group's age limit."

"Perhaps the Belief and Beauty Society would be of interest to you, then. Let me give you a pamphlet."

Lily reluctantly accepted the proffered paper.

"And here is the list of the League's summer activities, which I'm sure Sofia will want to participate in," said the officer.

Lily was sure that "wanting" to participate was not an option, and that taking at least some of the courses would be obligatory. But she just smiled politely and asked, "Where do we go to buy Sofia's uniform?"

"Just across the Ring at Warenhaus Gebrüder Barasch. I hope they still have Sofia's size. They must be overrun at the moment with so many new recruits."

Lily and a skipping Sofia made their way to Barasch Brothers, Breslau's largest and oldest department store established and run by Jews until, anticipating the worst, they had decided a couple of years earlier to sell their chain of stores and flee the country. Lily enquired at the entrance and they were directed to the children's department on the second floor, where a large Nazi banner announced the section they were looking for. After some searching by the assistant and trying on by Sofia, Lily and Sofia made their way out of the store, Sofia proudly clutching their purchases – a dark blue skirt, brown jacket, white blouse, and black neckerchief.

CHAPTER SIX

When the second week in August arrived, the family packed suitcases and drove for a week's vacation to the nearby spa town of Hirschberg. While he drove, Herr Müller related the history of the town to the children.

"Local legend has it that the town, then under Polish rule, was founded by Prince Boleslaw the Third after he had been following a wounded deer in the area. He was so enchanted by the beauty of the surroundings that he named it "Deer Mountain", known in German as "Hirschberg". Confusingly, the town lies in a valley, not on a mountain."

Johanna's eyes widened in wonderment. "A real prince, Papa? On a white horse, with a sword and cape and crown?"

"Yes, *Liebling*. Just like in the fairy tales that Lily reads to you. And the area is dotted with medieval castles and palaces which belonged to other princes and dukes."

As they neared their destination, Lily understood the prince's enchantment. The town's breathtaking location nestled in a verdant valley surrounded by majestic mountains – it was picture-book perfect. Lily had never been on vacation before and her excitement matched that of her young charges.

The journey had taken them almost three hours. Herr Müller had stopped on the way several times for short breaks and a picnic, to alleviate the children's squashed confinement on the back seat and their lack of patience. By the time they reached the guesthouse, which was to accommodate them for the week, they were all quite exhausted. Frau and Herr Müller retired to their room for a short rest, while Lily unpacked the children's suitcases and settled their dispute over who would get which bed.

When they were all refreshed, they strolled the short distance into the centre of town. The ancient Town Hall Square was very similar to Breslau's Ring, surrounded by colourful merchant houses and an arched arcade. The buildings' windows were adorned with festive window boxes and hanging baskets displaying a cheerful array of red and white blooms. The Town Hall itself was built in a very different style to Breslau's gothic masterpiece but was just as stunning. The exterior of the square building was fairly plain, but it was capped by a distinctive double red roof above which rose a tall green clock tower whose dome was topped by a golden orb sparkling in the sunlight. Little Armin was fascinated by the large fountain in front of the building with a sculpture of Neptune commemorating, according to the plaque on it, old trade relations with overseas lands. The Square was buzzing with people, live folk music and street artists. Lily was happy to see that there would be no shortage of ways to entertain the children.

After breakfast the following morning, Herr and Frau Müller left to spend the day at a nearby spa, to bask in the thermal waters famous for centuries for their therapeutic qualities. Lily and the children set out to explore the town. They started by tracing the old city defensive walls. Most of them had been destroyed over time, but they were still marked by a number of crumbling medieval towers from the top of which they had a good view of the town and the surrounding countryside. Johanna climbed up the remains of one of them and pretended to be a damsel in distress, calling out to Sofia, who took the part of her rescuing knight. Armin found a stick to use as a sword as he pretended to slay a dragon. When they became bored with the game, Lily sat them down and told them the story of Rapunzel.

"There once lived a man and a woman who always wished for a child, but could not have one. These people had a little window at the back of their house from which a splendid garden could be seen. The garden was full of the most beautiful flowers and herbs. It was, however, surrounded by a high wall and no one dared to go into it because it belonged to a witch who had great power and was feared by the entire world."

The children sat quietly absorbed as Lily narrated the fairy tale. The girls were enchanted by the length of Rapunzel's hair, which reached from the top of her tower down to the ground. Little Armin snuggled in closer, losing some of his bravado when she described the witch and her cruelty, and how the Prince fell from the tower into some thorn bushes and lost his eyesight.

"He wandered the forest in misery for some months, and at length came to the desert where the witch had banished Rapunzel. He heard a voice singing and it seemed so familiar to him that he went towards it. Rapunzel fell into his arms and wept. Two of her tears fell on his eyes and the Prince could see again."

"And did they live happily ever after?" asked Johanna.

"Of course. All love stories have a happy ending," Lily assured her, wishfully thinking of Heinrich.

Lily's mother had been down-to-earth about fairy tales. Although she had read such stories to Lily when she was a small child, as Lily had grown older she had told her daughter not to believe "all that nonsense" about Prince Charming and happily-ever-after. Perhaps because of her own difficult life, she had not wanted her daughter to harbour any false illusions. "The only happy endings are the ones you make for yourself. Don't rely on others to make your dreams come true," her mother had told her. Sometimes Lily had resented her mother's cynical outlook, and while she'd wanted to believe that it was possible to make one's own destiny, she still thought a little magic would not go amiss.

"Perhaps we can produce a play about Rapunzel for our little theatre when we get home," Sofia suggested.

"Good idea, Sofia. You can start thinking about what we will need to make for it. Now who's ready for some ice cream?"

"Me!" they shouted in unison.

When they arrived back at the Square, they discovered a gathering of children and parents sitting in front of a tall booth. It was covered in red-and-white striped fabric and had a rectangular window cut out of the front. Above the window a sign proclaimed: *Wilkommen in Kaspertheatre*, and on the window sill sat a brightly coloured wooden clock notifying the audience of the time of the next performance.

"Come, children," Lily urged them excitedly. "Let's find a good place to sit."

The first puppet to appear was Kasper, a rather ugly red-faced jester with a bell at the end of his hat's tassel which jingled every time he shook his head. He carried a large, menacing stick. After a short speech, Kasper was joined by his wife, Gretel, who was angry at her husband for mislaying their baby. Grandmother appeared with the baby and Gretel hit Kasper on the head with a frying pan. All the while, a dialogue was going on between the puppets and the audience, and Lily and the children shouted and clapped, captivated by the show. Even Armin sat mesmerized without fidgeting. He especially liked the crocodile that threatened Kasper with its large snapping mouth and sharp teeth, and who stole a string of sausages from him. Kasper beat the crocodile off and retrieved the sausages by hitting it repeatedly with his stick. Lily couldn't help feeling that it was all a bit too violent for children, but none of the parents seemed to mind. They were disappointed when the show came to an end, but Lily promised them that she would bring them back the following day.

As they ate their ice cream basking in the warm sunshine, Lily took in the myriad of sights and sounds in the busy square and couldn't help but marvel at her good fortune. She had been granted the opportunity of a second childhood, to enjoy delights and treats she had missed out on as a young girl – first her visit to the zoo with Heinrich and now a proper family vacation.

Over dinner with their parents, the children described the details of the day's adventures. "That sounds wonderful, my dears," said Frau Müller. "I hope you thanked Lily for giving you such an entertaining day."

It's I who should be thanking all of you, Lily thought.

The week passed all too quickly. Herr Müller took them for short car rides to nearby parks and palaces. Lily returned with the children almost daily to the puppet show in the town square, where they also enjoyed performances by acrobats, magicians, and troubadours, who travelled from town to town throughout the summer.

The highlight for Lily came on the final day of the vacation: an organ recital in the spectacular Church of the Holy Cross. She gasped as she entered the enormous three-story building, her breath taken away by the domed ceilings covered with Baroque paintings depicting scenes from the Bible, majestic marble columns, and enormous chandeliers, and a spectacular altar flanked by massive organ pipes ascending to the ceiling in the arms of sculptured cherubs. She had never seen anything like it. Nor had she ever heard such music. Her pulse raced madly as Bach's Toccata and Fugue (she later discovered its name) possessed her, producing a euphoric reaction in her body. She was moved to tears of ecstasy.

If only Heinrich could have been with me to share the joy of this moment, she thought. Never mind, she would take pleasure in reliving her experiences when she told him about them. He was away again on maneuvers, and although he had promised to join her if he could, he had not made an appearance. Her confidence was shaken once again, as she wondered whether he really had been unable to get away or if his interest in her was fading.

She did not have to brood on his absence for too long. The Sunday following their return from vacation, Heinrich came to call, presenting her with a posy of delicate fragrant freesia. No one had ever given Lily flowers before. As she inhaled their heady scent, Lily could not believe how lucky she was to have met this man who was revealing himself to be quite the romantic.

"Let me take those for you," said Frau Müller. "I'll put them in water. Where are you taking Lily today, Heinrich?"

"It's the perfect day for a leisurely boat ride on the Oder to Malt Island," he said, steering Lily out of the apartment.

When they arrived at their destination, they found a space on the lush grass among all the other picnickers, and they spent the afternoon chatting and laughing and enjoying an outdoor concert of Mozart and Haydn.

"I seem to be developing a taste for classical music," said Lily, describing the effect the organ music in the church had had on her.

As evening fell and they made their return river journey under the Sand Bridge and past Cathedral Island, Lily was bewitched by the gas streetlamps lighting up one by one and the illuminated double spires of the magnificent Cathedral in the distance. It was very romantic. The day which had been truly magical was sealed by a fleeting kiss when Heinrich bid her goodnight, leaving her wanting more. *My mother was wrong about fairy tales,* she said to herself. *There are Prince Charmings in this world.*

CHAPTER SEVEN

The current round of his regiment's training had been particularly strenuous, leaving Heinrich little time for more than a hurried meal and a few hours of sleep. But a fierce disagreement on strategy among the higher military echelons had resulted in the cancellation of exercises for a few days, and he found that this unexpected lull, alone with his thoughts, had caused him to seriously reflect on his life.

Heinrich found himself questioning his army career, with concerns on several levels. Recent months of rigorous training and maneuvers had kept him apart from Lily much more than he had expected, and certainly much more than he liked. He treasured his meetings with her, and her bashful delight in being with him, which she could not disguise, was both charming and intensely arousing. It was taking all his willpower and strength of character to keep his hands off her. He was not a promiscuous man, but he enjoyed sex and was not one to reject opportunities when they presented themselves.

Whenever his platoon returned to the city after training, his army buddies would make a beeline for Breslau's brothels and sleazier clubs, attempting unsuccessfully to persuade him to accompany them. Eventually, they gave up pestering him to join them and stopped fishing for details of his exploits. Some of them, he knew, even wondered if he preferred boys.

Heinrich had neither need nor desire for prostitutes. Before he had met Lily, he had discovered the laisscz faire attitude to adulterous sexual encounters among well-to-do matrons, and he had been drawn to these non-committal arrangements with older women rather than to complicated entanglements with young fräuleins looking for a husband. He had also not been averse to juggling two or more affairs simultaneously, facilitated by his unpredictable schedule and the familial obligations of his mistresses, who had made no impossible demands on his time. He had honed his sexual skills and repertoire under the greedy hands of some of his more adventurous and imaginative conquests. They'd known they could count on his discretion and it had never ceased to amaze him how insatiable and uninhibited some of them were.

Heinrich found his mind wandering involuntarily away from his military concerns to some of his more unconventional sexual partners.

Clarissa's husband continually demeaned and belittled her, making her feel small and powerless. In the bedroom she assumed the role of leather-clad Kassandra the Dominatrix, brandishing an impressive arsenal of whips, chains, and other playthings. Helga, whose husband criticized her weight and forbade her cakes and sweets, liked to spread melted chocolate over his body and gradually lick it off, lingering luxuriously on one particular part of his anatomy. Ilse's husband was a tight-fisted Scrooge, mean with both the money and the time he allocated his wife. Her revenge was to spend extravagantly on sexy silk and satin lingerie to titillate and tantalize her lovers.

If he was honest with himself, Heinrich had to admit how much he enjoyed these games, while being simultaneously turned on and repelled by them. In moments of self-recrimination, he had justified these liaisons by seeing himself as the provider of much-needed escapism from these women's miserable marriages. Since meeting Lily, however, he had shied away from these escapades, fearing how disgusted she would be if she found out about them.

As he pictured Lily in his mind's eye and conjured up memories of their meetings, Heinrich felt his pulse quicken, and he was struck by the surprising force of his emotional connection with her, which had been instantaneous and unexpected, and had driven thoughts of all other women from his mind. He was determined to win Lily's trust and affection, and would, therefore, take things slowly, even though he was fairly certain that she wouldn't reject his advances if he were insistent. The extended periods of time away from her were taking their toll on him as well as slowing the progress of their romance. But for the time being, he would have to make do with the erotic Lily fantasies of his wet dreams.

Aside from his longing to spend more time with Lily, more pressing military concerns were weighing on his conscience. The army, the *Wehrmacht*, as it was now called, had been undergoing massive changes over the past several years. New warfare tactics had been introduced, replacing old methods and trench warfare with mobile operations combining units of infantry, artillery, tanks, and air power. Training for this type of warfare necessitated combined maneuvers which had become far more frequent than in the past. He fervently believed in Germany's need to recover from the humiliation of its defeat in the Great War, and to restore the people's morale by rebuilding and strengthening its armed forces so that it would not appear weak and easy prey to its neighbors. But he couldn't shake off the troubling suspicion that Hitler was preparing for an offensive rather than a defensive engagement. As he had told Lily, he would defend the Fatherland at all costs, but preparing for the launch of an unprovoked war was a different matter. And the signs were all there.

And then there was the issue of his religion. A couple of years previously, mandatory conscription for the over eighteens had been introduced, creating a huge influx of new recruits. In order to train them all, many non-commissioned officers had been promoted to the rank of lieutenant, including several of his subordinates, many of whom he did not get along with, particularly Bauer, who had taken a fancy to Lily on the evening Heinrich had met her. The only requirement for promotion was an Abitur, a high school diploma and university entrance qualification, but a recently introduced restriction banned promoting non-Aryan candidates, in particular Jews. While

Heinrich did not fear for his current position he worried that because of his heritage, however tenuous his connection to it, he would be denied any further advancement up the military ladder.

In the past, his Jewishness had never been an issue among his comrades-in-arms, but with the arrival of these newly commissioned officers, he had become aware of a noticeably chilly atmosphere in the Officers' Mess and at social gatherings. His hostile relationship with Lieutenant Bauer, who had not forgiven him for whisking Lily away from under his nose, continued to be fueled by snide remarks and taunts by some of the men wondering how Bauer could have let the Jew boy get the better of him. On top of these personal affronts, rumours and insinuations were circulating and gaining momentum about Jewish servicemen in general in the Reich's army, calling into question their loyalty. He wasn't surprised, since such ugly remarks had been rife before and after the last war, when Jews had been accused of avoiding enlistment, dodging front-line service, and profiteering. Heinrich found this particularly painful, since he knew that thousands of Jewish servicemen had been decorated for bravery, including his two deceased brothers.

Later, when he looked back, he wondered if he could have foreseen or predicted what would happen. Had he been blinkered or just plain arrogant?

All of these thoughts, and more, swirled in his head, leaving him unsettled and unsure of his own future, his future with Lily, and the future of Germany.

CHAPTER EIGHT

1938

Silvester nacht heralding 1938 was freezing cold, but this did not stop Breslau's residents from converging on the Ring to hear the clock on the *Rathaus* strike midnight. Lily thought that everyone needed this opportunity to get out and celebrate in these worrying times of uncertainty, growing unrest and violence in the city. Like many others, she supposed, Germany's situation made her nerves taut and her mood somber, brightened only by her meetings with Heinrich. She prayed that the new year would bring stability and hope for the future.

Lily had been afraid that Frau Müller would ask her to babysit and ruin her plans to meet Heinrich, but her employers were hosting a New Year's Eve party for friends in their apartment and had told her she would be free to go out.

"You go and have a lovely evening with your admirer," Frau Müller had told her. "Tonight is a night for young lovers."

Heinrich had booked a table at a cozy restaurant hidden away down a few steps in a basement on *Rouchenstrasse*. Expecting the place to be dimly lit and airless Lily was happily surprised to find a festively decorated high-ceilinged cavern, with natural stone walls and intimate niches where couples could dine in semi-privacy. The square tables were covered in starched tablecloths checkered in black, red, and yellow, the colours of Germany's flag. A small vase with a sprig of edelweiss sat at the centre next to a red glass tumbler holding a short thick candle whose flickering flame produced a romantic red glow.

A plump, heavily whiskered man dressed in traditional Silesian costume sat at one end of the restaurant on a slightly raised dais from where he serenaded the diners with accordion music, from time to time asking for requests.

A waiter came to take their order.

"For our first course," began Heinrich, "we will have the lentil soup and a shared portion of your traditional New Year's dish of herring with carrots and cabbage."

"I know some people believe that eating them will bring wealth in the coming year," said Lily. "But I'm afraid I'm not much of a believer."

"What are you going to have for your main course, Fraulein?" asked the waiter. "May I suggest our signature dish of slowly braised veal shanks?"

Heinrich ordered Holsteiner Schnitzel, a veal fillet breaded and browned in butter and topped with a fried egg and an anchovy. Noting Lily's raised eyebrow when the waiter set the heavily laden plate in front of him, he explained that the dish had been created in Berlin for Baron Friedrich von Holstein, a high-ranking nineteenth century German diplomat in the service of Kaiser Wilhelm the Second, who had liked to have a variety of foods on one plate.

"Something to drink, Sir?" inquired the waiter.

"Certainly. Kindly bring us two glasses of Sekt," said Heinrich, choosing the traditional sparkling wine with which to toast the New Year.

The food was delicious and their conversation flowed easily. Heinrich took pleasure in watching Lily eating heartily and relishing her food. He couldn't bear women who ordered next to nothing and then fiddled with their food leaving half of it on the plate. As he watched her lick her sensual lips, he was aroused and shifted uncomfortably in his seat. Before he knew what he was doing, he leaned across the table and jabbed his fork into a piece of meat on her plate, lifting it to his mouth as he stared into her eyes. Lily seemed shocked by this unexpected raw act of intimacy, and as she watched a drop of gravy trickle down his chin she blushed and looked away quickly.

The spell was broken by the approach of their waiter carrying two slices of *Käsekuchen*, lemon-scented cheesecake topped with toasted almond slivers and whipped cream.

"On the house for a sweet New Year," he proclaimed as he set the desserts down on the table. When she couldn't eat another morsel, Lily pushed her plate away and leaned back in her chair, her cheeks flushed and her eyes sparkling. Heinrich, too, was pleasantly full from the simple but sumptuous meal and was surprised to find himself slightly lightheaded from the wine.

After a few minutes, the waiter returned to the table carrying a tray holding a bowl of water and a pot of something hot.

"May I interest you in this New Year tradition?" he asked Heinrich.

"Of course. Let's have a go."

"You don't really hold any store by this, do you?" asked Lily laughing.

"Not really. It's just a bit of fun. But let's see what the future holds for each of us, shall we? You go first."

Lily took a spoonful of the hot molten lead and dropped it into the water. They waited to see what shape it would form as it solidified so that they could work out its prediction.

"I do believe it has formed the shape of a heart," the waiter said. "You are going to find love." Heinrich looked up to see her response. Again, she blushed.

"I bet you predict that for all the young ladies," she said quickly, her heart pumping wildly.

Then it was Heinrich's turn.

"That looks like a sword to me, Sir, predicting danger or harm. I hope for your sake that I'm mistaken."

"Well, I am a soldier so I suppose it's not so far-fetched. Not to worry," he added, seeing the stricken look on Lily's face. "It could just as easily be a bird in flight, which I imagine predicts a journey." While he was not a superstitious man, this prediction unsettled Heinrich more than he was prepared to admit. Travel and danger went hand in hand in his profession, and with the growing bellicose atmosphere enveloping Germany, both of these predictions might become concrete possibilities, sooner rather than later.

When the waiter moved on to the next diners, Heinrich took Lily's hand across the table to reassure her. He put his other hand in his coat pocket and withdrew a small black velvet box, which he placed in front of her. Although their romance was still young, mainly because of his long absences, he had wanted for some time to give her a token of his affection, to show her that his intentions were serious. He had never suffered a lack of self-confidence with other women, but with Lily he was always anxious when he went away that she would be swept off her feet in his absence by some other lucky fellow. He hoped he was not being too hasty or presumptuous.

Lily's heart skipped a beat. She couldn't breathe.

"It seems the prediction has some truth," Heinrich said and smiled. "This is a token of my love for you, Lily."

Lily picked up the box with trembling fingers, her heart racing so fast she thought she might faint. Heinrich had called her "my love". She was sure she hadn't misheard. How she wanted to tell him she loved him, too. But it was too soon. She was afraid that despite his declaration it would frighten him off.

She lifted the lid and gave a little gasp. For a moment, she was speechless.

"Oh, Heinrich, it's beautiful!" she exclaimed, lifting the exquisite brooch from its silk-lined resting place. It was a work of the most delicate craftsmanship. Seven bells sparkling with diamonds cascaded from two entwined white gold stems, which rested against a leaf of yellow gold encrusted with emeralds. It was a perfect lily-of-the-valley.

"I'm afraid the gold is plated and the gems are Swarovski crystals. One day I hope to be able to afford solid gold and real gems," said Heinrich.

"It's perfect as it is," said Lily with tears of joy in her eyes. "I will treasure it always."

She lifted her hand to stroke his cheek.

It had taken every ounce of strength not to display her initial disappointment that the box did not contain a ring. What was she expecting? Lily berated herself. Why would she even suppose that this was a proposal? There had never been anything in their relationship to suggest that one would be forthcoming. For now, she could only hope.

As midnight approached, they left the restaurant hand in hand and hurried to the nearby *Wachtplatz*, where several droshkies waited in line at the stand. Heinrich helped Lily up on to one of the carriages and the driver covered them with a pile of furry blankets to protect them from the freezing weather. Light flakes of snow were falling as the horses began to clip-clop their way around the square towards the Ring. Heinrich put his arm around Lily and drew her towards him. She thrilled at his touch and his kisses, which were tender at first, and when he began to gently probe her lips with his tongue, she opened her mouth to invite him in with a fiery passion and hunger she could not deny. The droshky slowed as they neared the town square and the countdown to midnight began. The clock struck twelve and the crowd raised an enormous shout as the deep chimes of the church bells of St Elisabeth and St Maria Magdalena rang out.

Fireworks exploded above the square, lighting up the winter sky and the sparkling snowflakes which were beginning to settle on the ground.

Drawing her closer, Heinrich kissed Lily deeply once again.

"*Prost Neujahr*, Lily. Happy New Year."

This is the happiest evening of my life, Lily thought, resting her head on Heinrich's shoulder as she watched the magic of the fireworks display. She would not allow the promise of a new year and a future with her newfound love to be spoiled by the sinister atmosphere pervading Germany or the ominous predictions at their dinner table.

CHAPTER NINE

Winter blossomed into spring, but Lily felt none of the usual uplifting promise of renewal and rejuvenation. The growing tension in Breslau became even more palpable and oppressive as the city gladly embraced and implemented Nazi propaganda. She was appalled by the thuggish Brown Shirts who swaggered through the streets, picking indiscriminately on anyone who took their fancy, making lewd remarks to women young and old, and encouraging willful vandalism against Jewish-owned businesses. Billboards were erected next to the Town Hall in the Ring and elsewhere across the city, whose messages aimed at creating hostility against Jews, other non-Aryans, homosexuals, and the disabled. Fliers littered the streets, spreading similar malicious slogans. The atmosphere was such that Heinrich chose to wear his uniform rather than casual clothes on their dates in order to avoid intimidation by the hateful hooligans.

One afternoon on the way to the park with Johanna, Lily noticed a group of men gathered in front of one of the billboards. She tried to hurry by and avoid them, but Johanna broke away from her out of curiosity to see what was on show. The board's big bold headline read: *Die Juden sind unser Unglück* – The Jews are our Misfortune – and to her horror Lily discovered that it was plastered with ugly cartoons, photographs, and articles portraying the Jews as pigs and monkeys, or with fists full of deutschmarks, or trampling small babies. She was revolted and wanted to get Johanna away as quickly as possible. The girl was not tall enough to read the notices for herself, but she could overhear the men's nasty remarks and raucous laughter directed at the object of their hostile contempt.

"Sofia says a girl called Miriam used to sit next to her in class. She told me she's happy Miriam doesn't come to school any more because she is Jewish and, being non-Aryan she might pass on horrible diseases to her classmates. What is Aryan, Lily? Why does Sofia not want to be her friend when she used to like her a lot?"

Lily didn't know how to answer. Sofia was obviously being brainwashed by her teachers, and while Lily's natural reply would be to criticize and contradict these teachings, instinct made her wary of expressing her opinion, especially to Johanna, who would no doubt repeat what she had said at the first opportunity either to Sofia or to her parents.

"It's complicated, Johanna. I think it would be better if you asked your mother or father to explain it to you."

Lily took Johanna's hand and they began to walk home. Hoping to distract her from what they had just witnessed, Lily took the little girl into a sweet shop and let her choose an assortment of candy from the large glass jars arranged on shelves behind the counter. They left the shop and clutching her paper bag full of treasure, Johanna skipped along, leaving Lily to her thoughts.

Although she sensed that Frau Müller at least was not a Nazi sympathizer, Lily was not willing to put her job on the line by making her own sentiments known. She really liked her work. The children were fond of her, as she was of them, and Frau Müller appeared to be more than satisfied with her work, treating her more like a member of the family than a servant. Lily tried to give much more work than was expected of her, but even so, she found herself with plenty of spare time when the children were at school. She used it to practice her sewing techniques on the scraps of material left over from the alterations she made to the girls' clothes. Frau Müller was so impressed by her outstanding needlework that she even asked her to make some modifications to refresh one or two pieces in her own wardrobe. Best of all, she had allowed Lily to take a couple of her discarded outfits and revamp them for herself. Now, Lily would feel elegant and sophisticated on her dates with Heinrich.

She wondered if her employer regarded her as her protégé and she was flattered. Frau Müller was fashion conscious, dressing tastefully in the latest styles. She kept up to date with the current trends, subscribing to all the important fashion, film, and society magazines which she passed on to Lily when she was finished with them, rather than throwing them out as she had done in the past. "Here you are, Lily," she'd say. "Perhaps you can find some ideas for when you take up a fulltime position of seamstress somewhere in the future. I don't suppose you will stay with us indefinitely and when you leave I sincerely hope you will pursue your dream."

Lily now had a treasured pile of *Elegant Welt, Sport im Bild, Die Dame,* and her most cherished, *Vogue.* Browsing through them, she was transported into a magical world of glamour and beauty, a world of which she was determined to be a part. She spent many hours of her free time in the library scouring the shelves for books on fashion history, styles, and fabrics. She wanted to be well prepared when the opportunity eventually presented itself.

At first, Lily had been shy about confiding in Heinrich her dreams for the future, fearing that he might consider her foolish fantasy unrealistic, but when she did, he listened attentively and surprised her with his encouragement. The next time he came to call, instead of bringing chocolates or flowers, he presented her with a sketchbook and pencils. "For you to create your own designs, Lily," he said. "I can't wait to see them."

She thought she could never love him more than at that moment.

Tonight would be her first opportunity to impress Heinrich with her handiwork. She dressed carefully in one of her newly recreated outfits. The two-piece ensemble consisted of a jacket-style blouse with well-defined shoulders and a tight waist extending into a peplum over the matching bias-cut skirt, which was snug at the hips and then flared out below the knee to mid-calf. The simple style and soft navy-blue material complemented her figure beautifully. Giving the outfit a personal touch, she had added a red-and-white striped trim on the collar and cuffs and at the belted waistline, and had replaced the original navy buttons with red ones. She even had a red felt pillbox hat to match. As a final touch, she pinned her lily-of-the-valley brooch on the front above her heart. Looking at herself in the mirror, she could hardly believe the transformation the outfit produced. She hoped Heinrich would be suitably dazzled.

Checking her watch, she saw that her preparations had taken longer than planned. She was running late. They had so little time together these days that every minute counted. Heinrich had warned her repeatedly to stick to major thoroughfares and well-illuminated side streets when she was walking alone after dark, but Lily knew a shortcut which would hopefully get to her to the rendezvous on time. She dashed into the dark alleyway and ran as fast as she could, her heart beating wildly. The dark narrow passage was more frightening than she had expected, and she began to feel quite anxious. Almost there, she told herself to relax, but as she rounded the corner, she came face to face with the drunken officer from whom Heinrich had rescued her on that fateful night in the bar when they had first met. The Lieutenant stank of alcohol and looked just as threatening as she'd remembered him.

"Well, well," he snarled. "If it isn't the filthy Jew-loving whore."

Lily froze.

"What brings you down this way, slut? Looking for more kosher cock to suck on?"

Lily was confused. What was this ugly brute talking about?

Before she had time to move out of his way, he grabbed her and pushed her against the nearest wall. Stabs of terror ran down her spine. She tried to scream, but his large hand covered her mouth while the other began to tear at her clothes. The red buttons scattered in every direction. He managed to free one breast and began to suck on it greedily. Terrified, Lily squirmed but she was pinned down and no match for his size and strength.

He released her breast and she prayed that he was done with her. In horror, she realised that he was unbuckling the belt of his uniform pants. With one swift move, he whipped the belt away and let the pants fall to the ground.

"Here's your chance to sample a real man. You're going to enjoy this much more than the Major's circumcised little knackwurst and you'll be begging for more."

He pressed against her and Lily could feel the hardness of his erection. He ripped at her undergarments as he began to lift her on to his swollen penis. But in his drunken euphoria he released her mouth and Lily let out an earsplitting scream.

"Shut up, you cow," came his response, accompanied by a stunning slap on the face.

Sobbing and deprived of all her strength Lily gave in to the inevitable.

But, with a sadistic smirk on his face on the verge of penetration, Bauer suddenly found himself hurtling backwards away from his prey.

"Let go of her, Bauer, you dog!" Heinrich shouted as he fell upon the Lieutenant and hauled him away from Lily. He was no match for Bauer in height or weight, but he had the advantage of being sober and fueled by rage. He rained down punch after punch on his rival's face, beating him into submission and unconsciousness.

Lily sat huddled against the wall, holding together the shreds of her clothing in an attempt to cover her nakedness. Discovering that her beautiful brooch had fallen off, she began to crawl around on all fours, scraping her knees and weeping as she desperately searched for it in the darkness. She almost missed the brief sparkle as the moonlight momentarily illuminated it lying in a small puddle, thankfully undamaged. Her hand closed around it, and she rocked back and forth holding it tightly in her fist.

"I'll kill the bastard," Heinrich raged.

"Leave him be, Heinrich. It will only make matters worse for you. You got here in time. He didn't manage to finish his assault."

"Then I'll report him and make sure he gets the punishment

he deserves," he threatened as he gave the comatose man one final kick.

Heinrich draped his jacket around Lily's shoulders and held her close until her sobs began to subside.

"Please forgive me, Heinrich."

"This is not your fault, Lily. There's nothing to forgive."

"But I promised you I would keep to the main well-lit streets. I should never have come down this alley. And now you will be in trouble. I'm so sorry … so sorry."

"No, I should never have asked you to meet me here. I should have called for you at the apartment."

"You're not angry with me? Please tell me you're not angry with me," she said through her tears.

"Of course I'm not angry. I love you. You've done nothing wrong. The only person at fault here is Bauer, and I'm not going to let him get away with it."

They sat in silence punctuated only by her sporadic sobs and his gentle whispers of comfort. When she had calmed sufficiently, he gently helped her to her feet.

"Let's get you home."

"But how will I explain my appearance?"

"Leave that to me."

When they reached the Müllers' apartment, Heinrich asked to speak with Frau Müller. He gave her a watered-down version of the evening's events, leaving out the attempted rape and attributing the attack to mindless violence or mistaken identity.

"Oh, you poor girl. I think a brandy is in order for both of you," said Frau Müller, heading to the drinks trolley.

When they had downed the warm and comforting schnapps, Frau Müller turned to Heinrich. "Thank you for getting her home safely. Don't worry, we'll look after her. Let's get you out of your ruined clothes, Lily, and into a warm bath."

Heinrich retrieved his jacket, and whispering, "I'll see you soon", he placed a light kiss on Lily's cheek and left her in her employer's care.

"I'm not a fool, Lily," said Frau Müller as she led Lily to the bathroom. "I can see there was more to this attack than Heinrich told me. Should I call a doctor?"

"No. I'll be fine, thank you."

Although she was in a state of shock, Lily was determined to avoid attracting any attention to herself, and certainly not to Heinrich, who she feared might get into serious trouble for fighting with a fellow officer.

"Your hand is bleeding." Lily unfurled her fingers to reveal the brooch she was still clutching. The pin had pierced her skin. She winced as Frau Müller gently removed it and put it to one side.

"You are sure you were not violated? You don't need to be embarrassed. I'm not easily shocked."

"I'm sure. Heinrich saved me from the brute." The shock hit Lily and once again, she crumpled. She started to tremble violently, the tears she had been suppressing flowing down her cheeks.

"There, there, Lily. Let it all out." Frau Müller rocked her as if she were one of her children needing comfort after a fall or a nightmare. *If only my own mother was here to soothe my pain,* Lily thought. *How I long for the warm safety of her embrace.* "You get into bed now and I will bring you some hot chocolate. Tomorrow morning I will get the children ready. You need time to heal, and I think the bruises on your face might alarm them. Best you take the day off and stay in your room. I'll get Cook to bring you your meals."

Lily was overwhelmed by her employer's kindness and compassion. She was unbelievably lucky to have this job thanks to Heinrich. A lot of other employers would not have shown such understanding. In fact, they might well have shown her the door.

The brandy, warm bath, and hot chocolate had the desired effect, and surrendering to exhaustion, Lily fell into an uneasy sleep. She tossed and turned as frightening scenarios sullied her dreams: Heinrich being court-martialed and imprisoned for having struck a fellow officer; Heinrich telling her their relationship was over now that she was spoiled goods; the Müllers terminating her employment for bringing shame on the household.

Sometime just before dawn, Lily woke up gasping for air. A nightmarish image of Bauer's ghastly face loomed over her, triggering a panic attack, which catapulted her out of sleep in a cold sweat and unable to breathe, choking on her own acid bile, which burned her throat and nostrils.

She slowly registered her dimly lit surroundings and her heartbeat gradually returned to normal. She felt stiff and sore all over. Frau Müller was right. She would be useless with the children today, but would one day off be enough to restore her to normality? How long would it take for her to put the awful episode behind her and begin to feel safe again? She wanted to bury herself under the covers forever.

Mid-morning, Frau Müller knocked at her door. "How are you feeling, Lily?" she asked as she entered the room.

"Much better, thank you."

"I have explained to Cook that you were attacked, but I spared her any details. The children believe that you tripped and had a bad fall. This should explain your bruises, which hopefully will look less angry by tomorrow. My husband asks whether you or Heinrich would be able to identify the assailant, and he has offered to go to the police on your behalf."

Panic started to well up again and constrict Lily's throat.

"That is very kind, but we would not be able to identify him," Lily choked out. "I don't wish to stir up any unnecessary trouble and waste police resources. Please thank Herr Müller for me."

"Well, if you are sure. This note and these flowers came for you," Frau Müller added, passing Lily an envelope and placing a vase on her night table. "I will check in on you later. Try to get some rest."

My dearest Lily,
Frau Müller assures me that you are recovering from last night's dreadful episode. I will make sure nothing like that can ever happen again. Please believe me when I say that I am not in the least angry with you, nor do I blame you in any way for what happened. My love for you is unchanged. I can only hope that your feelings towards me remain constant. Miserably, I must go away again, but I hope it will not be for too long. I can't wait to be with you again.

Your loving Heinrich

Lily hugged the letter to her breast. Heinrich's words were comforting, but she worried that he was going away once again. The general feeling in Germany was that war was imminent and, recalling the New Year's Eve prediction, she feared for his safety.

CHAPTER TEN

The first days of July saw an unprecedented rush of activity and preparation as Breslau was transformed into an Olympic-style city fit to host the German Sports and Gymnastics Festival to be held during the last week of the month. The streets were cleaned, planters were filled with vibrant shrubs, and hanging baskets overflowed with colourful blooms. Spectator stands were erected in and around *Schlossplatz* where a procession of the competing teams would parade in front of the visiting dignitaries, including Adolf Hitler himself. Posters around town proclaimed *Der Führer Kommt*, heralding his arrival. The city became a forest of swastikas with banners adorning the facades of buildings, lampposts, and specially erected flagpoles along the banks of the River Oder. The Sportfest was to take place in the huge Herman Göring Stadium, and the organizers anticipated the arrival of the finest gymnasts and athletes in all of Germany and beyond. While this was being touted as a friendly sporting event, its military overtones were indisputable, almost, thought Lily, like a declaration of intent. Heinrich had not shared his thoughts with her on the probability of war, but of late she had sensed an uneasiness in his manner which unnerved her.

There was much excitement in the Müller household because Sofia's League of German Girls group would participate in the processions through the centre of town. Sofia had become indoctrinated with Nazi ideology and was waiting with worshipful anticipation for the arrival of her beloved Führer. Herr Müller had secured preferential places for all the family at the opening ceremony and had kindly included Lily.

While she was very grateful for his generosity and thoughtfulness and she was eager to witness this once-in-a-lifetime spectacle, Lily's abhorrence of Hitler and all things Nazi was making her uneasy. She was careful to keep any signs of ambivalence well-hidden from the family, especially from Sofia who might report her to her counsellors. She had sensed that Heinrich was also uncomfortable with recent events following the Anschluss in March, when Hitler had annexed neighboring Austria as part of his plan for a Greater Germany, but they had avoided discussing it in any depth.

Lily had not seen Heinrich for some time, as the Breslau garrison was also involved in the preparations. Many of its officers, decked out in full ceremonial uniform, complete with tall tasseled helmets, would make up the guard of honour outside the *Hauptbahnhof* to welcome Hitler and other officials upon their arrival.

When the Sunday of the Sportfest opening arrived, Herr Müller gathered the family together and they set off towards the *Schlossplatz*. As they jostled the crowds in order to take up their places, Herr Müller remarked, "How fortunate that we are enjoying *Führerwetter*," referring to the bright sunny day which was pleasantly warm rather than stiflingly hot. "Being squashed among all these spectators would be unbearable if the temperature was any higher."

When they had claimed their positions, Herr Müller lifted Armin up and pointed in the direction of the dignitaries' rostrum. "You are witnessing history, my boy. That is our Führer, Adolf Hitler, and the two men standing just behind him are Reichsführer Heinrich Himmler and Dr Joseph Goebbels. They are very important men."

Lily shuddered and felt physically sick at being in close proximity to such evil men whose reputation for vicious cruelty and hateful bigotry was no secret.

She couldn't help scanning the hundreds of spectators nervously, anxious that Lieutenant Bauer might be in the crowd, even though the chances of her picking him out, or rather him picking her out, amid the throng were next to nothing. Hopefully he was at the train station as part of the Führer's reception. Heinrich had said nothing further to her about any disciplinary action which had been taken against him, and she preferred not to bring the subject up when they met, but the terrifying encounter haunted her dreams and made her jittery when she was unaccompanied in the street. What if he came looking for her to finish what he started? She never went out in the evening alone.

A band was playing marching music creating an atmosphere of pomp and ceremony. The crowd's excitement was palpable, almost electric. Above the hubbub of the crowd, Lily suddenly became aware of a far-off noise coming from the streets near the square. It got louder and louder until it felt like an approaching tidal wave, reaching skywards, ready to sweep everyone away. She experienced a sensation which was simultaneously terrifying and fascinating.

On the rostrum, Hitler turned towards the direction of the noise, his face registering a look of tense uncertainty, causing his bodyguards – several gigantic men in black uniforms and steel helmets – to surround him and close ranks. All the onlookers seemed to hold their breath as one. And then it happened. A marching column six rows deep emerged from the *Schweidnitzer Strasse*, identically dressed men in grey suits and Tyrolean hats.

"Who are they?" Lily asked Herr Müller.

Pointing at the flag held high by the leader of the procession, he answered, "They must be from the Sudeten Gymnastic Association in Czechoslovakia. I believe there are representatives of many Eastern European German ethnic minorities as well as athletes from South Africa, Italy, and even Argentina."

As the flag bearer spearheading the delegation came level with the Führer, Hitler stepped forward, stood at the edge of the balustrade, raised his right arm, and greeted the Sudeten Germans' banners. A colossal roar exploded from the spectators, building up into a crescendo of mass hysteria. Suddenly, Lily made out a new sound amid the shouting, a mantra passing from mouth to mouth in an insistent rhythm until it was voiced by the whole crowd – as if by one enormous throat: *Ein Volk, Ein Reich, Ein Führer* (One People, One State, One Leader). Lily registered in speechless horror the surge of right-arm salutes and the sea of ecstatic faces. Girls and young women dressed in colourful folk costumes broke away from the procession, reaching out their arms towards their leader and weeping in adulation. *Heil Hitler.* It was as if the Führer had cast a spell over the entire crowd.

After the competing teams had passed in front of the dignitaries, it was the turn of the Hitler Youth, firstly boys and young men, and then the League of German Girls. The Müllers clapped in excitement when they saw Sofia proudly marching by in her smart uniform. Herr Müller held up Armin, who waved and shouted, but Lily couldn't help noticing the frown on Frau Müller's face as she drew Johanna closer to her side.

When the excitement was over and the crowd began to disperse, Lily left the Müllers and hurried to her pre-arranged rendezvous with Heinrich. Her thoughts were in turmoil after the distressing spectacle she had witnessed in the square. Could she express her fears and her disgust to Heinrich? How would he react if she did? He was, after all, serving in Hitler's military. Was his loyalty absolute? Unquestionable?

Her uncertainty evaporated as soon as she saw him in the distance. He looked even more dashing than usual in his ceremonial uniform and she felt the heat rise in her body as her desire for him threatened to overwhelm her senses. Running into his arms, she drew him towards her and kissed him with a desperate passion which surprised them both.

The feel of his mouth on hers caused a surge of fiery heat between her legs, and the sensations of pleasure he aroused in her wiped out all negative thoughts.

Heinrich looked deeply into her eyes and registered the distress she could not completely conceal. "Lily, what is it?"

In a bolder voice than Heinrich had ever heard from Lily, she responded, "I am afraid for Germany and for the future. Today's events have shown me that life is uncertain and we should live for the moment. You have treated me with the greatest respect and waited patiently, but I don't want to wait any longer. I had hoped to be your wife, but if that is not to be, I will give myself to you willingly without the benefit of a ring."

"Oh, my beautiful Lily," he replied. "How I love you."

Wasn't this what he had been longing for since the first time he had set eyes on her? Had he not fantasized a million times about her naked body at one with his? How many times had he wanted to get down on one knee and propose?

But *racial infamy* – mixed marriages and even sexual relations between an Aryan and a Jew – was prohibited by the Nuremberg Laws and punishable by prison, labour camp, or worse. He might possibly be protected because of his military status but he would not risk Lily's safety. He didn't believe that she condoned Hitler's racial policies. She spoke with affection and respect of her mother's employers, Herr and Frau Schwartz, and she had voiced her concern over Sofia's indoctrination. But what if he was wrong about her attitude towards Jews? Perhaps, if he revealed his Jewish heritage to her, however loose his ties to it, she would sever all connection with him. And that, he could not bear.

"Of course I want to marry you, Lily. How could you doubt my intentions? I want you desperately, but you deserve to wear my ring first. Unfortunately, as a soldier I am not at liberty to do whatever I please, so we will have to be patient for now while I try to get the necessary permissions."

Somehow, he promised himself, he would find a way for them to be together despite the law.

CHAPTER ELEVEN

Following Bauer's attack on Lily, Heinrich had deliberated long and hard over how to deal with the situation. He had every right – and even a duty – to report the Lieutenant's behavior to his superiors, who would no doubt throw the book at him. He did not fear Bauer's retribution, but he was determined to preserve Lily's anonymity and avoid drawing attention to their relationship.

In the end, it wasn't necessary for Heinrich to make the report. Another officer had come across the unconscious drunken Lieutenant lying in his own blood, urine, and vomit, with his pants down around his knees. The officer had dragged Bauer back to barracks and filed a report of his own. Heinrich assumed Bauer must have known he was in enough trouble for being involved in what would be presumed to have been a drunken brawl, and he would have had no intention of risking the addition of attempted rape to his misdemeanors by accusing Heinrich of attacking him. Bauer alone knew the identity of his assailant, who was also the only witness who could testify to the vicious attack on a defenseless woman. As such, Heinrich's name was kept out of the disciplinary proceedings.

Heinrich made no further mention of it to Lily, but assured her that she was safe and that Bauer would not bother her again. His own relationship with the Lieutenant, however, was now even more hostile than before. There had been talk of transferring some of the regiment to Dresden, and Heinrich recommended to the disciplinary committee that Bauer be relocated as part of his punishment. He hoped that it was only a matter of a few weeks before the threat was permanently removed from Breslau.

At the beginning of September, the transfer list was published, and sure enough Bauer's name was at the top. Heinrich would finally be able to tell Lily the good news when he met her later that day. He had kept their recent meetings low-profile, choosing discreet venues away from prying eyes, and Lily had begun to wonder why they needed all this secrecy if Bauer really couldn't make any more trouble. Eventually, Heinrich knew, he would have to tell her he was Jewish and that their relationship was taboo.

He left the barracks for their rendezvous and hopped on a tram towards the Museum. He was surprised to see several of his fellow officers heading in the same direction and he gave a friendly salute in acknowledgment. When he alighted from the tram, he made his way to the small park in front of the museum to wait for Lily. Walking along the secluded side street, he felt a menacing presence behind him and heard shouts of *"Yid"* ... *"Jude"* ... "Filthy Jewish pig, traitor to the Reich". Heinrich looked around to see at whom these insults were aimed but he seemed to be alone. He walked on. Suddenly, a violent push from behind sent him stumbling forwards. He turned to confront his assailants, shocked to recognise his fellow officers.

"What is this? What are you doing?"

In answer, they set upon him, their punches knocking him to the ground. He was pummeled by the kicks of their steel-tipped boots, every blow accompanied by their jeers. "This one's from Bauer," snarled one of them. Heinrich registered a bright flash of metal, screamed in agony as the knife pierced his side, and then merciful oblivion.

Huddled in the shadows at the far corner of the park, Lily made out the sounds of a brawl on the street. She heard the word "Jude" and realised that some poor Jew had been attacked by hooligans. Caution and fear prevented her from intervening. Memories of her encounter with Lieutenant Bauer made her legs turn to jelly and she crouched down out of sight.

When all was quiet and she was sure the attackers had left, she made her way gingerly towards the street. The victim was lying face down in a puddle of blood. Next to him lay a knife. She lifted the poor man's shirt to reveal the wound. Fighting the urge to vomit, she untied her scarf and pressed it against the hole in an attempt to staunch the flow of blood. Keeping pressure on the wound, she gently turned him over. The world stood still. She heard screams and then realised they were her own. Heinrich was unconscious, his face was ashen. He must have tried to intervene and protect the Jew, she thought, who appeared to have escaped, leaving her beloved to face the attackers alone.

"Heinrich, wake up ... It's me, Lily ... Please be alive." She kissed his pale lips and stroked his hair, calling his name over and over. After a few moments, which seemed like an eternity, his eyes fluttered open.

"You need help," Lily said quickly. "I will get you to a hospital."

Heinrich answered groggily. "No, Lily. My brother...Martin... lives a few meters away...on Garten Strasse. Help me get there. He will help."

She struggled to get him to his feet and, summoning all her strength, dragged him, with his body leaning heavily on her, across the street. Her knees were starting to buckle as she reached the apartment building and pushed her way inside.

"Leave me down here in the corner under the stairs out of sight and take the elevator to the second floor. He lives in Apartment Four," Heinrich instructed weakly.

Lily closed the elevator's decorative wrought-iron doors and slid the scissor gate across. Pressing the second-floor button with trembling fingers, she willed herself to keep calm and in control. Heinrich had told her that he was estranged from his brother and had not spoken to him in years. Would Martin be willing to listen to her and help, or would he just slam the door in her face?

She rang the doorbell. From the other side of the door, Lily could hear a woman ask, "Moshe, are you expecting anyone?"

A man's voice responded, "No." And then he opened the door.

Lily thought she must have got the wrong apartment. Standing in front of her was a tall gentleman with flecks of gray in his luxuriant beard and curling side locks. His head was adorned with a large black velvet yarmulke and white strings peeped out from under his shirt and fell over the belt of his black trousers. Nothing about him spoke of a resemblance to Heinrich. But then she noticed his eyes. They were Heinrich's remarkable kaleidoscopes. Behind him stood an equally tall, unfashionably dressed matron, her hair obscured by a severe black head covering.

"Are you Martin Graber?" Lily asked hesitantly. "Please don't turn me away," she pleaded when they just gaped at her. "I need your urgent help. My name is Lily. I am your brother Heinrich's girlfriend. He has been badly injured and needs a doctor. He wouldn't let me take him to hospital and insisted I bring him here."

The man took in her tears and shaking hands and then the streaks of blood on her clothes. "Where is my brother now?" he asked.

"Hiding in the ground-floor stairwell. Please hurry. He has lost a lot of blood."

"Golda, please fetch Dr Feldheim from upstairs. I will help this young lady bring Heinrich up here."

Heinrich lay semi-conscious on his brother's couch while Dr Feldheim attempted to clean and stitch the knife wound and check for other injuries.

"I've done as much as I can, Moshe, but he needs a hospital and a transfusion to replace the lost blood. And I can't guarantee that the wound is not infected or that he is not bleeding internally. Legally, I am no longer allowed to practice medicine so I cannot refer him. You must decide what to do under the circumstances."

"Thank you, Doctor," said Martin, "for all your efforts. Please tell me what I owe you for your services this evening."

"A brandy will be payment enough."

"I think we could all use a stiff drink," Martin agreed, pouring shots for everyone.

"Your brother needs rest and plenty of fluids. I will check back on him in the morning, but please don't hesitate to call me if he spikes a fever or becomes delirious."

The brandy had a calming effect on Lily. She gathered her bearings and looked around the apartment. Despite the horrors of the evening, she was intrigued. One long wall held floor-to-ceiling bookshelves which heaved under the weight of a library's worth of huge volumes whose titles were unfathomable, printed in letters she recognised from her childhood with the Schwartzes as Hebrew. On another wall stood a large glass display cabinet filled with religious artifacts, a pair of ornate silver candlesticks, an eight-branch *Menora*, a ram's horn Shofar, wine goblets, and more. An array of framed photographs showed a number of elderly people and four children, three boys and a girl. She assumed these were Heinrich's nephews and nieces. Several coats hanging by the front door were evidence of young family members, as well as a scattering of school books on the table and a couple of dolls in a play pram.

Everything suddenly fell into place. Heinrich was the "poor Jew" being attacked, reasoned Lily, not the heroic rescuer. Lieutenant Bauer's foul words on the night of her near-rape now made sense. Why had he never mentioned his heritage to her? Surely he knew she held no anti-Semitic prejudices. Was this the real reason he failed to commit to her, because the Nuremberg Laws forbade it?

Golda came over and took Lily's hand.

"You must be exhausted, my dear, and in shock from this horrific episode. Let me give you some warm soup and fix you a bed for the night."

"You are very kind and I can't bear to leave Heinrich in this state, but I'm afraid I must get home or else my employers will be worried about me and may involve the police. Heinrich refused to let me take him to hospital so I can only assume that he would not want the authorities involved, directly or indirectly through me."

As she prepared to leave, Lily told Martin and Golda briefly about her background and her employment, and her relationship with Heinrich. "I had no idea he was Jewish."

"Well, Judaism has played a very insignificant part in his life," explained Martin. "Our family, like many in Breslau and in Germany generally, was completely assimilated into society and disregarded the trappings of religion. I was drawn back into spirituality after the death of my brothers, and I am the only one who keeps the *mitzvoth* – God's commandments. My wife, Golda, is descended from an important rabbinical family. It was the luckiest day of my life when her father met me by chance in the synagogue of a town I was visiting on a business trip."

"Why do your wife and the doctor address you as 'Moshe'?" Lily asked.

"That is my Hebrew name. Heinrich's name is 'Chaim', which means life."

"If you are Jewish, how is it possible for you to carry on with your business? Have the Nazis not confiscated everything you own?"

"My business is an old established one, which for years has supplied fish and other foodstuffs to the military. My services are deemed valuable to the German economy and war effort, so I have the status of *Honourary Aryan*."

Lily glanced over at the couch, where Heinrich was lying, before saying, "I realise your relationship with Heinrich is strained, but can you find it in your heart to help him? If his would-be murderers discover he is alive, he will be in mortal danger. Heinrich whispered the name Bauer to me, which can only mean that he was attacked by fellow officers he recognised. If they find out he isn't dead, they will come back to finish the job and silence him permanently."

"I have already lost two brothers who tried to prove their loyalty to the Fatherland by rejecting their birthright. Did they learn nothing from the Dreyfus Affair in France? The elite are not immune to anti-Semitism; in fact, jealousy of their position often fans the flames. Every year on the anniversary of the meaningless fruitless deaths of my brothers, I make a solemn visit to the cemetery to say Mourner's *Kaddish* at their graveside. I am not willing to lose my last remaining brother. I will use my connections to get him out of the country and to safety. Now it's getting late, Lily. You had better be getting home. My eldest son Erich will accompany you part of the way. Come back in the morning when both you and Heinrich have rested. But be discreet."

As she neared home, Lily forced herself to put aside the mental image of Heinrich's wounded body and concentrate on her plan of action for the following day's escape.

CHAPTER TWELVE

Lily rose at sunrise after a fitful night of dreams peppered with violence and death. She had tossed and turned in her sleep, jolted awake from time to time by her own moans and bathed in a cold sweat. Now, Lieutenant Bauer's smirking face flashed before her eyes and then the lifeless body of her beloved Heinrich.

She dressed hastily and threw some clothes and her most precious belongings into a bag, deliberately leaving some items in order to give the impression of her intention to return. Scribbling a hasty note to Herr and Frau Müller, she explained that regretfully she had been called away in an emergency and apologised for leaving in such a hurry. She would be back as soon as she could, but she would understand if they felt obliged to terminate her employment and seek a replacement. Thanking them for their kindness and understanding she concluded, *"I will miss the children with all my heart and hope to be reunited with you all in the very near future. Love Lily."* She hoped that this would convince them that all was well, and that this would quash their concern and efforts to try to find her. Most importantly, she hoped to deter them from reporting her to the police.

Time was of the essence. Soon the children would be up looking for her. As Lily made her escape, she could see Hedwig the cook pottering about in the kitchen preparing breakfast. Praying that Hedwig wouldn't look up from her chores in the direction of the hallway, Lily made a quick dash to the front door. The heel of her shoe caught on the Persian rug which decorated the entrance hall and she momentarily lost her balance, her bag banging lightly against the wall.

"Is someone there?" called Hedwig.

What should she do? Stay perfectly still and silent until she heard the cook carry on with her work, or answer? Her ears rang with the racing beat of her heart as it pounded her chest. What if she were discovered? Would Hedwig give her away? Could she rely on her amicable relationship with the woman? She decided to hold her tongue. The seconds ticked by.

"Must have imagined it," she heard Hedwig mumble.

As soon as the silence was broken by the clatter of dishes and pans, Lily took her chance and slipped out of the door and into the semi-darkness of the street.

Knowing she mustn't draw attention to herself by hurrying along too fast, she willed herself to walk at a normal pace. The streets were fairly quiet given the early hour, but she kept looking over her shoulder, terrified of an attack or surveillance. How had this city, her home, where she had spent her whole life, suddenly become so threatening? Turning the corner into Garten Strasse, she came face to face with a policeman.

"What are you doing out and about at such an early hour, Fräulein? Planning a trip?" he said, spotting her bag.

Lily blinded him with her most beguiling smile and then, modestly lowering her eyes, she answered tearfully, "Yes, Officer. I am on my way to the train station. My grandmother is sick and I am needed to take care of her."

Since the *Hauptbahnhoff* was situated further down the street, this seemed to satisfy the policeman, who allowed her to pass without further interrogation. Lily walked on in the direction of the station. As soon as she saw the policemen's back disappearing down a side street, she quickly doubled back to the Grabers' apartment.

When Golda opened the door, Lily rushed to the couch where Heinrich lay still as a corpse. His breathing was shallow, his complexion pallid.

Golda tried to reassure her. "He has passed a quiet night with no need to summon the doctor. Moshe has gone to morning prayers and will bring Dr Feldheim back with him. He has made some plans for Heinrich's escape, but it will not be easy." She cast an inquisitive gaze at Lily's bag.

"I intend to go with him," Lily said firmly. "I cannot bear us to be parted. And I too am in great danger if I stay. My employers know of my relationship with Heinrich. I believe that Frau Müller is quite fond of me, but if they find out he is Jewish, they may feel obliged to report us to the authorities – or at the very least terminate my employment with no reference. And the elder daughter Sofia is a fanatical member of the *Bund Deutscher Mädel*. She would be proud to denounce me to her leaders."

Martin returned with the doctor. As soon as Dr Feldheim began to check his patient, Heinrich opened his eyes with a groan and tried to sit up.

"Hold on. Take it easy. We don't want you undoing all my fancy stitch work."

"You should have let Lily do it," joked Heinrich weakly. "She's a wizard with a needle and thread."

Lily's spirits rose and she gripped his hand tightly. He was able to take a few sips of tea, but refused food. He was very weak and ached all over.

"It is imperative that you keep your movements to a minimum and drink plenty of fluids," instructed Dr Feldheim as he redressed the knife wound.

Golda told them of Lily's plan to accompany Heinrich.

"If you are to be his nurse, Lily, you must endeavour to keep the wound clean and dry. I will give you iodine and some replacement dressings. I no longer have access to drugs, which he may require if he develops an infection. I wish you both the best of luck."

After the doctor took his leave, Martin laid out the escape plan.

"I have spoken to my contacts in Stettin. There is a ship captained by a man with whom I have had many dealings and who owes me a favor or two, which is sailing tomorrow to the Far East. Yes, it's a long way," said Martin as he saw Heinrich's eyebrows shoot up, "but, under the circumstances, it is your only chance of getting away from here before you are missed. I will send Erich to the station to buy two tickets on this morning's train to Stettin. You must get away before your absence at the barracks is noticed."

"I imagine my attackers won't be bragging about their misdeed, especially if they think I died from my wounds. Others will probably assume I had a successful night with the ladies and am just late in getting back. It has happened in the past," he added sheepishly, averting his eyes from Lily. "By this afternoon, however, they will start trying to track me down."

"Since you both have legitimate documents," continued Martin, "there should be no problem getting past the guards and on to the train. My driver will take you from here to the station and help Lily get you aboard. You will be met at the other end and taken to the wharf, where the ship is awaiting departure. If you make the voyage safely to its destination, the captain will help smuggle you off the ship. After that, it will be up to you."

Martin helped Heinrich wash and shave. He dressed him in one of his own suits, shirt, and shoes, which more or less fit him. Golda packed a small bag with more items of clothing and other necessities. Then it was time for them to leave.

"Moshe," said Heinrich, using his brother's Hebrew name for the first time in many, many years, "I fear for you and the family. You must get away from here while you still can. What we have seen till now is nothing compared to the dark times I foresee for the Jewish people in Germany."

"Don't worry. Some time ago I decided that my conscience no longer permits me to serve and supply the German army. I have liquidated many of my assets and am poised to leave in the next few weeks."

"Thank you for everything, Moshe. I know I haven't been a very good brother, but I love you and wish you well."

Golda gave Lily a package of sandwiches, fruit, and a flask of coffee for the journey, and Martin added an envelope full of Deutschemarks – "in case you need to bribe someone".

With tears in their eyes, the brothers bade each other farewell.

"*Eine Sichere Reise*, a safe journey. I pray God will bless us with the opportunity to meet again in better times."

CHAPTER THIRTEEN

When they reached the station, Heinrich gathered his strength to make his way to the platform where their train was almost ready to depart. He leaned heavily on Lily while the driver carried their bags. The guard eyed them suspiciously as they reached the gate.

"Papers!"

Lily handed over their documents. The guard seemed to take an inordinate amount of time inspecting them and looking Heinrich up and down. Lily sensed her pulse quickening, and she could feel Heinrich sweating under his clothes. Finally, the guard seemed satisfied and waved them through.

Heinrich was weakening and beginning to drag his feet. Lily prayed he would be able to make it up to their compartment. With only a few meters to go, she felt his legs give way and he began to stagger. Martin's driver handed her the bags, and supported Heinrich, practically carrying him up the steps into the carriage. As soon as they were seated, he wished them farewell and jumped off the train just as the guard blew his whistle and the train pulled slowly out of the station.

Once they were settled and Lily had stowed the bags on the overhead shelf, she checked Heinrich's wound. A little blood had seeped through the dressing, but it didn't appear too serious. Lily dabbed it with her handkerchief. It seemed the leakage had now stopped.

The first half of the journey was uneventful. Heinrich slept and Lily tried to relax by looking out of the window at the unfamiliar countryside. Much of the landscape was covered in thick forest, but this gradually opened out into stretches of agricultural land dotted with small holdings at first, and then, as the train pulled further away from the city, these gave way to much larger farmsteads. Lily couldn't identify the crops, but here and there she spotted horses and herds of long-horned cattle roaming in the fields. Their air of freedom gave her hope and comfort.

She must have dozed, because she was suddenly jerked awake by the braking of the train as it entered the central station at Posen. They had been travelling for over two and a half hours. Passengers began to get down from the train and there seemed to be something of a commotion on the platform. Lily was alarmed to see several police officers and soldiers interrogating those who had already disembarked, while other officers boarded the train and began to pass from compartment to compartment. There was a lot of shouting. She heard the word *"Jude"* several times and she willed herself not to panic. Through the window, she witnessed an elderly well-dressed couple being dragged out of the carriage on to the platform just a few steps away from her. Two soldiers were manhandling them while another threw their luggage out of the train.

Heinrich woke up disoriented. Lily whispered in his ear and shoved her handkerchief into his hand. The compartment door slid open and a soldier menacingly demanded to see their documents. He eyed Heinrich suspiciously. Surely news of the disappearance of an army officer could not have already circulated to all the major train stations. Was it possible that they were on the lookout for him?

"What is the purpose of your journey?" barked the soldier.

"I am taking my patient to the Hohenkrug Tuberculosis Sanatorium in Stettin," said Lily, refusing to be intimidated.

On cue, Heinrich coughed into the handkerchief, making sure their inquisitor saw the blood on it. Alarmed, the soldier threw the papers at them and backed hastily out of the door. Lily saw him gesticulating to his colleagues in the corridor, who blanched and hurried along the train to get away from them. Heinrich squeezed Lily's hand in admiration of her quick-wittedness.

The train seemed to be delayed interminably at the station and Lily's nerves were taut with anxiety. Perhaps a more suspicious soldier would summon up courage and come back to double check on the sickly passenger. Or perhaps the railway authorities would have them thrown off the train for fear of him infecting other travelers. Heinrich would not pass a physical examination and they would be caught in their lie. Lily fixed her eyes on the station clock, watching the minutes tick by.

Finally, all signs of the disturbance disappeared and the train moved off. Lily managed to persuade Heinrich to take a few bites of Golda's sandwiches and drink some coffee before he drifted off to sleep again. The journey continued for another three hours. They passed by picturesque little villages and towns, and lowland areas punctuated by a myriad of rushing rivers and silver lakes. Eventually, the open landscape became urban again and the pastoral fresh air became thick and polluted with the smoke of industry. They had reached Stettin, the first destination on their escape route.

Having rested for most of the journey, Heinrich had regained enough strength to disembark from the train unaided. Lily looked around nervously for their contact, praying that the long delay at Posen hadn't jeopardized the arrangement.

"Lily?"

She turned and was surprised to see a young woman standing behind her.

"I am Magda, a secretary at the offices of Graber and Sons here in Stettin. Let's not hang about and raise suspicions. Come with me, please."

Outside the station, Magda summoned a taxi, which drove them to the wharf.

When they arrived, she ushered them up a flight of metal stairs and into a small office.

"It's best if you wait here out of sight until dark. Keep the door locked and admit no one. When it is safe, a trusted crew member will come to get you. The ship sails after midnight."

Magda made some fresh coffee and offered to get them some food, but Lily declined. Heinrich wasn't well enough to eat and her nerves had made her stomach feel like a clenched fist. Exhausted from the effort of the journey, Heinrich had collapsed on a chair and laid his head on the desk. He fell asleep immediately. When Magda left, Lily locked the door as instructed and took the other chair. Too frightened to sleep, she kept watch over him, stroking his hair and checking his breathing every so often.

As night began to fall, Lily heard footsteps ascending the stairs. She shook Heinrich awake gently. "It's time to move again, my love," she whispered. From outside the office came the sound of muffled voices. Someone was jiggling the door handle. The beam of a flashlight swept across the frosted glass door panel, illuminating in reverse the signage Graber and Sons. The door handle rattled again, more insistently. This couldn't possibly be the person they were expecting, thought Lily. Panic enveloped her. How easy it would be to smash the glass with the flashlight and unlock the door. Instinctively, she fell silently to the floor behind the desk, dragging the half-conscious Heinrich with her. She trembled violently. Out in the corridor two men raised their voices and appeared to be arguing.

"But we do not have a permit to break into this office, Sergeant," said one.

"There is something suspicious going on here, I'm sure of it," came the reply.

"The owner is highly thought of by the Reich. We could get into a lot of trouble by investigating without the proper authority."

There were more footsteps, and a female voice.

"Can I help you, officers?" asked Magda.

"And who might you be?" the Sergeant's tone was aggressive.

"My name is Magda Becker. I am the office manager here."

"What are you doing here at such a late hour?" he persisted.

"I forgot some important papers on my desk, which I must give to the captain of one of our vessels this evening."

"Then we will come in with you and take a look around."

"Do you have a search warrant?" Magda asked. "No? I didn't think so."

"Are you denying me entry, Fraulein?"

"On the contrary," Magda replied. "I will be happy to show you around whenever you come back with authorization."

"You will regret this," he threatened.

"Not as much as you will when you are prosecuted for trespass and warrantless search. Now, please leave."

Lily could not believe how calm Magda sounded, and how courageous she was, standing up to these men. Having seen the way in which soldiers had treated passengers on their train she was sure the officer was capable of shoving Magda aside and breaking down the door. What would become of them if that happened?

"You will be hearing from us again, Fraulein. Mark my words."

When she heard the men retreat down the stairs, Lily slowly let out the breath she had been holding.

After several more minutes, Magda opened the door and reentered the office, locking it behind her. "That was close," she said. "We had better get you out of here as soon as possible.

"You were amazing. So calm and in control," said Lily.

"Well, I'm shaking now. I have never been so frightened in my life," Magda admitted.

"What made you come back?" asked Lily.

"There seemed to be more than the usual police and military activity in the vicinity of the port when I left, and I had an uneasy feeling. I decided to stay nearby and keep my eyes open for anything threatening near this part of the wharf."

"Thank goodness you did," said Lily, giving Magda a hug. "You have saved our lives."

"I am going to look around downstairs and when I'm sure it is all clear I will come back to get you."

After some time, Magda returned and led them out of the office to a secluded spot in the shadows next to one of the large warehouses.

"You will be safe here until someone comes to get you. I don't know how long it will be. The captain doesn't want to take any unnecessary chances. Stay hidden and don't move. You will be spirited on to the ship as soon as the coast is clear. Goodbye and good luck."

Lily breathed in the salty, fishy air and listened to the music of the wharf – the creak of wooden crates, the shouts of stevedores, the groan of hawsers, the trundle of wagon wheels. When it was completely dark, the human element quietened, leaving only nautical noises, the screeching of seagulls, and the lazy lapping of the waves against the quay.

After about an hour, a man materialised out of the darkness.

"I will carry Herr Graber; you bring the bags. Stay very low and completely silent, and don't stop until I tell you to."

The ship was moored two berths away. Keeping close to the warehouses within the shadows, they proceeded quickly until they were level with the gangplank, which was illuminated by the wharf lighting. Giving Lily a stevedore's cap, the man said, "Here, tuck all your hair inside this cap and listen carefully. I am going to put 'our cargo' in this wagon. You go in front and pretend to pull. I will push from behind. Keep your face hidden. The wagon should conceal your clothes and the fact that you are a woman. Let's go!"

They made their way across the wharf and up the gangplank onto the ship in safety, where the Captain was waiting for them.

"Permit me to introduce myself. I am Captain Stuart Jameson, at your service."

"But you're English. What are you doing on a German cargo ship?" said Lily in amazement.

"My crew is made up of many nationalities, including other English merchant seamen. The ship is chartered and has no nationality of its own. The crew goes wherever people are hiring. I have captained many ships for many years and my relationship with Herr Graber is longstanding. He uses me and my crew for his import business whenever possible. However, with the rumours of a brewing conflict, I fear that this happy arrangement is going to come to an end very soon. Please follow me, if you will."

Captain Jameson, supporting Heinrich, led the couple below decks.

"I'm afraid this is no luxury liner, but I can give you a cabin to yourself. It's a bit spartan. I hope you will be comfortable."

"What about Heinrich?" asked Lily.

"I prefer that he spends the first couple of nights in the infirmary under the watchful eye of the ship's doctor. His health is now my responsibility. Don't worry, he will be in good hands. The Chief Cook has prepared a healthy broth for both of you. I suggest you take some nourishment and then settle down for the night. You both need your rest."

Lily accompanied the Captain to the infirmary. When she was sure Heinrich was comfortable, she gave him a lingering kiss. Heinrich stroked her hair.

"I love you, Lily. I promise you nothing will keep us apart," he whispered. "Tomorrow I am going to ask the captain to marry us and soon we will be able to start a new life together."

Reluctant to leave him, but feeling exhaustion overcoming her, Lily allowed the captain to lead her back to her cabin. She lay down and, despite the hardness of the unfamiliar mattress, she immediately fell into a deep sleep.

CHAPTER FOURTEEN

Lily awoke to the rhythmic chant of the ship's engines. How long had it been since they had set sail? She had been so tired she must have slept for hours and hours. Her rumbling stomach suggested just that. Looking out of the small porthole window, it was hard to discern whether it was still dark out or daylight, since the ship appeared to be cocooned in a blanket of thick fog. She made out the mournful moan of a distant fog horn and gave an involuntary shiver. Climbing down from her bunk, she stood up, slowly trying to adjust to the motion of the ship and get her sea legs. She had never been at sea and hoped that she wouldn't suffer sickness. She needed all her strength for Heinrich. She hurried to get dressed so that she could go and check on him.

Lily smiled as she remembered his parting words last night. Today she would become Mrs Graber. Although it would be nothing like the wedding day of her dreams, she allowed her imagination to wander and conjure up the scene. She and Heinrich would be up on the top deck. The sun would be shining down on them and sea birds would lend a happy chorus to the proceedings. Captain Jameson would wear his official uniform and the crew would cheer when they exchanged their vows.

Ich nehme Dich, Lily, zu meiner Gattin. I take you Lily, to be my wife.

Since neither she nor Heinrich had living parents, their physical presence would not be missed, but perhaps they would be watching from above. She was saddened that her mother had not lived to see her settled, even under these most unusual circumstances. Not unusual, unique, she corrected herself, and truly romantic. Heinrich's brother Martin would not approve of the match, of course, nor of the absence of a rabbi to conduct the ceremony, but he and Golda had witnessed their devotion to each other, and Lily hoped that Heinrich's happiness was important to them and would not destroy their newly rediscovered relationship.

Part of her dream had been to design and sew her own wedding gown. *Elegant* magazine had run a feature on Hollywood bridal glamour and the innovative figure-hugging bias-cut dresses of French designer Madame Vionnet. Inspired by these fashion trends, Lily had sketched her own dream dress: ivory satin cut on the bias to produce a long and fluid silhouette; a dropped waist bodice with bateau neckline edged in narrow delicate lace; and long sleeves narrowing towards the cuffs edged in matching lace. A Juliet veil and a posy of sweet-smelling lily-of-the-valley completed the picture. She closed her eyes and imagined herself standing before Heinrich in her creation. But it was not to be. She had packed one of Frau Müller's smart outfits which she had remodeled, and that would have to be her trousseau. Her treasured lily-of-the-valley brooch would add the finishing touch. There was no mirror in the cabin, but she was sure that Heinrich wouldn't be disappointed. She couldn't wait to see him.

As she opened the cabin door, she felt a resounding bump followed by a sudden lurch which flung her backwards into the room. Regaining her balance, she listened for noises in the eerie silence, aware of a change in the engine's rhythm. The silence was rudely broken by the shrill rings of the ship's siren and the clatter of running feet. Trembling with fright, Lily pushed her way out of the cabin.

Last night's exhaustion had made her disorientated and she had not paid attention to the layout of the ship. Which way to the infirmary? The passageway was barely illuminated. She felt her way along and reached a staircase. She could hear shouting coming from the deck above. As she placed her foot on the first step, the ship lurched again, the door at the top of the staircase burst open, and she was drenched by a waterfall of bone-chilling seawater, which made her gasp and gag, and tossed her backwards.

She began to claw her way back to the staircase, screaming for help. It took every ounce of her strength to reach the top step, but then the ship listed even further to the side. Flailing helplessly, she was saved from falling by the captain's strong arms.

There was pandemonium on deck.

"Captain Jameson, what's happening?"

"A freak storm pushed us off course. We have rammed into some rocks. Didn't see them in this darned pea souper fog. Gouged a huge hole in our side. We have to abandon ship. Put on this life jacket and get into the lifeboat."

Lily had no idea what a pea souper was, never having experienced any form of fog, let alone such a thick one. The air had an unfamiliar unpleasant metallic smell and she could barely see further than the captain's face.

"Let me go. I won't leave without Heinrich," she shouted trying to make herself heard over the deafening noise of the siren and the clamor made by the crew.

"I am going back for him. It's imperative that you get into the lifeboat and away from here before the ship starts to go under and sucks everything down with it. We have transmitted mayday messages and help is on its way."

Lily struggled against him. "No, I won't go without him. You can't make me."

"I'm afraid I can. Take this in case we are separated." He shoved a leather pouch into her hand. "We are not too far from the British coast. Our rescuers will come from there. I expect you have no contacts in England. My sister's address is on the letter inside this pouch. Take it to her. She will help you until I arrive with Heinrich. I promise I won't let you down."

With that, he picked her up and deposited her in the lifeboat as it was being lowered into the water.

Lily began to whimper like an injured animal as they rowed away, her teeth chattering in the freezing air. A sailor threw a blanket around her shoulders, but it was no comfort. How would Heinrich survive in these conditions? Hadn't the doctor specifically told her to keep the wound dry? Surely he was too weak to withstand the icy conditions. One of the crew held up a large flashlight and was scanning the area in the hope of being spotted by a rescue boat. It cast a ghostly haloed light. Here and there, she saw flotsam and jetsam in the water, litter from the floundering ship. Horrified, she realised that there were also men in life jackets bobbing up and down. Some were hoisted into the lifeboat. Others were not so lucky. One man with a gash in his head floated past her and drifted lifelessly away.

"Where is the Captain?" she screamed.

"He will be the last one to leave the ship, lady. He will make sure everyone else is safe first. But don't you worry; the captain is a resourceful man. You'd be wise to stop your screaming now and save your energy."

"Heinrich!" she sobbed. "Where are you?"

Her only answer was the lapping of the waves against the lifeboat and the distant death throes of the sinking ship.

Captain Jameson fought his way down to the infirmary. The door was jammed shut, probably obstructed by a heavy metal cabinet or dislodged bed. The water level was rising rapidly. He would have to act fast. He ran back along the passageway until he found the metal container screwed to the wall. Pulling it open, he grabbed the crowbar which was kept there for emergencies. The infirmary door was stubborn as a mule, refusing to budge, and Jameson was weakening with every attempt to prize it open. Then the ship changed angle once again and the obstruction fell away. Jameson pushed his way inside. Heinrich was not in his bed and was nowhere to be seen. Perhaps the doctor had managed to get him to a lifeboat. As he turned to leave the infirmary, he caught sight of a body wedged in a corner pinned under some equipment. As he reached it, the ship heaved once more and freezing water flooded the room. The door slammed shut as the vessel plunged to its final resting place on the seabed.

CHAPTER FIFTEEN

Lily was sick from fear and the rocking of the boat. How much longer till someone found them? She could feel hypothermia overcoming her body. *I must stay alert and in control*, she willed herself, *for Heinrich's sake*. She had never been religious, but she prayed to God that the captain would keep his promise, silently repeating over and over the Hebrew name Martin had used for his brother – *Chaim* ... Life.

She was brought out of her trance by the sound of distant shouting and a motor engine. The weak beam of a searchlight illuminated the lifeboat momentarily. One of the sailors launched a flare, which lit up the sky and reminded Lily of New Year's Eve, precipitating another bout of tears. She fingered her brooch. Thank goodness she had decided to wear it. Her only keepsake from Heinrich.

A boat emerged out of the fog. Lily could just make out the letters "RNLI" and a white flag with a red cross painted on the bow. It drew alongside and a hefty rope was thrown over, neatly caught by the sailor next to her. The rescue team pulled the rope taut and they held the two vessels together. A large man in yellow oilskins and thigh-high boots leaned across with outstretched arms. "Over you come, lads, one at a time." Raising an eyebrow in surprise at the sight of Lily, he corrected himself. "Sorry, lads, ladies first."

In a rather ungainly manner, being shoved from behind by one of the crew and hauled across by her rescuer, Lily found herself on the deck and smothered in warm blankets.

When all the crew had come aboard, the rope was released and the rescue boat sped back towards the coast and the safety of the coastguard station.

So it was true what people said about the British and their tea, mused Lily. No sooner was she inside the coastguard station than she was being plied with cups of tea. It was thick and dark with far too much sugar, although somehow the sweetness didn't take the edge off the bitter taste of the brew.

"Drink up, dearie. It's for the shock and to take the chill off you," said a round-faced man in a chunky dark grey fisherman's sweater and matching knitted hat.

She clutched the tin mug to warm her hands and obliged him by taking a few sips, trying as best she could to hide her grimaces.

The crew members were being questioned by the coastguard for details of the ship, its ports of departure and destination, and the circumstances of the accident. Lily couldn't understand all of it, but when he turned to look at her inquisitively, she realised he wanted to know what a woman was doing on a merchant ship. They shook their heads or shrugged their shoulders. The escape had been a private arrangement between Martin and Captain Jameson, with Magda as the go-between, and the crew must have been ignorant of her and Heinrich's presence on board.

The coastguard approached her.

"Do you speak English, Miss?"

"A little."

"What were you doing on the ship?"

Lily thought carefully before she answered. What would be the best explanation that would cause her the least trouble?

"Refugee." She began to sob. "Is there news of Captain Jameson and my fiancé? Have they been rescued?"

The coastguard sat beside her and took her hand. "Fiancé, you say? I'm sorry, but we haven't picked up any other survivors, and no other boats in the area responded to the Mayday call. The captain probably went down with his ship. Anyone not here is missing presumed drowned. No one would have survived long in the freezing water. I am very sorry, Miss." He turned to the tea man. "Fred, could you see your way to taking this young lady home? I'm sure your missus won't mind giving her a hot bath and a change of clothes. I'll come by in the morning after I've made some inquiries about procedures in this type of case."

"Aye, aye, Sir," said Fred, giving a comical salute.

Lily felt too wretched to protest. She needed time to digest all that had happened and a friendly female face would be welcome.

"Come on, dearie. Can you walk? It's not far. You can lean on me."

Fred's wife fussed over her like a mother hen. After a hot bath and a plate of soup, Lily found herself snuggled up in bed in a flannel nightdress under a cozy eiderdown, but despite her exhaustion, sleep eluded her. What had happened to Heinrich? Had the Captain reached him in time? Could the coastguard be wrong about other survivors? With these and more unanswered questions buzzing in her head, Lily finally succumbed to her overwhelming tiredness.

Next morning, she awoke confused and unsure of her surroundings. She heard the squawking of seagulls and the distant chatter of English voices. Although she had slept deeply, she felt drained and unrefreshed, and she was wracked by uncontrollable tears as she recalled the events of the day before. A light knock on her bedroom door brought her back to the present. The kindly Mrs Fred poked her head around the door.

"Morning, Miss. Did you sleep well? How are you feeling, luv?"

"Fine, thank you," Lily replied, wiping her eyes and trying to put on a brave face.

"Will you come downstairs for some breakfast and, if you are up to it, a chat with our coastguard? You can put these on for now," Mrs Fred said, pointing to a pile of clothes at the end of the bed.

"Please give me a few moments," said Lily.

Her hostess had a completely different build and the clothes hung unflatteringly on Lily, but she folded and tucked here and there and succeeded in making herself look halfway presentable. Downstairs, she discerned the muffled voices of the coastguard and her hosts.

"I reckon by her accent that she's German, which was where the ship departed from."

"What do you think, Doris?" Fred asked his wife.

"Poor thing. Must be one of them wretched Jews we keep hearing about. Nasty business. She's definitely posh, though," observed Doris. "Her clothes were in a bit of a state, but even I can tell that her outfit is top quality, and that brooch is not off a market stall, I'll bet."

"She said something about traveling together with her fiancé. But we didn't pick him up, and as far as I know there weren't any other rescue boats in the area."

They stopped talking as Lily walked into the kitchen.

"Come and sit down, luv, and have a nice cuppa," offered Doris.

"Coffee?" Lily inquired hopefully.

"Sorry, luvvie. We only do tea."

After she had managed to stomach another cup of the strong overly sweetened brown liquid and eaten a slice of toast slathered with butter and homemade jam, Lily asked, "What will happen to me?"

The coastguard had been in touch with the authorities. "They will have to discuss your case and see if you are entitled to asylum here or if you must be returned home. Do you have any relatives in England or someone who can vouch for you? You will have a better chance of staying if you do."

"I have a contact," said Lily, producing the letter from the leather pouch Captain Jameson had thrust into her hand, and which she had clung to during her ordeal. Her only hope was to reach the captain's sister, otherwise how would she find Heinrich?

"Well, that could be useful," said the coastguard. "I'll see if we can get in touch with Mrs Cooper and find out if she will take responsibility for you."

Then he and Fred headed back to the coastguard station.

Lily sat at the kitchen table, her shoulders slumped, tears burning her tired eyes.

"Let's you and me take a walk into town," offered Doris, "and see if we can't find you something more suitable to wear. Margate is a lovely seaside resort, although it's a bit off season now, so not so many visitors about."

They walked in the direction of the seafront. As they turned into The Parade, Lily caught sight of the water and immediately began to feel shaky. She held onto Doris for support, hoping she was not about to faint.

"Get back up on the horse, luv," said Doris encouragingly. "That's the only thing to do."

Lily wasn't quite sure what she meant, but she straightened up and tried to pull herself together.

"That's it. Only way to conquer your fear is to look it straight in the eye, as my Fred would tell you."

The previous day's fog had cleared, and although the sky was mostly cloudy, the sun peeked through from time to time, casting a sparkle on the water. A number of small boats bobbed up and down in the harbour, while a couple of much larger ones were moored alongside the pier. They continued on into Marine Drive and Lily was surprised to see quite a lot of people on the beach despite the cool weather.

"That's nothing. In the height of the summer you can't make out a grain of sand for the crowds on the beach. Holidaymakers have been coming here for over two hundred years. It's under three hours by train from London, so many visitors come just for a day out. But mostly they come to stay for a few days, as you'll see by the number of hotels and guest houses. That hotel over there, the Metropole, is one of the more fashionable establishments."

"You have a Metropole? Where I come from we also have a Metropole. The last time I saw it, Adolf Hitler was standing on a balcony making an impassioned speech to a huge crowd of spectators. He was screaming and shaking his fist and everyone was clapping or shouting *Heil Hitler*. It was frightening. I think the man is mad and I think he means war."

"Well," said Doris, "our Prime Minister Neville Chamberlain thinks he can keep us out of it. He's just come back from meeting Hitler in Munich, telling the country that he has made peace in our time."

Lily was about to tell Doris about Heinrich being in the military and fearing the worst, but she decided it would be wiser to keep her own counsel. The less they knew about her, the better.

They strolled through the ornamental gardens into the High Street until they reached the frontage of a large department store.

"This is Bobby's," said Doris. "I'm sure we can fit you out here with some suitable clothes."

"But I don't have any money," protested Lily.

"I will be your Good Samaritan today and you will pay me back when you get settled."

Lily squeezed Doris's hand in gratitude, too overwhelmed with emotion to speak. How warm and accepting these people were, nothing like the reputation the British had for being cold and unwelcoming. She agreed to accept only the most basic necessities and simple items. She didn't want Doris to spend too much money, firstly because she had seen how modestly they lived, and secondly because she didn't want to have too large a debt to repay. Who knew when she would be able to earn some money?

CHAPTER SIXTEEN

It had been three days and still there was no word from Captain Jameson's sister. As each day passed, Lily became more and more anxious, and the uncertainty of her future weighed heavily on her mind. As the hours and then days went by, Lily increasingly despaired of ever seeing her dearest love again. She repeated his name over and over like a mantra, Chaim, Life, Chaim, Life, praying for God or the Fates to save him. Even if he survived the wreck, she knew he was very weak and that his wound was in danger of becoming infected and fatal.

On the fourth day, the coastguard reaffirmed that no other boats had reported picking up survivors or casualties from the sinking ship and her faith in being reunited with Heinrich was beginning to falter. But she willed herself not give up hope. What was there to live for without Heinrich? She had to believe he would be found.

Doris seemed quite comfortable having another female presence in the house, but Lily didn't want to be treated as a guest and offered to help out whenever she could. Nevertheless, the hours passed slowly with very little to occupy her or distract her from her morbid ruminations.

"It's a lovely day today, Lily. Why don't you go out and explore the town? There's lots to see and a breath of fresh sea air will do you good," suggested Doris.

Lily felt that this was an order rather than a suggestion and, not wishing to offend her hostess, she reluctantly agreed, even though she felt she'd had enough sea air to last her a lifetime.

Since she had never been to the seaside in Germany, Lily had no idea what to expect and she was fascinated by the town's unfamiliar out-of-the-ordinary environment. She decided to walk along the pier, a long walkway on stilts which reached out into the sea and boasted amusements and entertainment in the pavilion at the far end. At the start of the walkway located opposite the Metropole Hotel stood several shops selling ice creams, sweets, beach items, and souvenirs. Lily was drawn to a stand of postcards, and was taken aback to see that, in addition to panoramic photographs of Margate, there was a large choice of rather rude ones featuring cartoons of holidaymakers, particularly women with large exposed breasts and bottoms. Although she didn't fully comprehend the wordplay on the cards, she had a pretty good idea of their meaning and understood that they were meant to be humourous. These were so very different from the venom-spewing cartoons depicting Jews as pigs and monkeys that were circulating all over Breslau. How amazing, she thought, that one type of art could be used for such different purposes.

While she was looking at them, the shopkeeper came outside.

"Can I help you, Miss?"

Lily blushed scarlet with embarrassment at being caught looking at the smutty postcards. She quickly pointed to a bucket containing what looked like pink magician's wands. "What are these for?"

"That's rock, Miss. Never seen it before, then?"

She shook her head.

"It's a sweet made of sugar. Look. The middle is white with the word *MARGATE* embedded on it in red letters. As you suck the rock *MARGATE* remains legible all the way through it to the very end. It's one of the most popular seaside souvenirs."

Lily started to move on, but the thought of the long walk to the end of the pier over the waves below made her feel threatened and shaky. She hadn't recovered from the horror of the shipwreck and despite Doris's words of wisdom about facing her fear, she decided to turn her back on the sea and explore the centre of town instead. Turning into Duke Street, she found herself in Old Town, a maze of narrow cobbled streets lined with quaint houses built from small uneven bricks or lumpy stone, giving the neighbourhood a medieval feel. She smiled as she imagined flinty fisherman and seasoned seafarers filling the pubs with the smoke from their briar pipes and swigging tankards of rum, singing sea shanties and entertaining one another with tall tales of their adventures. There certainly didn't appear to be a shortage of pubs. She passed some small shops selling fishing tackle and boating equipment, a hardware store, and a pharmacy.

As she walked on, Lily had to admit that Doris was right. It was good to be out in the fresh air. After about another ten minutes, she came to a lovely ornamental park. There were several elderly people occupying wrought-iron benches at the edge of the manicured grass, and some young mothers with small children and infants were enjoying the open space. A few people were walking their dogs. The scene reminded Lily of Breslau and her excursions with the Müller children. It seemed like years had passed since those innocent afternoons, rather than just a few days. Lily sat down on an unoccupied bench next to a pretty fountain surrounded by colourful flowerbeds. What was she going to do? What would happen to her if the captain's sister couldn't be found or refused to help? She forced back her tears, not wanting to make a public spectacle of herself. She would have to find a job. Perhaps Doris and Fred would let her stay on in their house a little longer if she could somehow pay them for the room. She had passed a number of hotels and guesthouses where she might be able to work and there were shops and restaurants that might need staff, but as Doris had pointed out, this was the off-season and most of the establishments were probably letting go rather than hiring employees. She would have to find something. There was no going back.

Downhearted, Lily began to retrace her steps. After a few minutes, a sign advertising the Shell Grotto caught her eye and aroused her curiosity, and she decided to take a look. The minute she entered the underground cavern, she was enchanted. The entire surface of the walls and ceiling was covered in exquisite mosaics created from thousands upon thousands of different shells. The ornate subterranean serpentine passageway was decorated with intricate patterns depicting flowers, trees, stars, and more. It snaked its way under archways and around corners until it reached a rectangular room crowned, cathedral-like, by a tall shell-encrusted circular dome. Rays of light specked with motes of dust shone down through an opening at the top of the dome, magically illuminating the lustrous artwork. Lily marveled at the beauty of the astonishing grotto, amazed by the handiwork and the effort it must have taken to create it. She took a deep breath, feeling spiritually uplifted for the first time in days.

Emerging back out into the open air, Lily felt re-energized and ready to meet her challenges. She had been at rock bottom once before when her darling Heinrich had come to her rescue. This time she was alone, but she would not let him down. She would make a new life for herself once again, and hopefully in time the pain of her lost love would become bearable.

When she got back to the cottage, it seemed that Doris had guests.

Lily entered shyly. "Excuse me. I don't mean to interrupt," she said, making her way to the stairs.

"Come back, luv. There's someone here for you to meet. This is Sally, your Captain's sister."

Lily thought she might faint with gratitude as she extended her hand towards the young woman who bore little resemblance to her brother. She was slim and attractive, with blonde curls and blue eyes. Lily guessed she was in her early forties. Sally ignored the outstretched hand and enveloped Lily in a hug, which triggered a fresh bout of tears.

"I'll leave you two to get acquainted," said Doris, picking up her shopping bag and heading out. "I'm sure you have lots to discuss."

"I understand that you have a letter for me from my brother,"

Sally began, her eyes brimming with tears, her bottom lip trembling slightly, "which can mean only one thing."

Lily rushed upstairs to her room, returning with the leather pouch. Sally held it tightly to her breast for a few moments, breathing in the lingering odour of sea and salt, and then slowly withdrew the letter as if delaying the inevitable.

Dear Sis,
Old habits are hard to break so I have prepared this letter "just in case", an instruction us Royal Navy sailors were given whenever we set off, as you well know. You have received this sort of letter once before and I am truly sorry to put you through it again and cause you the pain of losing your brother as well as your husband. This time it is not in the service of King and country, although I fear another war is brewing.
I have made this voyage many times, carrying goods from Europe to the Far East and back again, and I do not anticipate any problems, but you never know.
Before this voyage, I received an urgent request for help from a longtime business associate and friend. I have taken on board two fugitives. I do not know the full details of their story, but my friend would not have asked me to do this if it weren't imperative to get them out of Germany. If they reach you with this letter, please give them any assistance you can. If all goes smoothly, I will be depositing them safely at our destination in Shanghai and will be seeing you myself as soon as I can, but if not ...
Everything I own, which isn't much, I leave to you and the children.

Love you always,
Stu

Sally gave up trying to control her tears, and passed Lily the letter to read.

"But the Captain promised me he would save my Heinrich and bring him to your house," insisted Lily once she had read the letter.

"If I am reading this letter, then it means neither Stu nor your man will be coming home."

Lily sat down heavily, cradling her head in her hands. When Sally had regained her composure she continued, "My late father served in the Royal Navy and Stu followed his example. Dad was invalided out during the Great War. Stu didn't see active duty until the war was nearly over. He was one of the lucky ones. My late husband, Rob, knew Stu from school, although he was three years younger. Stu was the sort children looked up to and tried to emulate. Rob was too young to serve in the war, but when the hostilities were over, he signed on as a merchant seaman, following in Stu's footsteps. It was Stu who introduced us. We were married a couple of years later and life was good, although Rob spent a lot of time away from home. One day, when our son was three and our baby girl just a few months old, there was a freak accident; his ship hit and detonated an unexploded mine. I received the farewell letter he had been instructed to prepare 'just in case'. The situation on your ship must have been pretty bad if Stu made sure to give you this letter for me. I'm so sorry."

They sat in silence for a while.

"Would you like to tell me your story, Lily?"

Lily carefully chose the parts of her story she thought she should tell Sally, leaving out how she had met Heinrich and the near-rape. She described the perfect officer and gentleman she had fallen in love with and how amazed she had been that he had felt the same way about her. She told Sally about her job with the Müller family and how painful it was for her to leave the children. She tried to describe the threatening atmosphere which had overtaken Breslau and the terrible things that were happening to the city's Jews. Finally, she described the night Heinrich was attacked and their flight from Germany.

"His fellow officers discovered he was Jewish and that he was romantically involved with a gentile – something forbidden under Hitler's Nuremberg Laws. They call such couples *Mischlinge* – the name given to mongrel dogs. Until that night, I had no idea he was Jewish, not that it would have made any difference to me. Our escape was arranged by Heinrich's brother, the owner of an important import business who knows – knew – your brother well. All I know about the accident is that there was thick fog and the ship hit something. Your brother threw me into a lifeboat and went back for Heinrich. I didn't see either of them again." When Lily finished, she gave a deep sigh. "I don't know what I am going to do now."

"You are going to come home with me, Lily. Stu's instructions were for me to help you and that's what I intend to do."

CHAPTER SEVENTEEN

Heinrich could no longer feel his legs and didn't know how much longer his arms would have the strength to grip his makeshift raft. What had happened while he'd slept in the infirmary? He had been roused from a deep sleep by the sound of the siren, uncertain of where he was. He slid off his bed, but the floor moved violently under his feet making him stagger. Grabbing a life jacket which lay by the door, he weaved his way drunkenly out of the infirmary. Where was Lily? He had no idea where the cabins were situated. Surely the Captain would have made sure she was safe? He called her name, but his weak voice was drowned out by the wailing of the siren. The boat pitched and threw him against a wall, sending a shaft of searing pain through his body. He knew he had to get out, but where was the way up? He felt a blast of salty air and crawled towards its origin. Desperate to rest, he willed himself to keep going. With a last-ditch effort, he pulled himself out onto the deck where he lay exhausted. He couldn't see anything through the thick fog and all sound was muffled. The ship swayed again, shooting him helplessly along the deck and over the edge into the water. The impact took his breath away. He floundered about in the icy water until a large plank of wood floated towards him. With his last ounce of energy, he pulled himself onto it.

While he drifted in and out of consciousness, his thoughts turned to Lily. What had he been thinking allowing her to come with him on this futile journey? He should have persuaded her to leave Germany and make her way to France or Belgium. No one would have looked for her there. If he had managed to reach the Far East, he could have sent for her. He should have put up more of a fight, but he had been too weak to argue with the plan which Martin had contrived, or to dissuade Lily. Now they were both doomed. He was so very cold. What was the point of surviving without Lily? And, if he did survive, how would he ever be able to live with her death on his conscience? His last thought before he passed out for the final time was reuniting with Lily beyond the grave.

"There you go, laddie. Welcoom back. Deep breaths noo."

The intake of air assaulted Heinrich's nostrils with an overpowering stink of fish. He leaned sideways and retched painfully. He couldn't remember when he had last had food in his stomach and the combination of seawater and bile burned his throat and mouth. He tried to sit up, but his body refused to comply. He appeared to be weighed down by a mound of blankets and tarpaulin. Looking to his left, he came face to face with nets filled with flapping fish, gasping for air almost as desperately as himself. The glassy eyes of those already dead stared back at him. He turned to his right in the direction of the voice which had greeted him and discovered that it belonged to a leathery fisherman. For a moment Heinrich was gripped by a ridiculous thought: Could this be the River Styx ferryman transporting him to the Otherworld? No, he wasn't dead, and by some miracle he had been rescued from the icy water. He studied his savior more carefully. The fisherman's rough and weathered face was deeply lined, a testament to a life at the mercy of the elements, and his hands were calloused and scarred. Heinrich thought that he was probably younger than he looked, although his beard was almost white. Fragrant smoke curled upwards from his pipe but did nothing to alleviate the smell of the fish. His bright blue eyes were friendly and had a sparkle to them inviting trust and friendship.

"Get a wee sup of this doun yer thrapple. It'll help stop yer chitterin'," the fisherman ordered, lifting Heinrich's head and tipping something very alcoholic into his mouth. The fiery liquid made Heinrich cough and choke, but slowly he managed a few sips and felt it warming his body as it reached his stomach.

"I thought ye were deid, sure ah did," said the fisherman. "Ye look well knackered. Nae to wirrie, we'll soon have ye on dry land and oot of them slevvery claes."

Heinrich couldn't understand a word, although it sounded friendly. He had no idea where he was being taken, but the language certainly wasn't German so he wasn't being repatriated for the time being. His rescuer began to sing a shanty which reminded Heinrich of the lullabies his mother used to sing to him and he drifted into sleep.

Having been warmed and bathed and offered another swig of alcohol Heinrich was put to bed. He slept for thirty-six hours, often fitfully thrashing and moaning much to the alarm of the fisherman and his wife. When he finally awoke, he was disorientated, unable to identify the room or the sounds around him. He tried to get up with no success. He couldn't make his body do his bidding and his wound was throbbing painfully.

He called out and after several moments, a round, grey-haired woman poked her head around the door. She smiled, and called over her shoulder, "He's woken up, McFee."

The fisherman entered the room.

"Well noo, laddie, you'se feelin' better?"

Heinrich guessed what was being asked and nodded his head.

"Dis ye have a name?"

"Heinrich Graber."

"German, eh?"

"Yes."

"A'm Alasdair McFee. Ye can call me McFee. Awbody daes. Dis ye speak English?"

"Yes. Do you?" asked Heinrich in all seriousness.

McFee gave a huge guffaw, not in the least offended, and switched from his Scottish vernacular to a more formal version of English to which Heinrich was better accustomed: "When I was cleaning you up last night I noticed a nasty wound in your side. Stabbed, were ye?"

"Yes."

"I've asked the doctor to come in and have a wee look at ye."

"Thank you," said Heinrich. He decided he was not going to offer any more information than was absolutely necessary until he had appraised his situation and the danger he may be in. The short conversation had left him surprisingly weak and he lay back on his pillows.

McFee left him to rest and a little later his wife waddled into the room holding a tray. Heinrich was starving after three days without proper food, and the smell of the freshly scrambled eggs and thick buttered toast made his mouth water and his stomach gurgle. He summoned the strength to sit up, and wolfed down everything on the plate, much to Mrs McFee's delight.

As she was taking the tray away, Heinrich asked, "Where am I? Is my fiancée here, too?"

"Lowestoft, on the coast of East Anglia. It's a fishing town. There's no woman here with you."

"You speak a different English to your husband. I can understand you."

"I'm what my husband would call a Sassenach. English, from south of the border. He is Scottish. McFee came down from Scotland with his father and brothers every year for the herring fishing season. We met by chance one summer and fell in love. His family weren't pleased that he chose a Sassenach for a wife, I can tell you."

My story's not so different, thought Heinrich, *since I, a Jew chose a gentile woman to the displeasure not only of my family but also of the State.*

"You get your rest now," Mrs McFee said. "The doctor will be along by and by to check on you."

Heinrich dozed again. When he awoke he could just make out muffled voices outside his bedroom door.

"What do you know about him, McFee?" asked Dr Finlay.

"Nothing, except he's German."

"What about other survivors?"

"I didna find any. Ma radio's bin shot for a few days so I didna pick up any Mayday calls. I have noo idea how he ended up in the water or what ship, if any, he came from. It was a miracle he got tangled up in one of ma nets. I would nivver have spotted him in the fog."

Heinrich wondered how much information he should give them. Obviously he wouldn't mention his military career or the exact circumstances of his flight from Germany.

McFee came in with a man carrying a black bag.

"Heinrich, this is Dr Finlay. He'd like to take a look at ye."

"Thanks, McFee, you can leave us to it," said the doctor as he lowered the covers and began to examine his patient. "This wound looks nasty. When did you get it?"

"A few days ago," said Heinrich, wincing as the doctor prodded at it.

"Looks infected, I'm afraid, but not too serious. This will sting a bit," the doctor said as he poured iodine on the open, raw skin. "I think I'll leave the stitches be for now. They were obviously done by a professional and should do the job." As he put on a fresh dressing, he asked Heinrich how it had happened.

"I was attacked by some Nazi thugs. I fought back and injured one of them before I managed to get away. I don't suppose you know much about the situation of Jews in Germany under Hitler."

"You're wrong there. We have heard some of the terrible stories, and you aren't the first refugee to cross the shores of England seeking safety. But how did you manage to get away?"

"Well, it wasn't safe for me to stay there. My brother has contacts with a shipping company and managed to get me on a boat to Shanghai. I was smuggled on with my fiancée, Lily, at night, barely conscious, so I have no details of the ship's name. I was put in the infirmary while Lily was taken to a cabin. I don't know what happened, but I suddenly found myself falling off the deck and into the water. Please, Doctor, can you tell me if they have managed to locate Lily yet?"

Dr Finlay chose to ignore the question and concentrated on listening to Heinrich's chest. "I'm not too happy with your lungs and I can't rule out pneumonia. But you seem a fairly fit specimen, so I hope with a lot of rest and good nourishment you will be able to fight it off. That's it for now. I'll call back in a couple of days to see how you're doing."

"Thank you, Doctor. I appreciate your help."

Before leaving, the doctor repeated Heinrich's story to the McFees.

"Ah racken he fell off the ship and naebodie noticed. If, as he says, he was a stowaway, the crew wouldna have known he was on board so he wouldna be missed. The Captain certainly wouldna turn back to look for him, as he wasna supposed to exist in the first place," McFee concluded.

"His clothes were in a bit of a state, but I could tell they were good quality," said Mrs McFee. "A smart suit and leather shoes. He certainly seems to be a gentleman."

"Just another one of those Jewish refugees we've seen on the Pathé News."

"Are you up to looking after him for the time being?" said Dr Finlay. "He's in no state to move at the moment."

"We're happy to help, Doctor," McFee assured him. "Nivver bin one to turn away a stranger in need."

A little later, Mrs McFee took Heinrich a cup of tea and some biscuits. "Has there been any news of other survivors?" Heinrich asked her, trying to sound composed, but unable to disguise the anguish etched on his face.

Mrs McFee stroked his hand gently. "I'm afraid it seems that there weren't any. I found this in your pocket. I've dried it out and it's a bit worse for wear, but I expect you'll be wanting to hang on to it."

She was shocked when Heinrich started to keen and wail as he looked down at the photograph of Lily. She held him to her ample breast and cradled him like a baby until his sobbing subsided.

"There, there, now. I'm so sorry ... I didn't mean to upset you so. She's a beautiful girl."

"The love of my life. Lost to me now," he choked.

CHAPTER EIGHTEEN

Having heard Lily's version of her forbidden love affair and escape from Germany, Sally decided on a plan which she hoped would ensure her safety.

"It seems that war with Germany is inevitable. In the last war, 'British' Germans were rounded up as enemy aliens and sent to detention camps. I'm sure it will happen again, so you can't be German. I will say you are from Switzerland, a distant cousin on my mother's side, and you've come to stay with me to improve your English."

When Sally had brought Lily "home" after a circuitous route on several trains, Lily had been immediately enchanted by The Waves Guesthouse, a boarding house run by Sally in Bournemouth not too far from the town centre.

The three-story guesthouse stood at the end of a row of Victorian terrace houses. Standing sentinel on both sides of the front door were two splendid pinkish-blue hydrangea bushes. Below the pretty stained-glass window imbedded in the front door, a *Welcome* sign invited guests over the threshold.

"You are really welcome," said Sally, putting an arm around Lily's shoulders as they entered the house.

"Mum, is that you?" Two sets of feet came bounding down the stairs and two sets of arms flung themselves around Sally.

"Lily, I would like you to meet Rob Junior and Gracie. Children, this is Lily who has come to live with us."

Rob's jaw dropped as he looked at Lily and he blushed scarlet. "Pleased to meet you, Miss," he mumbled and shifted nervously from one foot to the other. "Got lots of homework," he added, and quickly retreated back upstairs to the safety of his bedroom.

Sally chuckled. "Fourteen's an awkward age, but I'm sure Gracie, who's twelve, will be happy to show you around. Gracie, we will give Lily the blue room in the attic."

Gracie grabbed Lily by the hand, seemingly chuffed that she had been given the honour of welcoming the new guest, and said, "Let's go."

The first room on the ground floor, Gracie called "the sitting room". On one wall, a set of bookshelves displayed an eclectic choice of titles, both fiction and non-fiction. There were a number of classics, Dickens, Austen, Brontë, side by side with a collection of Mills and Boon romances, and a few well-worn Beatrice Potter children's tales sitting next to some local guide books. On the opposite side of the room, a mantelpiece above the cast-iron fireplace exhibited framed family photographs and a collection of cheap knickknacks. The fireplace itself was decorated with pretty floral tiles which matched those on the hearth in front of it. To one side, stood a coal bucket and a wrought-iron stand from which hung a poker, a shovel, brush, and tongs. The wooden floor was polished to a shine, but much of it was covered by a rather drab brown carpet which, for Lily, diminished the room's charm.

The dining room was an altogether much brighter space with a large bay window looking out onto the back garden which was surprisingly large and carefully tended. Boarders could enjoy the view while they took their breakfast at one of the four tables arranged strategically around the room.

"Everyone gets a full breakfast for free but tea is extra," Gracie proudly showed off her catering knowledge.

Lily wondered why Sally would charge extra money for a cup of tea. Only later would she understand that "tea" was what they called supper and was actually a proper meal.

There was a hatch built in to the wall shared with the kitchen from which plates of food were distributed, shortening the distance from cook to diner, thereby preserving the food's heat, Gracie explained. Breakfast was served early so that the children could help before they left for school.

Sally's kitchen was small but efficient. It was quite obviously her domain, and although the food she prepared was standard fare, it was tasty and plentiful, Gracie told Lily. Sally, Gracie said, took pride in making her guesthouse a home away from home.

The house was far more spacious than it had appeared from the outside. The first floor boasted four bedrooms and a shared bathroom. Sally and the children occupied the two larger ones and the boarders the two small ones. A second set of narrow stairs led up to the top floor which Sally called "the attic", divided into two small rooms under the eaves. The furnishings were basic and the décor simple, but the house had what Lily could only describe as a homely atmosphere.

Lily sat down on what was to be her bed, and she couldn't help but recall her arrival at the Müllers' apartment. While this accommodation was not prettily decorated, it reminded her nonetheless of the room she had left behind. After all she had been through, she marveled that once again she had been taken in to a stranger's home and made welcome. She had very little to "unpack" so, rather than dwell on unhappy thoughts, she made her way back downstairs to the kitchen.

Sally had put the kettle on. "Cup of tea, Lily?"

"Do you by any chance have coffee? The only beverage in Margate seems to be thick brown tea. I tried to get used to it, but I would really like a coffee."

Sally laughed. "Of course I have coffee. We are quite continental here at the Waves."

Lily sat down at the table and Sally offered a plate of assorted biscuits to accompany their drinks.

"What made you decide to open a guesthouse, Sally?"

"The house belonged to Rob's family. After we got married, we moved in and Rob had the idea of turning it into a guesthouse. He said it would provide extra income, and also he liked the idea of me having company and an occupation while he was away at sea."

"Who exactly are your guests?" Lily asked as she scanned the dining room that evening, taking note of one young woman and two single men.

"Bournemouth is a holiday resort, but the sort of folk who come down here mostly stay in the posh hotels. Because of its relatively mild weather, it's an all-year-round resort. During the summer, the town is really crowded, but throughout the year, there are still visitors at weekends and Christmas and the like, and the hotels are always looking for staff. Many of the employees are local, but others come here from all over the country seeking work and they need lodgings. Miss Williams over there is a chambermaid at the Royal Bath, and John and Ralph are porters at the Metropole."

"There's a Metropole here?" asked Lily, astonished. "There's one in Margate too. And in Breslau." She repeated what she had told Doris about Hitler's appearance there and shuddered as she recalled it.

"Are there many hotels here in Bournemouth? Perhaps it would be possible for me to find a position in one of them? I won't be able to pay you until I find a job," Lily apologised.

"Don't worry your head about that. I will find you plenty of jobs to keep you busy so you will earn your keep, starting with helping the kids with their homework. How's your French, by the way? Rob could certainly use some tutoring."

Lily soon discovered that Sally had not been exaggerating. Running a guesthouse was a full-time job and Lily was happy to take some of the load. Unlike her job at the Müllers, she didn't have to find extra things to do to fill her time and she was grateful to be busy. Only at night when she was alone in her room did she allow herself to grieve for Heinrich, soaking her pillow with tears she feared would never stop.

From the day of Lily's arrival, Gracie had adopted her and taken charge of familiarizing her with local life. Lily was amazed by the free spiritedness of Sally's children – so different from the formal decorum of Johanna and Sofia. Rob and his friends played out in the street, kicking a ball around, or flipping and swapping cigarette cards. Since Sally didn't smoke, Rob was always trying to cadge cards from the boarders. Sometimes Miss Williams would find discarded packets in the hotel and bring the cards back for him. Gracie also liked to collect things, many of which she picked up on the beach. One afternoon, she took Lily down a nearby chine, a heavily wooded gorge leading down to the sea. Lily felt like Alice in Wonderland having fallen into a deep hole. One minute they were on the street in broad daylight, and the next, they had plunged into a damp jungle rich with thick vegetation, which echoed with the distant gurgling of running water and the chirping of birds. Lily hesitated. She felt threatened by the muggy darkness and goose pimples rose on her arms.

"What is this place? Is it safe?" An image of the dark alley and Lieutenant Bauer flashed before her eyes and she froze. Her ears rang with the throb of her palpitations and her mouth went dry, the heady fragrance of the pine trees mingled with the sour stench of rotting undergrowth causing nausea to rise in her throat.

Gracie laughed. "This is a chine. There are lots of them along the coast. They cut through the cliffs all the way down to the beach. Don't be afraid – it's quite safe. Just watch your step because it can be a bit slippery especially when it's raining."

Lily took a few deep breaths to calm herself and followed Gracie's lead as they wound their way down along the twists and turns of the path. Then, just as suddenly as when they had entered, they were all at once out in the daylight again on a stretch of beautiful sand. Lily slowly breathed in the fresh air and took in the view.

"Over there," said Gracie pointing to the left, "is the pier. Those white cliffs in the distance are the Needles on the Isle of Wight. And France is just over the horizon. You can actually see it on a very clear day."

They walked leisurely along the sand, Gracie stopping now and then to pick up an interesting shell or investigate a piece of debris. "I once found a pretty bracelet and a packet of sweets right here," she boasted.

The sea was calm and the sun sparkled on the gentle waves, and Lily thought that in time she might be able to look at it in peace without associating it with the horror of the shipwreck and Heinrich's death.

A week later, Lily made her first foray into the centre of town. The two resorts she had now visited, Bournemouth and Margate, couldn't be more different from each other. Bournemouth had an elegant air to it. The hotels were grand and the shops fashionable. Even the Bobby's Department Store on the Town Square looked fancier than the one she had shopped in with Doris. She was particularly enchanted by the Gervis Arcade, a grand Victorian-covered row of shops between Beales Department Store on Old Christchurch Road and the cinemas of Westover Road. She had a feeling that the beach shops here probably wouldn't be displaying dirty postcards.

"Sally, how is it that Bournemouth is so different from Margate?" she asked on her return to the boarding house.

"Well, the people appointed to oversee the development of the town at the beginning of the century wanted to maintain it as a resort for the elite, because they thought it would be financially advantageous. So they developed facilities which would continue to attract the right sort of holidaymakers. They invested in a range and quality of entertainments to draw people to a tourist destination which would rival not only the English resorts but also those of the Continent, especially the French Riviera. The author Thomas Hardy, a native to Dorset, described Bournemouth as 'a Mediterranean lounging place on the English Channel'."

That evening as she got ready for bed, Lily reflected on the day. She could be happy here, she thought. She didn't miss the Germany she had left behind. It had changed beyond recognition from the pleasant hometown of her childhood into a hellish, frightening place. Even if she and Heinrich had not been forced to leave, they would never have been able to build a life together in Breslau.

Now she would have to be brave for his sake, pull herself together and get on with life.

CHAPTER NINETEEN

Life settled into some sort of routine. Lily helped serve and clear the breakfasts and tidy the house. The boarders were responsible for the daily upkeep of their own rooms, but once a week Lily would give them a good clean and change the bedlinen and towels. Her conversations with the family and the boarders were helping to improve her English and she was working hard at trying to lose her German accent. She borrowed books from the local library – Agatha Christie, Daphne du Maurier, CS Forester – and browsed their collection of fashion magazines and newspapers.

When the children came home from school, she helped with their homework if they needed any. As Sally had hinted, French was Rob's weakest subject, but he seemed to be uncomfortable being tutored by Lily, and she soon guessed he may have a schoolboy crush on her.

Sally had quite a lot of friends, but as a widow, she always felt like the fifth wheel when she went out with other couples. She was delighted to have a partner for an evening at the cinema or very occasionally at a restaurant, and for the first time in her life Lily had a girlfriend to hang out with. Sally had fun introducing her to English quirks: eating fish and chips wrapped in newspaper; weighing things in stones and ounces; using weird phrases such as the "bee's knees", "kick the bucket", "stiff upper lip". Sally commented to Lily that heads turned whenever she was out with her, wryly adding that Lily seemed to be oblivious to her own beauty and the effect she had on men.

Now that she felt settled, Lily decided to write to Frau Müller. She felt she needed to explain to her former employer, who had always treated her well, why she had disappeared so suddenly.

Dear Frau Müller,

I hope this letter finds you and the family well. I am writing because I feel I owe you an explanation for my sudden departure. As you know, I had been seeing Heinrich for quite a while and we had fallen in love. You met him and seemed to approve of our liaison. What I didn't know was that Heinrich was Jewish, although completely alienated from his religion and heritage. Even if I had known, it would not have changed my feelings for him.

The night before I left, Heinrich was brutally attacked by some of his fellow officers and left for dead. We had to get away. I won't give you details of how we escaped. It is better that you know as little as possible. I had to leave with him for several reasons. Firstly, because of my deep feelings for him. Secondly, the officers knew of my existence and I would have been a juicy Mischlinge target for Nazi punishment. Lastly, I did not want to endanger or disgrace your family in any way by my association with you. I hope you will understand and forgive me.

Unfortunately, our escape plan foundered. We were smuggled on to a ship which sank in bad weather soon after we sailed. I was rescued, but my darling Heinrich lies in a watery grave at the bottom of the sea.

I have found a safe haven with an English family and hope to be able to rebuild my life somehow, when the profound pain of bereavement lessens.

It seems war is coming, and I hope that you all stay safe.

I miss the girls and little Armin.
Yours,
Lily

In mid-November, Sally and Lily went to the cinema to see Jezebel starring Bette Davis and Henry Fonda. Lily still idolized the glamour of Hollywood's leading ladies and registered every detail of costume and design in the films she saw. She made mental notes of styles and fabrics, and paid close attention to accessories and makeup. Before the start of the main feature, a short Pathé Newsreel presented some of the notable current affairs stories from around the world. Quite often the snippets were amusing or featured celebrities, and Lily enjoyed them. Tonight, though, was different. After the trademark cockerel gave its familiar crow, Lily sat bolt upright in her seat. On the screen were pictures of shop windows daubed with the Star of David and the word Jude in large letters. More shots showed Nazi soldiers on a vandalizing rampage, smashing windows and setting fire to synagogues. The narrator's deep voice described the images of *Kristallnacht*, the Night of the Broken Glass, as a wave of destruction and violence in cities throughout Germany against the property of Jews.

Sally squeezed Lily's arm as she watched tears roll gently down her friend's face.

"This must be happening in Breslau too. I fear for Heinrich's family. Why does the world do nothing about this? It's monstrous," said Lily through her tears.

For several days, the news lay heavily on her heart and she tried to find something to distract her and lighten her mood. Christmas was just around the corner and she wanted to give Sally and the children gifts. All her savings had gone down with the ship, and although Sally gave her a small remuneration for her work on top of board and lodging, Lily couldn't afford to be extravagant.

Sitting in the lounge one evening helping Sally to repair some torn bed linen, Lily watched her needle going in and out of the fabric and had an idea.

"Sally, how would you and Gracie like to have smart new dresses for Christmas?"

"Well, I haven't had anything new for quite a while and I would be happy to go shopping with you one afternoon. You could do with a few more items in your wardrobe as well."

Sally suggested they go to Boscombe where the prices were much lower than in Bournemouth, but Lily persuaded her to accompany her to Beales. "I would be petrified to go in there by myself, but I'd love to have a look."

A uniformed doorman opened the huge doors of the department store and ushered them inside. The ground floor was enormous and Lily was momentarily speechless. It was magically beautiful. Counter after counter presented their wares in sparkling glass display cases: perfumes and soaps, trinkets and scarves, leather purses and gloves, embroidered handkerchiefs and fashion jewelry, and much more. The polished wooden floor between the counters was covered in a rich carpet runner which muffled their footsteps, and the huge space had an air of decorum and elegance. Almost automatically, Lily and Sally began talking to each other in lowered voices as they looked around.

They took the escalator up to Ladies Fashion on the first floor and browsed until a saleslady approached them.

"May I help you ladies?"

On a whim, Sally pointed to a dress that had taken her fancy.

"Good choice, madam. Would you like to try it on?"

"You must," Lily urged Sally on. "It looks like it was made for you."

Sally hesitated, but a nudge from Lily spurred her on. "Yes, please."

The saleslady showed her into a dressing room.

"The fit isn't quite right," Sally declared as she nervously emerged wearing the dress.

"Don't worry, madam, we have seamstresses who will make any necessary alterations."

"I think I would prefer to buy a dress that fits me perfectly. One never knows with alterations how the finished article will look," said Sally, as if she were in the habit of coming to fancy stores to buy her outfits.

Having changed back into her own clothes, she hurried Lily away.

"Did you see the price of that dress?"

"But did you like it?"

"Who wouldn't like it? It was beautiful."

A few days later, Lily braved her first ride on a double-decker bus. As she took in the lovely view from the top, she felt excited and motivated for the first time in ages. Disembarking in Boscombe, she made her way to the market and found a stall with a good selection of reasonably priced fabrics and sewing accessories. She also discovered a secondhand stall selling cigarette cards and a pretty engraved wooden box. Proud of her purchases and the relatively small outlay of money, she returned home with renewed energy and a sense of purpose.

CHAPTER TWENTY

Lily had given up hoping for a reply from Frau Müller. Then, shortly before Christmas, a letter arrived.

> **My dear Lily,**
> *I was saddened to receive your letter and learn of your terrible ordeal. I did indeed like Heinrich and you made a beautiful couple.*
> *Things here in Breslau are tense. The brutality of the Nazis is unforgivable and the winds of war are definitely blowing through Germany.*
> *I must ask you not to write to me again. Sofia is deeply entrenched in the youth movement and would find our correspondence suspicious, if not criminal.*
> *Johanna misses you and wants to know who is going to make pretty clothes for her and her dolls now that you are gone. Whatever else, don't give up your dream of becoming a dressmaker.*
> *I wish you well in your new life.*
>
> *May God protect us all.*
> *Elsa Müller*

Reading Frau Müller's lines brought tears to Lily's eyes. Her mention of Heinrich and how they made a beautiful couple was almost more than she could bear. Lily bristled with anger at Sofia's indoctrination. How could a mother be so afraid of, and intimidated by, her own child? It was sickening. And Lily couldn't help but feel guilt at abandoning Johanna. Above all, and despite everything, Frau Müller, generous of spirit as always, voiced no resentment at her disappearance and was still encouraging her to pursue her dream.

Lily hated what was happening to Breslau and to all of Germany, and she was inwardly ashamed on behalf of her countrymen and women who were allowing the systematic destruction of values and morality. The newspapers and radio had recently been full of stories about Jewish children from Germany and Austria being sent away by their parents on something called Kindertransport, a rescue mission which was bringing these young refugees to Britain. Lily could fully understand the parents' concern for their children's safety, but how could they bear to part with them and send them off to an unknown future?

Luckily, she did not have much spare time to dwell on these events as preparations for Christmas at The Waves were reaching a crescendo, and she was hurrying to finish her sewing. Sally was also running around like a whirling dervish, sourcing all the ingredients for a festive meal and purchasing gifts for the children, which she stowed away from their prying eyes. The children's excitement was palpable, even though Rob tried to pretend that he was too old for "all these Christmas goings-on" and not in the slightest bit interested in trying to guess what presents he would get. Bournemouth was all aglitter. Shops large and small decorated their window displays in the Christmas spirit, and festive lighting weaved its jolly way between lampposts in and around the Square. Greetings cards began to arrive at the guesthouse from far-flung relatives and previous boarders who had happy memories of Sally's hospitality.

Finally, Christmas Eve arrived. Once she was certain that Rob and Gracie were in bed, Sally asked Lily to help her get the sitting room ready. A small tree was already standing on one side under the front window where it could be seen from the street, in keeping with the rest of the neighbors along the terrace. It had been decorated by the children with tinsel and a few beautiful glass ornaments. Gracie had made a sparkling angel, which looked out over the room from its perch on a star at the top of the tree. The tree diffused a pleasantly relaxing outdoorsy scent, complementing the smell of the open fire which burned brightly in the fireplace. The weather had turned bitterly cold over the past few days, and the warmth of the fire was welcome and comforting.

"Let's do the stockings first, Lily," said Sally, holding up two large embroidered ones.

"These are lovely. In Germany, children place a shoe outside their bedroom door on December the 6th – *Nikolaustag*, or St Claus Day. If they have behaved well throughout the year, the shoe will hold gifts when they check in the morning."

"What happens if they were bad?" laughed Sally.

"Supposedly they'll find a rod instead. Although I don't believe that really happens."

"These stockings were mine and Stu's when we were kids. I have lots of fond memories of Christmas growing up. What about you?"

"I don't remember much festivity as a child. My home was not a happy one. After my father died, there was little money to spare for elaborate Christmas celebrations. We did not have a tree, but my mother tried to make our tiny apartment festive with tinsel and homemade paper streamers. We were not religious, so we didn't go to Christmas Mass. My mother worked extra hard leading up to the holidays, and even though her employers were Jewish, they gave her a generous bonus, which she spent on special food and sweets. My last employers were well off. In their living room stood a magnificent tree hung with exquisite glass baubles and chocolate treats. The floor underneath it was piled high with a heap of packages. Things have changed in Germany, though. In the last few years Hitler has tried to Nazify Christmas. Rather than focusing on the religious origins, the Nazis try to emphasize celebrating the supposed heritage of the Aryan race. Sofia, my employer's older daughter who joined the Hitler Youth, tried to persuade her parents to adopt this version, but her mother would not hear of it and they continued to celebrate Christmas as they had in the past."

Sally began to fill Gracie's stocking: two Yardley lavender bath cubes; a Shirley Temple paper cut out dress-up doll; and a bag of her favourite pick-and-mix penny sweets – aniseed balls, dolly mixture, fruit pastilles, jelly babies, and vanilla fudge. Lily took care of Rob's stocking: a harmonica; the latest edition of Modern Wonder magazine; a tube of Rolos; and a bag of pear drops. When they were finished, Sally added a clementine to each stocking and a few small items donated by the boarders. She placed some packages under the tree and they stood back to admire their efforts.

Sally watched as a tear slid slowly down Lily's face.

"What's the matter, Lily. Do you miss home?"

"I have no home except this one. It is warm and loving, and exactly as I pictured my life with Heinrich. I'm not crying for the past, but for the future which will never be."

When Lily came downstairs the following morning, she found Sally and the children sitting on the floor next to the tree.

"We were waiting for you to join us for the present-opening ritual," said Gracie. "We thought you'd *never* get down here."

She took a package marked *For Everyone from Mum*. The two children ripped off the paper to reveal a game called Monopoly.

"The man in the shop assured me that this is the new game everyone is playing," said Sally. "We can all play it together later on. This is just for you Gracie, and this is for Rob," Sally added handing them each another present.

A huge smile lit up Gracie's face as she revealed a pair of roller skates.

"This is amazing," said Rob, examining the ivory-handled pocket knife.

"It was your father's. He bought it somewhere exotic. I think you are old enough to have it now. Just be careful with it," Sally said, and Lily could tell she was choking back tears of emotion.

"And these are from me," said Lily, giving a small package each to Gracie and to Rob. "A box for your treasures, Gracie," she explained when Gracie threw herself into her arms.

"Wow, thanks, Lily," said Rob as he unwrapped a wad of cigarette cards.

Next, it was Sally's turn to open the gifts from her children – a tin of Nivea Cream and a box of Cadbury's Roses.

"And this is for you, Lily. It's not much, but we hope you like it," said Gracie.

The package contained a set of three delicate pure cotton handkerchiefs with Lily's initials embroidered in one corner, and a leather-bound diary.

"You will be able to keep a record of your new life here in England," Gracie said with a shy smile.

"A perfect gift," exclaimed Lily, trying to hold back the wave of tears threatening her eyes. "But I will use the pages of the diary for my sketches."

"Sketches? What do you sketch?"

"You'll see," said Lily as she handed Sally her gift.

For a moment they all stared in silent amazement as Sally held up the dress.

"But how on earth could you afford this?"

"I didn't actually buy it. I made it based on the dress you tried on in Beales."

"You made it from scratch? This is unbelievable. Why have you been hiding such a talent?"

"It's a long story, which I will tell you later. Meanwhile, this is for you Gracie."

Lily had made the young girl a crisp white blouse with puffed sleeves, a lace-edged Peter Pan collar, and imitation pearl buttons.

"I love it!" Gracie exclaimed. "My friends are going to be *sooo* jealous. Thank you so much, Lily, it's beautiful."

"I don't have much experience with men's clothes," Lily said, looking at Rob. "But maybe we can come up with something you'd like me to make for you."

Rob blushed and mumbled something, which Lily couldn't quite catch, but she took it as agreement.

"Off you go, children," said Sally as she collected up the wrapping paper. "And take your presents with you," she added, piling her and Lily's gifts neatly on the sofa. "Lily and I are going to get on with Christmas dinner. Miss Williams has gone home for the holiday, but Ralph and John will be joining us."

Later, Lily looked round the dining table and, although she was not religious, she silently thanked God for finding her sanctuary in this warm and loving family of strangers. They chatted and joked as they ate Sally's wonderful meal of turkey, roast potatoes, and Brussels sprouts, followed by a flaming Christmas pudding and mince pies. They pulled crackers and wore silly paper hats, toasted one another with blessings for the coming year, and joined in with the carol singers who braved the cold weather to bring Christmas cheer to the neighbourhood.

Nineteen thirty-eight was coming to an end, and underneath all the jollity, Lily had a feeling that they each were wondering fearfully what 1939 would bring.

CHAPTER TWENTY-ONE

Heinrich surrendered himself to Mrs McFee's ministrations, and after three weeks of nourishing food, lots of rest, and fresh sea air, he began – at least physically – to feel like his old self again. Emotionally, his feelings continued to roller-coaster between abject misery at the loss of Lily and gratitude at having been saved. He followed the news coming out of Germany and was sickened by what he heard. He prayed that his brother had managed to get his family to safety, and although he knew he was unlikely to receive a reply, he wrote a letter updating him on the disastrous outcome of his escape.

Dear Martin,
I hope this finds you and the family well, although in my heart of hearts I hope this letter does not find you at all in Breslau, and that by now you are safely ensconced somewhere far from Germany. There will be war, of this I am certain, and the fate of the Jews has never been bleaker.
I don't know if you received any news about the ship and your Captain friend. I myself know very little of what happened. There was an accident of some kind, the ship was mortally damaged and sank. I was swept into the icy water and had given up all hope when by some miracle I was rescued by a fisherman and brought back to life. Perhaps my name Chaim had something to do with it. My darling Lily was not so lucky. Putting this down on paper makes real what I have barely been able to acknowledge.
My beautiful, brave, and loyal girl is gone.
I was taken in by the fisherman and his wife and now, several weeks later, I am finally beginning to regain my strength.

Rumours of Kristallnacht have reached us, and I fear for you and for all Breslau's Jews, who are at the mercy of the Nazi scum.
I am ashamed that I once called myself an officer of the Reich.
I spit on Hitler and his henchmen.
Once again, I urge you to leave. If you can get to England, come to this address.
I am deeply sorry for the years we were estranged and hope you can forgive me.

Your loving brother,
Heinrich

One afternoon, Dr Finlay came to check up on him and brought a visitor.

"This is a colleague of mine, Dr Rothman. He is a member of the Great Yarmouth Jewish Community and Norfolk Fund for Refugees. I thought you might like a chat."

Heinrich once again told his visitor the tailored version of events surrounding his escape, and asked him for up-to-date news on the situation in Germany. Rothman asked Heinrich if he needed any help from the Fund, but Heinrich declined the offer, saying they should reserve their assistance for those in a more desperate situation.

"You have heard about Kristallnacht, the Night of the Broken Glass?" Rothman asked him.

"Yes. I am haunted by an image in my mind's eye of the Storch Synagogue, just a few minutes' walk from my brother's apartment, going up in flames."

"Well, immediately after Kristallnacht, a delegation of British, Jewish, and Quaker leaders appealed to Prime Minister Neville Chamberlain to permit the admission into Britain of unaccompanied Jewish children from Germany and Austria without their parents. Jewish relief agencies have committed to provide funds for this rescue operation and to find homes for the children. As yet, we do not know how the transport arrangements will work, but we expect several ports along the coast will be involved."

"If I can be of any assistance," Heinrich offered immediately, "please count me in. You may need German speakers and I will be happy to be of service."

Heinrich was anxious to repay the McFees' generous hospitality and to start pulling his weight in return for his board and lodging. He knew nothing about the fishing industry, except that his father had built up a successful fish import business now run by his brother, which was not very useful. But he told McFee he was a fast learner and would be happy to take on whatever tasks the fisherman would throw at him. He learned to tie knots, haul in the nets and repair them, gut the fish and sort them. The wintry sea was choppy and unpredictable, and McFee was reluctant to take such an inexperienced sailor out on his fishing expeditions. But one evening the weather forecast predicted favorable conditions for the coming few days, and he asked Heinrich if he would like to tag along.

In the early hours of the next morning McFee fired up the boat's engine, let the ropes go from the quay and they slipped into the darkness to start the day's work. "The early bird catches the worm," said McFee, "and it's true that to get the best catch of the day, you need an early start."

They chugged along for about two hours until they reached McFee's "lucky" fishing ground, and shot their nets as dawn was breaking in the east with the promise of a pristine clear winter's day.

"Time for a cuppa while we wait," said McFee, offering Heinrich tea from his Dewar flask.

Without warning, Heinrich had an uncontrollable urge to vomit and he rushed to lean over the side of the boat.

"You'll get your sea legs soon enough," laughed McFee.

Heinrich didn't want to tell him that his sea legs were fine. The sickness was caused by a horrific hallucination of his beautiful Lily descending in slow motion to a watery grave, her face drained of colour and her glorious titian hair fanned out and rippled by the current as she sank. He fought to recover his composure, taking great gulps of salty air into his lungs to steady his wildly beating heart. Once he was calm, he gratefully accepted the proffered drink, and they towed in companionable silence for about two hours until McFee gave the signal to start hauling the nets to the surface and on to the boat. Seagulls that had followed them from the coast circled overhead, squawking as the two men worked in unison to pull their catch onto the deck.

"'Tis a good sign, Heinrich. The louder they shriek, the better the catch."

Back at the quay, McFee and Heinrich joined the hubbub of crowded boats and noisy fishermen unloading their catch and competing for the best prices from the local fish merchants. Although they were competitors, the fishermen were a close-knit band of brothers who socialized together, fought together, celebrated, and mourned together – a little colony within the wider community. Just like the Jews, Heinrich couldn't help thinking, smiling inwardly.

The call came a few days later. Dr Finlay arrived at the McFees and asked Heinrich to accompany him to Lowestoft Central Station. A special train from Parkeston Quay had arrived carrying five hundred and twenty Jewish child refugees, mostly from Vienna, as part of the Kindertransport rescue initiative. The bewildered children stood crowded together clasping their paltry belongings, identity tags hanging pitiably around their necks on a length of string like pieces of lost luggage. The scene was heartbreaking.

The Mayor gave a welcoming address to the stunned young audience who Heinrich was sure could not understand a word he said. "The citizens of Lowestoft greet you and wish you all the best in your new life. We know the hardships you and your people have undergone and you can be certain that our sincere sympathy is with you. Great as must be the joy of feeling yourselves once more free, we hope you will soon know the greater joy of reunion with your parents. Till then, we say to you all, 'Good luck for the future'."

Heinrich did his best to translate the words of welcome as he moved among the children, patting heads and shaking hands with a smile plastered on his face, masking the profound sadness he felt for this motley crew of youngsters, who had been sent to an unknown future by desperate parents whom they might never see again.

The children, some as young as four, were housed temporarily at the nearby Pakefield Holiday Camp while they waited to be distributed to foster homes. Heinrich went to the camp each morning to chat to them and bolster their spirits, encouraging them to enjoy the adventure and be positive about their new homes. Many of them shared stories with him of SS brutality, parents who were doctors, lawyers, and professors thrown out of their jobs, and a life under the cloud of constant threat and fear. Heinrich's thoughts were plagued by worry for his brother who had children of similar ages to these refugees, and he prayed silently for their safety.

The weather turned freezing, making conditions in the camp's bungalows far from ideal, and by Christmas, the children who had not yet been placed in foster families were relocated to a boarding school with better conditions several miles away. Mrs McFee sensed that the interaction with, and separation from, the refugee children had thrown Heinrich into a dark mood. "Why don't we take him north for the festive season?" she suggested to her husband. "It will surely lift everyone's spirits."

McFee told Heinrich of their plans. "We don't make a big fuss out of Christmas, as it's not considered an official holiday north of the border. It was banned by the Scottish Presbyterian Church in the seventeenth century and it's still illegal to have public celebrations. But Hogmanay, well now, that's another story. The New Year can only properly be celebrated in true Scottish style."

McFee had not exaggerated. The revelry was of a scale that Heinrich had never experienced. After a hearty warming Scottish dinner of cock-a-leekie soup, venison pie, haggis, and tatties and neeps, followed by tipsy laird trifle, they took to the streets for the late-night celebrations. A parade of kilted marchers made its way down the high street; the first revelers were swirling balls of fire around their heads; they were followed by three rows of pipers and drummers; and bringing up the rear was the local bagpipe band. The noise was augmented by the whooping, singing, and cheering of the townsfolk who lined the street, many of whom were already tipsy from the evening's alcohol.

Mein Got, *what a terrible racket,* Heinrich thought. *And their balls must have shriveled to the size of raisins under their flapping skirts in this freezing weather.* He chuckled to himself. The scene could not have been more different from the sedate German celebrations which he was used to.

His feelings of jollity evaporated at midnight when the church bells chimed the hour and fireworks lit up the sky. Heinrich was transported back twelve months to the wonderful New Year's Eve when he had professed his love for Lily and they had shared their first passionate embrace. How lovely she had looked that evening. He vividly recalled the look of surprise and delight on her face in the warm glow of candlelight as she opened his gift of the lily brooch.

The celebrants formed a huge circle, joined hands and began to sing in unison. Heinrich was pulled back to the present. Making out the words of the song, he could no longer suppress his tears.

Should auld acquaintance be forgot,
and never brought to mind?
Should auld acquaintance be forgot,
and auld lang syne?

The partying continued until the wee hours of the following morning. Before dawn, McFee dragged a drunken Heinrich over the next-door neighbor's threshold, shoving a lump of coal, a black bun, and pieces of shortbread into his hands. "A Guid New Year tae ye, McGhee," McFee shouted. "I've brought ye a real Viking first footer to bring luck for the coming year. Lang may yer lum reek!" He explained to a confused Heinrich that it was customary for the first person visiting a household on New Year's Day to bring symbolic gifts for good luck, and that it was an honour to be a first footer. "My greeting means 'May you never be without fuel for your fire'."

More whiskey was poured and pieces of the rich and fruity black bun were passed around. Heinrich did not recall anything that happened after that, and spent most of New Year's Day sleeping off his drunken stupor.

CHAPTER TWENTY-TWO

1939–1940

Lily adored working at Beales. She got on well with her fellow employees, and was impressed by the work ethic and philosophy of the store. Inhaling the aroma of luxury each morning when she arrived at the store, she was assailed by a thrill of excitement which did not diminish as the days and weeks went by.

On her first day, her supervisor took her on a tour of the various departments.

"Let me tell you a true story, Lily, to give you a better insight into Beales. The store was founded in 1881 by John Elmes Beale, born a few miles along the coast in Weymouth. It started as a small family business run by Mr Beale and his wife, but when Bournemouth became a resort popular with large numbers of visitors and new residents, he expanded his range of goods and extended the premises. He was an innovative businessman, producing original special resort souvenirs including an album of views of the town, and is considered to be the first store owner to have a live Father Christmas parading the shop and showrooms during the festive season. He employed a shopwalker in tailcoat and striped trousers to welcome customers, recognising the well-known ones and conducting them from their carriages to the appropriate counter. The story goes that one day Mr Beale noticed a member of staff dealing with a customer. When the man left, Beale approached the employee to ask how he had got on. Somewhat embarrassed, he replied that unfortunately he had not made a sale, to which Mr Beale replied, 'But did you make a friend?' That's how Beales built up its name and reputation. And that is how we treat our customers, Lily."

It had all happened just after the New Year. Sally, audacious as ever, had marched into Beales, returned to the first-floor Ladies Department which she had visited with Lily, and asked to speak with the supervisor. The flummoxed assistant, fearing a complaint, had hurried to get the department manager and Sally had laid out in front of them the dress Lily had made her for Christmas.

"Well, that's very similar to one of our dresses, Miss, but you didn't buy it here," insisted the manager.

"And if I recall, it's like the one you tried on but didn't purchase," the assistant added.

"Correct," said Sally, "but please take a look at the workmanship."

They examined the dress, remarking on the precision of the cut and the stitching. "Where did you get it?"

"My friend created it from the one glimpse she had of it when I tried it on."

Manager and assistant exchanged looks of disbelief.

"I imagine you would have an opening in your department for such a talented seamstress. You should grab her before she approaches the competition."

Several days and one interview later, Lily was taken on as an alterations seamstress in the store.

"I can't believe it. Thank you so much, Sally," Lily said, when she arrived home after her interview to inform Sally of the good news. "This is the second time someone has pulled me out from the depths of desperation by finding me a job." Fighting to keep tears at bay, she forced down the lump in her throat and hugged Sally tightly. Why must everything continue to remind her of Heinrich and the Müllers?

The work itself was not particularly glamorous. When a customer required advice on the fit or finish of a garment while trying it on, the sales assistant would call upon a fitter to record any necessary alterations and then relay the information to the seamstresses in the basement workshop. Lily was surprised to find that they also served the Menswear Department, and might even be required to make adjustments to bed linen or tablecloths.

So, while this was not the longed-for couturier's salon, the job was certainly an apprenticeship, giving Lily an exceptional opportunity to experience and work with different fabrics from fur and leather to heavily beaded gowns, customised to fit clients of every shape and size. The salary was modest, but enough to pay Sally for room and board, thereby reclaiming Lily's independence and self-esteem. Her days had meaning and structure. She was sleeping better, and the nightmares of losing Heinrich and the trauma at sea were recurring less frequently.

As the year progressed, however, the rumbling threat of war was reaching a crescendo. After Hitler invaded Czechoslovakia in March, it was clear that war could not be averted, and in Bournemouth preparations accelerated at a fast pace, since its coastal location so close to France made it a likely target for the enemy. Public shelters were constructed all over town and Sally's garden now housed an Anderson shelter. The middle section of the pier was blown up by the Royal Engineers so that any invaders would not be able to use it to disembark troops or equipment, and the pristine beach was spoiled by coils of barbed wire entangled in steel scaffolding.

Lily had finally managed to conquer her fear of the chine, and frequently enjoyed a leisurely walk down to the beach alone without looking over her shoulder or panicking at every sudden noise, but now it was off limits to the public. The beach café had been demolished, the beach huts taken away, and the chine and cliffs were being used for commando training.

Despite the tension, though, life seemed to go on as usual. The summer saw a large influx of visitors bringing extra custom to Deales and more work for Lily. The boarding house was full, and now that Lily no longer helped out, Sally was always exhausted by the end of the day.

Lily was relaxing in the garden one evening when Sally came out of the house holding two cold drinks and sat down beside her.

"Lily, may I ask you a favor?"
"Of course, Sally, anything."

Sally showed her a colourful flyer. "The Bertram Mills Circus is coming to town and I promised the children I'd take them, but I just don't have the time or energy. How would you feel about taking them?"

"A circus! I'd love to take them. I've never seen one."

The children were just as excited as Lily when they set off on a balmy July afternoon for their outing, and were bubbling with enthusiasm when they got home and competed with each other to tell Sally about it.

"Mum, it was amazing," effused Rob. "There were these fantastic animal acts. Elephants playing football, performing dogs, fierce lions and tigers, and an Indian snake charmer."

Gracie joined in. "I loved the Great Wallendas, a daring high-wire act. And there was a trapeze artist called Federico who swung across the tent holding onto a rope with his teeth. It was really scary. And there were dancers and acrobats in beautiful costumes."

Smiling, Sally turned to Lily and asked, "What about you, Lily? What did you
enjoy most?"

"Definitely the clowns. There was a particular one called Wearie Willy, a hobo dressed in tattered tramp's clothes. He didn't utter a word, but just walked around the audience with a really sad expression on his face. He was so different from the other colourful cavorting clowns."

"And don't forget Leinert the Human Cannonball," Rob added. "Here, Mum, we brought you the program so you can see for yourself."

"Well," said Sally. "I can see you had a really good time. I'm sorry I couldn't come with you."

Later, after the children had gone to bed, the two women sat in the kitchen having a nightcap, and Sally told Lily how happy it made her to see her friend getting her life together and enjoying what it had to offer.

"Well, it's mostly because of you, Sally. And the children. I cannot thank you enough."

"Nonsense," Sally said with a wave of her hand. "Now let's get the blackout curtains up for tonight's practice run. It's lights out all over town from midnight till four am tomorrow."

To make up for Sally missing the circus, Lily decided to treat her at the end of summer to a concert at the Pavilion, given by the Municipal Symphony Orchestra. The orchestra played every weekend to full houses, offering a classical program in the afternoon and light music in the evening. Lily had not heard any classical music since the unforgettable organ Fugue which had enchanted her in the church in Hirschberg, and later the outdoor concert with Heinrich, and she was keen to expand her knowledge, but Sally preferred light music. Lily bought the tickets and they dressed up for an evening out on the town in their finery. Sally put on her "Christmas dress", as she had named it, and Lily also wore one of her own creations. They made a stunning pair as they entered the Pavilion's lobby arm-in-arm.

Lily had never been inside the Pavilion and she was delighted by the interior elegance of the art deco structure.

"Come on," said Sally, taking her hand. "I'll give you a tour."

The first stop was the beautiful Tea Room, painted in warm and relaxing pastel shades of pink and terracotta with gilt ornamentation.

"It's actually a ballroom with a special sprung floor," Sally explained. She led Lily to the vast window. "From here, you get some of the most magnificent sea views and sunsets. Over there," she said, pointing outside, "where you can see some people strolling, is the West Terrace. When the breeze comes in over the sea, you get a lovely strong whiff of the flowers in the gardens below. And underneath us, there are two restaurants, one posh and one more for the likes of us," she laughed.

As they took their seats in the Concert Hall, Lily looked up in wonder at the intricate glass chandeliers which lit the enormous space.

"I expect they'll have to come down for safety's sake when war is declared," mused Sally.

Sally's nonchalant reference to the threat of impending war unsettled Lily. How could she be so matter-of-fact about it? Lily had been following the news closely and wanted to believe that the politicians would manage to avoid a confrontation with Hitler. After all, it was barely twenty years since the end of the previous bloodbath, which had cost the lives of millions of British, French, and Germans. How could they allow themselves to fail to prevent a repetition? Hadn't Heinrich told her that the Great War was the war to end all wars? Her heart skipped a beat as she pictured him in his uniform. How ashamed he would be to be wearing it now in service of the maniacal Führer. She had shuddered as she'd read this morning's headlines which screamed Hitler Invades Poland. Would the allies renege on their promise to the Poles?

The orchestra struck up the first notes and Sally nudged her back into the present. Lily was determined not to allow black thoughts ruin her evening.

The music was a joy. The orchestra played an array of songs made popular by Glenn Miller and other big bands, the Andrews Sisters, Vera Lynn, Bing Crosby and others, and there was a lot of foot tapping and humming as the audience enthusiastically joined in.

At the end of the evening, the two women made their way home. They sang and laughed, and Lily chatted on excitedly about the orchestra and the music.

The following morning, Britain declared war on Germany.

CHAPTER TWENTY-THREE

During the first months of the war, life went along much as usual, disrupted only by the testing of air raid sirens, the mandatory blackout, and the introduction of food rationing. The Waves had been hit by the fall in visitors immediately after war was declared, but, by Christmas, Sally had hung out the No Vacancies sign and was as busy as ever. One afternoon, when the festive season was over and there was a lull in business, Sally and Lily decided to take advantage of the reopening of the cinemas. On their walk home, Lily had noticed two policemen escorting a couple of bewildered-looking gentlemen.

She turned to Sally, and said, "What will I do if they decide to send me away?" Lily's anxiety had been growing steadily over several days since the Bournemouth Police had started rounding up potential enemy aliens for internment.

"They are only taking men between the ages of sixteen and sixty. They say it's for the town's safety in the event of a German invasion," Sally tried to reassure her.

"But most of them are poor Jewish refugees who escaped from Hitler. What sort of threat can they pose?"

"I don't understand the logic either. How can anyone think they might be Nazi sympathizers? Some of the people who have been taken for internment have lived in Bournemouth for years and years. The ridiculous policy seems to be that it's better to be safe than sorry."

Lily looked into Sally's eyes and said, "So why am I so sure it won't happen to me?"

"They are only interested in German and Austrian immigrants and refugees. We did the right thing when I brought you back here. We went to the police station and registered you as my family from Switzerland. Switzerland is a neutral country. Britain is not at war with the Swiss, so you are not the enemy."

Nevertheless, a few days later, Lily received notice to report to the authorities to have her case assessed.

"I'm sure it's a mistake or just a formality," Sally tried to reassure her.

Lily remained unconvinced on the day they set out for her internment tribunal. The officer was sure to request her documentation which, surprisingly, she had never been asked to produce before. Sally had come up with a fabrication and she could only hope she would make a convincing case for herself. She was not a very good liar.

The tribunal officer looked up from his desk as Lily and Sally entered the room,

"Please take a seat, ladies," he offered.

Lily registered the look on his face, which in a split second transformed from bored indifference to a lascivious leer. In her mind's eye she substituted his British uniform for that of Lieutenant Bauer, causing her pulse rate to spike and her step to falter. She willed herself to stay calm and in control of her emotions.

"Now, Miss ..." he said, searching the list in front of him for her name.

"Please call me Lily," Lily interrupted.

"Yes, um, Lily. It says here that you are from Switzerland. Is that correct?"

"Yes, sir."

"Could you kindly explain to me why you came to this country?"

"My mother wished me to improve my English and arranged for me to stay with my cousin," Lily said, turning to look at Sally.

"I understand you own a boarding house, Miss ... er."

"Mrs Cooper," Sally corrected him. "I run The Waves Guesthouse."

"And you registered Lily when she came to live with you?"

"Not immediately, as the stay was supposed to be a short holiday over Christmas. But as the threat of war loomed, Lily's mother and I decided it would be safer for her to stay here rather than return to the Continent, with Switzerland being on Hitler's doorstep. Lily reported to the local police station to let them know she was extending her stay."

The officer turned to Lily again. "How do you intend to support yourself in Bournemouth?"

"I am living with my cousin and I have secured a good position at Beales, working as a seamstress. I am certain they will vouch for me if necessary."

The officer scribbled some notes.

"One more question, if you don't mind me asking. Are you Jewish?"

"No, I am not."

"Not a refugee then?"

"No."

"Didn't think so," he said with a smirk.

Lily didn't care for his tone and its veiled prejudice. She wondered what would happen if she asked him whether being Jewish would make a difference, but she held her tongue.

"Well, it appears that you have a roof over your head and steady employment which is commendable. So everything seems in order. I just need to see your papers and we are all done."

Lily hoped he couldn't see her hands trembling in her lap.

"Unfortunately," she said, trying to control the nerves in her voice, "there was a small fire at the guesthouse a few weeks ago and, among other things, my documentation was destroyed. I have written to my parents asking to have new ones drawn up and sent to me, but what with the war and everything, I'm afraid it all seems to be taking longer than I expected." Lily's face wore a very convincing damsel-in-distress expression to which she added a demure flutter of eyelashes and a bashful smile.

"That's all right for now. Pop it into the police station when it does arrive. Take this paper outside to my secretary and she will draw up your Internment Tribunal Card classing you as an unrestricted alien."

"Thank you very much, sir," said Lily flashing the officer a brilliant smile as she stood up to leave.

"I told you it was a piece of cake," said Sally happily as they walked back into town. "And you were fantastic."

Lily blushed. "I hope I wasn't too forward."

"Not at all. What's the point of having all that beauty if you don't use it to your advantage when the situation warrants?"

"But what happens when I don't produce any papers and they decide to dig deeper?"

"Believe me, Lily, they are overwhelmed and understaffed. An old mate of Rob's who's a local Bobby told me they won't be wasting their limited resources on one young lady."

Lily fervently hoped that Sally and her informant were right.

As they walked across the Square, they were greeted by the familiar wolf whistles, cat calls, and saucy remarks to which they had become accustomed in recent weeks. "'Allo swee'art. Come over 'ere and give a fella far from 'ome a propah welcome to yer luvverly tahn." Lily had been terrified at first. Her natural instinct to feel threatened would bubble to the surface and she would break into a run to get away from the attention as quickly as possible, which made the soldiers hoot with laughter and try even harder the next time she walked by. Sally had assured her they were just having harmless fun and that she should just ignore it. After all, they were serving their country. *Easy for you to say*, Sally, Lily thought. *You haven't been a split second away from rape by a man in uniform.*

For the past few weeks, there had been large scale billeting of soldiers and airman in hotels and boarding houses across Bournemouth and the adjacent towns of Poole and Boscombe. Car parks, open spaces, and the promenades became military parade grounds for initiating new recruits into foot drill, and it was hard to avoid them on Lily's way to and from work regardless of the route she took. She noticed that a lot of the local girls welcomed the attention and flirted shamelessly with the men in uniform, particularly the airmen, and gradually she learned to do as Sally suggested, maintaining her normal stride and keeping a safe distance without reacting or giving them any encouragement.

"Lily, I'm afraid I have some news you are not going to like," said Sally, when Lily arrived home from work a few days after the tribunal.

"They've changed their minds. I knew it. I am going to be sent away." Lily started to cry.

"No, no. Nothing like that. We have been commissioned by the army to take in soldiers. I couldn't refuse. Apart from anything else, I need the money what with the drop in holidaymakers, and the army pays well. And it means our food rations will be increased. There's just one thing. Don't get me wrong, I'm sure it will all be fine, but I don't like the idea of you sleeping alone up in the attic with strange men in the house, so I think you should bunk in with me for the time being. How do you feel about that?"

"This is your home. I will do whatever you think best, Sally. It will also make

an extra room available if you need it for more guests."

"That's the spirit, Lily. Let's move your stuff so I can let the army know tomorrow."

It was strange sharing a room with Sally. It was a novel experience, as Lily had never so much as had a sleepaway or pajama party with a good friend. In fact, she had never really had a close girlfriend growing up. At first, she felt awkward and self-conscious, almost an intruder in Sally's space, until her friend told her to stop being daft. The room was large and Sally rearranged the twin beds, separating them with a chest of drawers.

"There's plenty of empty drawers and cupboard space for you. I got rid of all of Rob's clothes and bits and pieces ages ago." Sally looked wistful but then checked herself. "It'll be nice to have them filled up again."

"I haven't got all that much, Sally. But thanks."

The room provided much more space than Lily had had in the attic room. She wondered how its new occupant, who must be at least five foot ten, was managing when she could barely stand up straight in it, and only right in the middle where the eaves were highest.

The soldiers who had moved in were well-behaved and polite, grateful for the food and hospitality and conscious of the unspoken boundaries set by their landlady. They left early in the morning for training and returned exhausted after dark, with just about enough energy to eat dinner and retire to their rooms. Young Rob was excited to have them as boarders and boasted to his friends, some of whom were hosting school children evacuated from Southampton, whose docks were a prime target for the *Luftwaffe*, which was not nearly as impressive. But for Lily, the round-the-clock proximity of men in uniform was a bitter reminder of Heinrich and all she had lost.

CHAPTER TWENTY-FOUR

"Winston Churchill said *what?*" Heinrich asked McFee in amazement.

"He called fish and chips *good companions* and said they are invaluable to the national morale and fighting spirit."

"A greasy meal wrapped in newspaper is his weapon of choice and his strategy for winning a war against a highly trained, highly disciplined, and highly efficient military machine?" Heinrich laughed.

"Don't ye mock, laddie. A fish supper and a stiff upper lip are a lethal combination," joked McFee. "Ah'm just happy he's not rationing fish and that our livelihood isna in jeopardy."

Heinrich helped McFee haul in the last of the nets. They had had quite a successful catch that morning, sailing further northwards than usual. Now that the war was in full swing, fishing vessel movements were severely restricted because of the dangers of mines, surface and submarine naval activity, and potential aerial attacks.

Several of McFee's fisherman friends had returned to Scotland in order to take their families to safer shores. Lowestoft was the most easterly point of Great Britain and the Royal Navy had established five naval bases in the area, including Sparrow's Nest, the headquarters of the Royal Naval Patrol Service and the closest British military establishment to the enemy.

"At the start of the last war," McFee recounted, "I was in me early thirties, fishing with me da' on a steam trawler. The Germans had been mining shipping lanes and our vessel was one of many converted for minesweeping duties as part of the Royal Navy Reserve. The Germans were causing havoc with their mines and later their submarines. Our fishing community paid a heavy price. Over one hundred and seventeen men and laddies killed, and an even greater number of fishing vessels were lost," he added solemnly.

"I clearly remember one afternoon when we were heading back to port. There was a huge explosion and a smack we had spotted in the distance was enveloped in a huge cloud of smoke. When the smoke cleared, there was no sign of the wee craft nor of any survivors. This time round I'm too old and my boat isna serviceable, so the Patrol Service has no use for either of us. But I'll be sticking around here just the same. Ye never can tell when ye might be needed."

This was quite a speech for McFee, who generally was not a garrulous man given to idle chit chat. Heinrich felt at ease in his silent company and found what McFee did say to be interesting or useful. Heinrich enjoyed the outdoor life and manual work. The fresh salty air had helped to hasten his recovery, and the watchful hours at sea distracted him from dwelling on his unhappiness. He had decided the best way to conquer his fear of the sea after his near-drowning was to address it head on, and he was grateful for his military training which had taught him perseverance, endurance, and resolve. More than a year of hard work had strengthened and filled out his physique, his face had lost its pallid hue, and his scraggy beard and wild hair helped him blend in with the other fishermen.

Heinrich had presented himself to the Internment Tribunal as a Jewish refugee, vouched for by McFee and Dr Rothman from the Norfolk Refugee Fund, and he was classified as Category C – "no security risk". But now several months into the war, he feared that the situation was about to change as "enemy alien" fever seemed to be spreading across the country.

"Don't ye fret, laddie," McFee assured him. "There's plenty o' folk will support ye."

"It may not be up to them, McFee. I know how groundless prejudice works and how fear fans the flames of enmity."

One day at the end of May, McFee knocked on Heinrich's door and burst in excitedly.

"Get yer gear, laddie."

"But we're not fishing today." Heinrich was perplexed.

"Different kinda fishing." McFee didn't elabourate.

Heinrich grabbed his things and followed McFee out of the house.

"Mr Churchill needs us. Seems thousands of our lads are trapped just across the Channel on the beach in France and need rescuing. This is our chance to do our bit."

McFee loaded the boat with several gallons of petrol, some sandwiches and soft drinks, and a couple of bottles of rum. They set off along the coast towards Ramsgate, where a fleet of little ships was assembling before making a run to Dunkirk. Heinrich was astounded by the sight of a motley collection of vessels of all shapes and sizes bobbing up and down on the gentle waves as they waited for the signal to depart.

The sea was fairly calm as the little armada made its way across the Channel towards France. As they neared their destination, Heinrich could see billowing smoke on the horizon and hear the distant sound of gunfire. The noise of explosions became louder and louder as they approached the coast. The water churned around them, and high above the dangerous dance of dogfights between the RAF and the Luftwaffe shook the sky. Bombs fell alarmingly close to the boat. They looked across the bay and saw dozens of masts of sunken ships sticking out of the water. It was a terrifying sight.

McFee would later tell Heinrich how amazed he had been by Heinrich's composure, wondering how an office-bound businessman could remain so completely calm under fire. Heinrich didn't even noticeably flinch at the sound of an explosion or seem scared by bombs dropping in the water nearby.

I am finally in the war for which I trained, thought Heinrich. How surreal that after years of rigorous training and preparation, and a hard-fought rise through the ranks to leadership, I am fighting for the other side and praying that Germany will lose.

The horn of a destroyer waiting offshore for its passengers let out three loud whoops as the flotilla of small craft passed by on their way to the beach to ferry soldiers to larger ships anchored in deeper water. The air reverberated with a huge cheer as the desperate soldiers saw them approach. Heinrich was stunned by the picture unfolding in front of his eyes. Row upon row of exhausted young men awaited rescue; bodies of the unlucky ones floated in the water or were washed ashore. There was death and destruction everywhere. It would be ironic, Heinrich laughed bitterly to himself, if having been miraculously saved from drowning he would now find his death at sea. Dredged up from the depths of a long-ago memory, he recalled a Yiddish humourism: *Der mentsh trakht un got lakht* – Man plans and God laughs.

Without warning, a huge flame leapt into the sky from the coastline. A fuel store seemed to have been set on fire and the shore line was illuminated in the most dramatic manner.

Now that they were only a few yards from their target, McFee turned to Heinrich. "You'd best keep ye mouth shut so that the soldiers don't get wind of yer German accent. It could cause us unnecessary problems."

Heinrich didn't need to be told. He'd already decided to mimic McFee and adopt a thick Scots accent to cover his own. Hopefully they would be too tired and scared to even try to understand him. He helped the first one onto the boat.

"Walcom aboard. Nem's Henry. Shift alang, wull ye."

The soldier looked at him uncomprehending, and McFee roared with laughter.

"I believe they are French, laddie. They probably wouldna have picked up on your real accent, and the French aren't known for their grasp of the English language however it's spoken."

They made several runs ferrying evacuees to the waiting destroyer, made easier when the afternoon wore on, darkness fell, and the German planes ceased their bombing raids. At last, they were instructed to head for home and they set off back to Ramsgate, their boat packed with a final load of soldiers. While McFee steered, Heinrich made tea laced with rum for the exhausted men. No one spoke. Each seemed lost in his own thoughts, surely thankful for having been rescued from the jaws of death.

McFee and Heinrich received a hero's welcome when they arrived safely back in Lowestoft along with the other locals who had made the journey to Dunkirk.

About a week later, Mrs McFee suggested an evening out to celebrate the amazing rescue. The local cinema was showing the film Convoy about a Navy cruiser sent to meet a convoy in the North Sea and escort it safely into British coastal waters. She would have preferred a romantic comedy, but knew the men would not agree. As always before the main feature, the signature crowing cockerel introduced Pathé News. This evening, the newsreel presented footage from the Dunkirk rescue.

"Seems the French soldiers were taken to Bournemouth," said Mrs McFee. "Maybe it's some of the lads you rescued. Look, there you are, McFee!" The film rolled on and showed pictures of said soldiers being welcomed by their south coast hosts. Heinrich sat bolt upright as he stared at the screen. Among the ladies fussing over the Frenchmen was someone who bore a striking resemblance to Lily. She only appeared momentarily on the screen, but it was long enough to cause his heart to pump wildly and make him feel as if he were suffocating. Was he doomed to seeing Lily in every pretty face? Would he ever come to terms with never again holding her in his arms?

Two weeks later, Heinrich was tying up the boat on the quay while McFee sorted the fish. A local policeman approached him.

"Mr Graber, sir."

"Yes, Constable."

"I'm afraid I have to inform you that your unrestricted alien status has been revoked and you are to be interned. Kindly pack your belongings and report to the station tomorrow morning."

"Surely there's been a mistake, George," said McFee. "He's a hero. Saved soldiers at Dunkirk under fire. Surely that counts for something."

"New rules, McFee. Didn't you hear Mr Churchill's order to 'collar the lot' of the aliens? Only doing my job and I can't make exceptions."

CHAPTER TWENTY-FIVE

Heinrich joined the throng of people on the platform waiting to board the train to an undisclosed destination. Men, women, and children carrying their paltry belongings were directed into the train's carriages, fear and bewilderment etched on their faces. Heinrich found it comforting to be among *landsleute*, fellow countrymen, and be able to converse in German for the first time in almost two years, apart from his short interaction with the *Kindertransport* children. Perhaps if he questioned them there was a chance someone would have news of the Jews in Breslau, of his brother's family. There was also a chance, however, that someone might recognise him and denounce him as an officer in Hitler's army. He would be arrested as a spy and then God knows what would happen to him. Best to keep himself to himself for the time being.

"*Wissen Sie, wohin wir gehen?*" asked a fellow passenger. *Do you know where we are going?*

"*Ich habe keine Ahnung,*" replied Heinrich. *I have no idea.*

"I have heard that enemy aliens are being shipped off to Canada and even Australia. I have lived in England for years. My whole life, friends, and family are here. How can they do this to us?"

Heinrich shrugged and turned to look out of the window at the passing countryside, nipping the conversation in the bud. It pained him to be unfriendly, but it was imperative that he look out for his own safety.

The train chugged into the station at Liverpool. The passengers disembarked and were driven, under escort of soldiers with fixed bayonets, to the nearby docks. Could the man on the train be right, Heinrich wondered. *Are we to be put to sea?*

As soon as everyone was aboard the waiting ferry, it pulled slowly out of the port and into the open sea. Heinrich had long since conquered his fear of the ocean, but he had heard reports about German U-boats patrolling the Atlantic and the havoc they were causing to Allied shipping. Was he doomed to endure another shipwreck? Would he be lucky a second time?

A loudspeaker crackled into life.

"Ladies and gentleman, this is your Captain speaking. Welcome aboard. I wish to inform you that we are heading for the Isle of Man. The ferry will dock at Douglas, from where you will be transferred to one of the island's internment camps."

Not Canada then, Heinrich thought with relief. But where and what was the Isle of Man?

The ferry docked at a long pier and Heinrich could see what looked like a holiday resort. The long promenade beyond the sandy beach was bordered by pretty hotels and boarding houses, but on closer inspection, he made out a fence of barbed wire running down the middle of the road, punctuated by sentry boxes manned by armed guards. This was certainly not to be a summer vacation.

The internees were split into groups, and Heinrich and other single male Jewish refugees were loaded onto buses for an onward journey. The summer evening was balmy and clear, and the slowly setting sun embraced the green undulating hills of the island in a warm glow. They passed through quaint villages with thatched-roof houses, and crossed over deep valleys shimmering with sparkling streams meandering their way towards the Irish Sea. The journey came to an end at the Internment Camp, which was to be his home for the foreseeable future.

The camp compound of the town was enclosed by barbed wire in a similar fashion to the one he had seen on his arrival at Douglas. Heinrich was escorted to one of the boarding houses and was allocated a room. Shrugging off the welcome of the house's veteran internees, he closed his bedroom door and flopped down on the bed. His spirits were at their lowest ebb since the first days in Lowestoft. He took out the crumpled photograph of Lily from his pocket. "I'll try to make the best of it," he promised her, "for your sake and for the sacrifice you made to keep me alive and safe."

Dear McFee,

I have arrived at the internment camp on the Isle of Man. The conditions are reasonable. The internees are billeted in boarding houses and small hotels. I understand that the previous tenants and owners have been relocated in order to make this accommodation available. This, I am certain, does not endear them to the enemy aliens. I have my own room in a house shared by eleven other Jewish refugees. Each morning I walk down to the barbed wire separating the camp from the sea and from the rest of the town. The view inland is like something you would find on a picture postcard to send home from your holiday. It is very picturesque. Less so the internees' laundry hanging from the windows of the boarding houses and flapping in the breeze. From my vantage point, the town's main street is visible and I can watch the townsfolk going about their daily business, seemingly oblivious to the prisoners in their midst. Women pop in and out of shops, children play in the street, and now and again a bus may honk at a dog which has crossed its path. Our needs are cared for by the camp authorities. We prepare and serve our own meals. More often than not, the lunchtime menu consists of herring and potato. As if I didn't see enough herring in Lowestoft! It is not exactly fish and chips, not quite Mr Churchill's good companions, but I am developing a taste for kippers, and I dare you to show me a German who does not like potatoes. The smell reminds me of you and Hilda, and once again I am grateful for all you have done for me.

I have been horrified and saddened by the stories, told to me by refugees recently arrived in Britain, about the persecution of Jews in Germany, Austria and elsewhere. Hitler and his henchmen must be stopped. The camp radio broadcasts the latest war news, which is not very uplifting. We are safe here from the Luftwaffe and pray that the RAF pilots can hold their own and protect Britain.

At first, I thought I would die of boredom, but I have taken up sketching. I was able to procure a sketch pad and pencils, and there are certainly many sights and scenes on which to practice my drawing.

He suddenly paused his writing, momentarily transported back to happier days in Breslau and the look of delight on Lily's sweet face when he gave her the gift of a sketchpad and pencils for her designs. She had a natural artistic talent he could never hope to achieve. With a sigh of longing, he returned to his letter.

I'm not very good but hopefully I will improve in time. Or not, since I hope I will not be incarcerated here long enough to hone my skills.

Perhaps you would be kind enough to write me a few lines when you have the time.

My best wishes to you both. Stay safe.

Yours,
Heinrich

As the weeks went by, Heinrich gradually started to let down his guard a little and made some friends. Seven of the internees in his boarding house were from Austria and the other four from Czechoslovakia, so there was no chance their paths would have crossed in Germany. When asked, he offered his fictitious background of a businessman stripped of his property and forced to flee after an altercation with a Nazi soldier. Everyone knew of similar stories, so no further elabouration was necessary.

At first, life in the camp was not as monotonous as he had imagined it would be and there were several opportunities for whiling away the time productively. One group of boarding houses was allocated to workshops where watchmakers, toymakers, and tailors could practice their professions, and many of them invited other internees to learn their trade. The camp was home to a number of esteemed academics who had established a sort of camp university offering lectures on a variety of topics. Several professional musicians gave impromptu concerts, and there was even an Austrian baker who prepared Viennese pastries and cakes. Daily newspapers were available as well as library books, and the editor of the camp's own newsletter was always looking for articles, poems, and stories from internees with which to fill the pages. As time passed, however, and the days repeated themselves over and over, offering few surprises with nothing to look forward to and no end in sight, Heinrich was finding it increasingly difficult to keep his spirits up. And the feeling of being incarcerated and under suspicion was oppressive.

When the weather was warm, the internees were occasionally allowed onto the beach for a dip in the sea. They were always accompanied by armed soldiers.

"Do they think we are going to make a run for it by swimming across to Ireland?" Heinrich joked humourlessly with Franz, a refugee from Austria.

One day, he discovered that internees were allowed to work beyond the confines of the camp as farm labourers, and he immediately signed up. While he was working in the open fields, away from the sentry boxes and barbed wire of the camp, he could almost taste freedom, an illusion easily shattered whenever he caught the vigilant eye of the guard who watched over him.

He didn't hear anything from the McFees for several months. The postal service was interminably slow and he worried that his letter had been heavily censored, or perhaps McFee had never received it at all. If he had, it was anybody's guess how long a reply would take to reach the camp. Finally, a small package arrived from Lowestoft.

Dear Heinrich,
McFee is not much of a writer, so I am answering your letter, which we were delighted to receive. We trust all continues to go well for you.

We haven't suffered any serious bombing, but the air raid sirens wail most days or nights, and the stress of ducking in and out of shelters not knowing what the next hours will bring is starting to strain people's nerves. Because of our proximity to the naval bases, we are sure to come under heavier bombardment soon.

I do have some good news. McFee made some inquiries and discovered that there is one certain way to secure your release. Volunteer for the British Army.

We know that anything military is completely unfamiliar to you, your being a businessman and all, but you have built up your physical strength working with Alasdair and it is a way out. From what we understand, you wouldn't be called upon to do any real fighting. But you would be making a contribution to the war effort and helping to beat Hitler, which we know you would like to do.

Do let us know what you decide. I enclose a few bits and pieces, which I hope will be useful. Sorry it's not much but this darned rationing is very limiting.

With affection,
Hilda McFee

Unfamiliar with the military ... Heinrich laughed wryly. If only they knew.

He unwrapped Hilda's package and was deeply touched as he looked over its contents: a pack of cigarettes, a small tin of coffee, a bar of soap, a Rowntrees Chocolate Crisp, a packet of Fisherman's Friend, and a hand-knitted scarf, no doubt her own handiwork. Mrs McFee's thoughtfulness brought a lump to his throat.

He mulled at length over McFee's suggestion before making his decision. Several days later, Heinrich strode to the camp commandant's door and knocked.

"Yes, Graber. What can I do for you?"

"I've come to enlist, sir."

CHAPTER TWENTY-SIX

1941–1942

It had been Sally's idea for Lily to volunteer her assistance when it was announced that the town was to expect an influx of French soldiers recently evacuated from Dunkirk. Members of the *Cercle Français*, to which two young women, Betty and Pam, belonged, were enlisted to work as interpreters, but there were too few of them to go around, and Lily's knowledge of French, although limited, was a resource they were delighted to accept.

All schools were closed immediately before the servicemen arrived, and turned into barracks. Sally and the children joined the hundreds of townsfolk who flocked to help make up beds and prepare food. They worked around the clock in the few short hours before the first trainload arrived, greeted by the Mayor and a small crowd of well-wishers who were there to welcome the exhausted, hungry men in their ragged uniforms. The interpreters worked tirelessly, going from school to school. Betsy and Pam took Lily under their wing and a firm friendship was forged between the young women.

Lily had been excited to see a glimpse of herself on the Pathé Newsreel which showed clips of the evacuees' disembarkation at Ramsgate and their arrival in Bournemouth. How brave and awe-inspiring were the boatmen who had risked their lives to save these poor men! One pair of weathered fishermen caught her attention. The frame was grey and grainy, but as the camera zoomed in, something in the younger one's eyes made her heart lurch with an inexplicable jolt of familiarity, setting her pulse racing and sending a shiver down her spine. Unable to shake off the unsettling effect those eyes had had on her, she surreptitiously crept back in to the cinema two days later and waited with bated breath for the newsreel to begin. She was on the edge of her seat in anticipation as the familiar music began and the cockerel crowed its introduction. But to her dismay, the newsreel had changed, and instead of showing the footage she was waiting for, the newsreader launched into a commentary on the visit of the King and Queen to Scotland. Lily left the theatre frustrated, and the disquieting feeling continued to unnerve her for several days.

Soon after the French evacuees had been relocated to camps in other parts of the country prior to their return to war, the Battle of Britain began, and Bournemouth was witness to dramatic dog fights in the sky above the town and the bay as the *Luftwaffe* flew over on its bombing raids. Air raid sirens wailed almost daily, sometimes twice in one day; the aircraft hummed as they flew over, bombs dropped, and then came the tense wait for the All Clear to sound. The air raid shelter became Lily's second home. After several months, Bournemouth became a reception centre for reinforcements in the shape of Air Force personnel from Canada, Australia, and New Zealand, and the visiting airmen were called for duty almost as soon as they arrived.

Feeling the need for more cheerful excitement, one Thursday afternoon Lily slipped out of Beales and rendezvoused with Sally near the Pavilion. King George and Queen Elizabeth were paying a royal visit to inspect the airmen from overseas who had come to fight for Britain. Lily watched as the men were paraded in Westover Road outside the Pavilion. How smart they looked in their starched uniforms. The King and Queen passed along the ranks, having a brief word with some of them. Although the visit was supposed to be secret, word had leaked out and crowds packed the pavements. The road from the station was lined with people, and windows and balconies of nearby hotels were also crowded. The people clapped and waved. Lily remembered Hitler's visit to Breslau for the Sportfest. What a contrast! Here the people showed their admiration for their leaders with dignified decorum – no histrionics, no fevered chanting, no mindless ecstasy.

Once it was understood that the Royal Canadian Air Force would be staying in the area for an extended period of time, the Anglo-Canadian Friendship Society was set up to arrange dances and other entertainments for the airmen. Betty and Pam joined immediately and they invited Lily to become a "society girl" and come with them to various social events, but for many months she had steadfastly refused.

"What are you frightened of Lily? It's only a bit of harmless fun. After all we owe them a lot for leaving their safe homes and coming over here, risking their lives to help us win the war. It's Christmas and they are far from home and their families. The least we can do is show them a good time."

"A good time?"

"It's all proper and above board, don't you worry. Plenty of chaperones to keep us out of trouble."

Sally also encouraged her to go out and have fun.

"You only live once, Lily. It's been over three years. You've pined long enough, and I'm sure Heinrich would want you to get on with your life. We've enough to make us miserable, what with rationing, the bombs, and bloody Hitler almost on our doorstep. Go out with your friends and let your hair down a bit."

Lily knew that Sally was feeling particularly low because, having celebrated his seventeenth birthday, Rob had joined the Home Guard and was training every day after school. Neither Sally nor anyone else was under the illusion that the war would be over before his fast-approaching eighteenth birthday when he would be conscripted into the army. So Lily had finally given in and agreed to go with her girlfriends to a dance at the Allied Services Social Club. But what was she going to wear?

She had been devastated when France fell and Paris was occupied by the Germans, cutting England off from the couture houses and their exclusive designs. Worse still, there was a shortage of lush French fabrics for glamorous clothes. While surprisingly the

Ladies Department maintained many of its wealthy customers and their demand for high-quality fashion, Beales now sought to boost their business among the middle classes. Notices at the entrance and around the store claimed: *If you can only have one outfit a year, you want to get the best value for it, so come and spend your coupons with us. We'll make them go as far as possible.*

Of course, less well-off families, especially those with children, couldn't afford to spend their clothing ration in a place like Beales, and most had to *Make Do and Mend*. This government campaign provided Lily with an opportunity to make a little extra money. Although magazines and posters featured Mrs Sew and Sew, offering dressmaking hints and tips, not all women had the time or talent to do anything but the simplest alterations. Lily, on the other hand, could turn a simple garment into something special. Her reputation spread by word of mouth, and she was particularly sought after for her bridal wear and mother-of-the-bride ensembles. She knew better than to ask her clients how they managed to get their hands on the material for her creations, and she turned a blind eye to their providence. Sally lent her an old sewing machine and she was inundated with requests. For herself, Lily frequented Bournemouth's many secondhand shops which were doing record business, looking for cast-offs she could revamp just as she had done at the Müllers.

Now, she stood perusing her wardrobe and, after considerable hesitation and indecision, she chose a remodeled slender-cut floral dress. The pleated bodice, puffed sleeves, and pussycat bow at the neck gave the demure dress a chic and feminine flair. She added flat pumps, a dash of lipstick, and left the house to join her friends before she could change her mind.

CHAPTER TWENTY-SEVEN

The three women made their entrance at the Social Club.

"Wow!" said Betty. "How lovely. Considering the limitations, it's amazing how festive they've made the place look."

A large hand-painted banner on the far wall proclaimed *Happy Xmas to our Allied Servicemen*. The blackout curtains were decorated with glittery cardboard stars and snowflakes, and the bar, set up at one end of the hall, was trimmed with tinsel. Colourful crepe paper streamers stretched outwards and downwards from the central light fixtures and were fixed to the walls, creating a circus tent atmosphere, and sprigs of holly adorning the tables which lined the room completed the seasonal picture.

While Betty and Pam scanned the hall, Lily was blind to everything except the bar. Her eyes were fixed on several uniformed men lounging casually with drinks in hand who were chatting to a couple of society girls. Her ears were buzzing, her legs turned to jelly, and the room swam before her eyes. Betty took her arm to lead her in, but an ominous sense of déjà vu made the back of her neck prickle and glued her to the spot. She was transported back to that fateful night in the bar when Heinrich rescued her from Lieutenant Bauer. Who would protect her now?

"Come on, Lily," said Betty. "Don't be shy. Let's get a drink and mingle. We'll look after you, don't worry." The spell was broken bringing Lily back to the present. Betty and Pam linked arms with her and they made their way across the room.

"Three glasses of punch if you please," Pam instructed the barman, her foot tapping to the music that had started up. Immediately the floor was packed with couples dancing to popular swing tunes. There were many girls like Betty and Pam who were regular attendees at these functions and had already made the acquaintance of some of the servicemen. Lily's friends were quickly approached and led on to the floor. Lily retreated to the sidelines, studiously refusing to make eye contact with any man who might consider asking her to dance.

"Excuse me, Miss."

Lily slowly looked up.

"May I have the pleasure?" Her eyes moved upwards from the outstretched hand to the mouth that had addressed her.

Her intended "no thank you" sat unuttered on her lips as she registered the handsome face in front of her.

"Flight Lieutenant Hughie Gardner, at your service. I would be honoured if you would accept."

Lily blushed and allowed him to take her hand and lead her onto the dance floor. "I'm Lily," she said, "and I'm afraid I'm not much of a dancer."

"That's okay. I'm no Fred Astaire either."

They danced to "In the Mood" and Lily began to relax and enjoy herself.

"You weren't entirely truthful with me, Lily, were you?" Hughie said to her. "You dance really well."

She wasn't in fact totally inexperienced. One afternoon, Lily had found Sally dancing alone in the living room with the radio blaring. "Come on," Sally had invited her. She'd pulled Lily in and they had danced until they collapsed laughing and exhausted on to the sofa. Sally had introduced Lily to the most popular dance tunes and taught her some of the basic steps.

Jiving now to the familiar Andrews Sisters, Lily felt her embarrassment slip away. Her partner was also more skillful than he had led her to believe and she knew they made an attractive, energetic couple.

"Another one?" he asked as the music came to an end.

Judy Garland's voice began to sing "Over the Rainbow" and Hughie tentatively took Lily in his arms. As they swayed to the ballad, Lily leaned against his broad shoulder and wondered what it would have been like to dance with Heinrich. She had never had the opportunity. And now she never would. The closeness of Hughie's body made her feel quite flustered, and gave rise to sensations she had not experienced for a long time. Her heart was pounding and it was not caused by the lively jiving of the previous dances.

When the song came to an end, Lily found she was reluctant to free herself from Hughie's arms.

"Ladies and gentleman, refreshments are now being served," announced the loudspeaker. This was her cue to break away.

"I'd better join my friends," she said to Hughie. "Thank you for the dances. It's been a while since I really enjoyed myself."

"The pleasure was all mine. I hope we can repeat it." Hughie enveloped Lily's hand in both of his before releasing it – a simple but electrifying gesture that sent her heart racing once again.

"Someone seems to have made a conquest," said Pam when Lily approached her friends.

"And what a dish," added Betty. "Looks like a film star."

Lily's eyes roamed the room, searching the groups of partygoers mingling while they enjoyed the light refreshments until she found Hughie standing with a couple of fellow airmen. He was talking animatedly and suddenly turned and fixed his gaze on her, causing his audience to look over in her direction. She turned away in embarrassment, discomfited that he had caught her staring at him and annoyed that he seemed to be discussing her with his companions.

Just like all the rest, she thought to herself, he probably wants to brag about making a score.

"I think I'm ready to leave now," Lily said to Betty and Pam. "But you stay and enjoy yourselves. Thank you for inviting me. I had a lovely time."

Before they could protest, she collected her coat, went out into the cold winter evening, her feelings in turmoil, and started to walk home.

"Lily, please wait." Hughie ran to catch up with her. "I hope I didn't offend you in some way."

Lily was instinctively wary of being out in the dark with a man she barely knew and she drew back.

"I just wanted to tell you what a great time I had and that I would like to get to know you better, if you'll allow me. I promise to behave like a gentleman." She had heard almost the exact words once before, and Heinrich had certainly kept his promise.

"I'll think about it," Lily said, unwilling to make a commitment but losing her battle against the undeniable attraction she felt.

"*Robinson Crusoe* is playing at the Pavilion. I've never been to a British pantomime and I understand it's a mandatory experience for foreigners. If I get tickets, will you come with me, Lily?"

She hesitated for a moment. "Would it be possible to get four tickets? I'll pay you back, of course. I promised to take my landlady's two children and I wouldn't feel right going without them." *And I would have chaperones*, she thought.

"It will be my pleasure and my treat – a small gesture to repay the kind hospitality I and my fellow servicemen have received over here."

Later, Lily clasped her beloved brooch as she lay in bed reliving the events of the evening, sleep eluding her. After an unsettling start, the dance had been really enjoyable. She couldn't deny that Hughie was gorgeous. Startling blue eyes were partially concealed by a blond forelock which he swept back nervously with long slim fingers. If she was honest with herself, she had decided it was time for her to leave the dance when she'd caught herself wondering what it would be like to feel those fingers on her body. His lopsided grin was enchanting and added to his boyish good looks, which had awakened in her feelings she had thought only Heinrich could arouse. She had been impressed by his good manners and he seemed respectful. He didn't call her sugar or sis, or babe like many of his countrymen who assumed instant familiarity with the local girls.

Was this meeting a coincidence, a matter of pure chance? *Hughie Gardner – H.G. – Heinrich Graber.* She didn't believe in fate, and yet...

CHAPTER TWENTY-EIGHT

Sally had immediately sensed the change in Lily. It was as if a heavy weight had been lifted from her shoulders, revealing the light-hearted young woman she must have been before tragedy laid her low. Hughie had made a favorable impression on her when he came to collect Lily and the children for their outing to the pantomime, and the children had waxed lyrical about him on their return.

"He's fab, Mum," confided Gracie, the colour rising in her cheeks as she avoided eye contact with her mother. Sally hoped this teenage crush wouldn't upset the wonderful relationship her daughter had with Lily.

"Yeah, he's a good bloke," said Rob. "I'd like to pick his brains about the RAF. You should ask him over for a meal, Mum."

"Well, that will depend on Lily. But I'm glad you had a good time and that she is in safe hands." Not so happy about her son's interest in the air force though, she thought.

Now that Japan's ignominious attack on Pearl Harbour had brought the United States into the war, Bournemouth's military population had been augmented by a large number of Americans, who had become a major topic of conversation among the town's womenfolk. Lily's coworkers in Beales' sewing room were no exception.

"It's as if the cinema has come to life," proclaimed Maud. "They're so handsome and well-groomed and clean, just like Hollywood heroes."

"And they use deodourant and aftershave," added Ethel. "If only my Tom would learn from them. He don't half niff by the end of the day."

The British soldiers who had been billeted at Sally's over the past couple of years had been shipped overseas, and the rooms were now taken by American servicemen. Sally was as captivated as the rest of Bournemouth's female population both by the men themselves in their beautifully tailored uniforms and by the chocolate, candies, tinned fruit and peanut butter of which they seemed to have an endless supply. Lily found them too brash and self-confident, swaggering with suave sophistication and liberal largesse.

"It's true they throw their money about," Sally agreed with Lily, "but it's a shot in the arm for local businesses." She didn't have to add that having them as lodgers at the guesthouse insured the family's extra income and rations. Sally, the children, and Lily had enthusiastically embraced the "Dig for Victory" campaign, and the garden, thanks to Bournemouth's amenable climate, flourished with cabbages, runner beans, beetroot, onions, herbs, tomatoes, cucumbers, and even strawberries. A neighbor had helped Sally build a chicken run, and now the early morning chorus of seagulls and other marine fowl was amplified by the clamorous crowing of the raucous rooster. It was Gracie's job to feed the chickens and collect the fresh eggs. All things considered, despite the rationing their meals were nutritious and satisfying. But the little extras provided by her guests were happily received. Sally accepted the packs of cigarettes they handed out even though neither she nor Lily smoked. "Don't look a gift horse in the mouth," she told Lily, adding yet another strange saying to the many Lily had accumulated since coming to England. "They may come in handy for bartering in the future."

Lily had other reasons for disliking the American lodgers. They habitually made suggestive remarks about her looks, often in front of Hughie. She and Hughie had become quite an item over the past few months. She was grateful that he was nothing like the Americans and that he bristled whenever they tried to engage him in their lewd banter. He generally ignored their comments, but one evening on their way out, she had sensed that he was close to punching one of them who suggested, "Come on, babe. Ditch the Mountie and I'll show you a real good time."

"Just ignore them, Hughie. I do," said Lily, glaring at the troublemaker as she hurried him out of the front door.

Hughie was by no means sure of himself when it came to Lily, who kept her feelings closely guarded. He was the polite gentleman he had promised to be and she felt secure in his company. Although she worked long hours and he was frequently out of town at the pilot training base, they managed to make good use of their limited shared leisure time and take advantage of the surprisingly considerable choice of entertainment on offer in spite of the war and the sporadic bombing of the town.

They were both great fans of the movies, and in the dark of the cinema Hughie would casually drape his arm around her shoulders and steal a gentle kiss. She longed for more, but was afraid of initiating, of seeming too forward, of launching a rollercoaster whose end she could not predict. And she still could not help feeling she was betraying Heinrich. One afternoon, they attended the Bournemouth Music Festival featuring the London Philharmonic Orchestra. Sitting on the beach, enraptured by the music, Lily was thrown back to her day out with Heinrich on the Oder River and the outdoor summer concert they had enjoyed. The memories were losing their vividness, but they still had the power to pull at her heartstrings and cast a shadow over a sunny outing.

They often went dancing, and Lily couldn't wait for the slow numbers to begin so that she could melt into Hughie's arms and feel his physical reaction to her closeness which mirrored her own arousal. The Pavilion ballroom was their favourite venue, but one evening Hughie suggested the Swiss restaurant, which he'd discovered was a popular and inexpensive destination for dinner and dancing, frequented by men in the Forces and their partners. The restaurant, located on the ground floor of a block of flats not far from the town centre, boasted large picture windows overhung by red-and-white-striped awnings, matching the colours of the Swiss flag which fluttered over the entrance. Several tables and chairs, shaded by large red-and-white parasols, were arranged on a small low-walled forecourt, offering outdoor seating and giving the venue a holiday ambience as befitted the seaside resort.

"I don't imagine there's anything authentically Swiss about the place," apologised Hughie as he escorted Lily inside, "but I thought it may remind you of home."

Lily smiled nervously, hoping that indeed there was nothing really Swiss about it, which she would be asked to explain or elabourate on. She had stuck steadfastly to her invented history and Sally was still the only person who knew her true background. As soon as they were seated, she quickly changed the subject.

"Hughie, you've never really told me the details of how you ended up in Bournemouth?"

"After my pilot training, I boarded a troopship at Halifax, Nova Scotia, bound for Liverpool. There were eighteen thousand servicemen on board and the crossing took a long seven days because we zigzagged to the Southern Atlantic in order to avoid U-boat concentrations. When we disembarked, I was transferred here. My first assignment was an aircrew course on survival techniques. The base's swimming pool had been turned into an aquatic training camp, where we learned to deploy and get into inflatable dinghies." Hughie smiled as he reminisced.

"Don't you miss home? You never really talk about it to me."

"I miss my family, but not Moose Jaw. The landscape is mile after mile of uninspiring prairie land. In contrast, here I wake up each morning to a breathtaking view of the sea; I can take a stroll on the promenade and watch the birds circle over the cliffs. I know it's a strange thing to say in wartime, but it's almost like being on vacation. And there are no extremes here. At home, the summers can be scorching hot with wild thunderstorms, and the winters freezing cold. Temperatures have been known to reach one hundred degrees in summer and drop to minus forty in the winter. And tornadoes are not uncommon."

"That sounds unbearable."

"I certainly don't miss the Canadian weather, but for all its charm Bournemouth's mild cloudy days of driving drizzle are hard to take. In Moose Jaw most days in the year see sunshine. And because of the clear skies, it was an ideal area to set up a pilot training school which is where I learnt to fly."

"And are there moose in Moose Jaw?"

"None at all," he chuckled. "The name comes from the Cree language of indigenous Indians who populated large areas of Canada. They called the town '*Moosoochapiskun*', which means 'where the white man mended a cart with the jawbone of a moose'. But you must be homesick, Lily. I'm sure you miss the snowcapped mountains and the tinkling of cow bells."

"I think you are confusing me with Heidi, the character in the children's novel," laughed Lily. "Not all of Switzerland is picture postcard beautiful. I am actually quite settled here now and happy to be away from Europe."

"Well, I'm really glad you are here. It's the only thing I can thank Herr Hitler for."

If only you knew, thought Lily, relieved that their meal arrived and conversation was cut short. When the music started up, they were the first couple out on the dance floor.

Towards the end of the summer, Hughie arrived at The Waves pushing two bicycles with plans for a day out and picnic in the Dorset countryside. The day was warm and balmy, the summer breeze fragrant with the smells of the outdoors. They cycled along the leafy lanes, bordered by colourful hedgerows enclosing meadows of grazing cattle and horses. Stopping at a pub in one of the small quaint villages for a rest and cold drink, they exchanged pleasantries with some of the local patrons. They continued on their way until Hughie announced, "Time for lunch, I think." They pulled off the lane into a shady coppice. Hughie laid out the picnic, while Lily gathered some wild flowers, thinking what a perfect day this was turning out to be.

They ate in companionable silence watched by a pair of inquisitive squirrels. Lily threw some crumbs in their direction, but before the squirrels gathered the courage to approach, they were chased off by a flurry of birds that swooped down to make claim to the tempting snack. The stillness was punctuated by the buzzing of bees, the chirping of birds, and the faint mooing of distant cows. For a while, all thoughts of the war were erased from her mind. Lily sighed with contentment.

"I haven't felt so relaxed and at ease for a very long time," she admitted.

"One could almost believe that the war was taking place somewhere else," Hughie agreed.

As if their conversation had tempted fate, the peace was suddenly shattered. The sky was resonating with the unmistakable hum of aircraft followed by the rat-a-tat of gunfire. Instinctively, Hughie threw Lily to the ground and covered her with his own body for protection. They lay in frozen silence until the noise dissipated in the distance. The threat over, he began to raise himself off her. "I hope I didn't hurt you, Lily."

In answer, she grabbed his head and pulled his face down towards her own, greedily seeking his lips. She longed for his touch and drew his hand to her breast, his fingers unleashing her long-suppressed passion. He looked into her eyes questioningly. "Yes, Hughie," she sighed, sliding her hands under his shirt to explore the rippling muscles of his torso. She could feel his erection against her hip, and, fueled with desire, she writhed and groaned under his caress.

"You are so lovely," he whispered in her ear as he lifted her skirt, aroused even further as he registered she was helping him slide off her underwear. Their kisses became more urgent and Lily arched her body to welcome him inside her.

Afterwards, as they lay spent side by side, Hughie gently stroked Lily's cheek and wiped away two lone tears which escaped her eyes – a tear of joy for the present and a tear of sadness for the past. She turned to face him sighing with pleasure as she planted a kiss on his open palm.

He looked at her questioningly. "Tears of happiness," she reassured him and herself.

CHAPTER TWENTY-NINE

Heinrich was becoming increasingly frustrated. This was not what he had signed up for. He had sworn allegiance to King George VI and received the King's shilling with the intention of taking his oath seriously. Admittedly, his decision to volunteer had been motivated more by his desire to leave the internment camp rather than by his eagerness to return to military service, but the step having been taken, he wanted to do whatever he could to reinforce Britain's resistance against Hitler. But, so far, he couldn't see how his service was making any significant contribution.

Arriving at the training camp, he discovered that he was to join the Army's Pioneer Corps. It felt strange to be back in uniform, although the ill-fitting khaki was nothing like his previous immaculate regimentals. To call the place a training camp was something of an overstatement. He and his fellow recruits practiced saluting and parade drills, commands, and army routines, but were not given arms or taught how to use them. Basic training was, indeed, very basic. Anxious to camouflage his military background, Heinrich copied some of the more incompetent soldiers, confusing left and right legs when marching and exaggerating clumsiness and tardiness during inspections.

To his amazement, he discovered that almost the entire company was made up of Jewish refugees, both recent and veteran. The only British soldiers were the officers. Equally surprising was the fact that the motley group of recruits included doctors, lawyers, bankers, academics, and other unlikely characters, whose only common denominators were their status as aliens and their loyalty to the British in the fight against the Hitler's forces. Having suffered persecution by the Nazis, they were horrified at the prospect of again falling into their hands, and they knew that if Britain succumbed, it meant certain death. Their fears were justified. Heinrich was not the only one who understood the ruthless force of the German war machine, the finely honed organization of the *Wehrmacht*, and the power of the *Luftwaffe*, and his knowledge was all the more intimate having been an active participant in the buildup to war over the past years.

All too soon it became obvious that none of the volunteers' personal expertise was to be capitalized on. Despite a lack of army medics, the qualified doctors were refused more suitable and meaningful service. Two Germans explained to their commander that they had fought for the Kaiser in the Great War and could contribute their experience to Britain's war effort. Their offer was refused. Heinrich was interested to know in which units they had fought and on which fronts. Perhaps they had served alongside his late brothers. One of them answered that the names were familiar, but he couldn't be sure. Heinrich continued to remain silent about his own military career; it was too recent, and he was afraid of being considered a security risk and sent back to the internment camp.

The duties of the Pioneer Corps were uninspiring and unchallenging. His company moved around the country to undertake manual labour wherever it was needed. They loaded and unloaded railroad cars; tested bailey bridges; mixed concrete; put up barbed wire defenses; cleared airfield runways of rocks and stones; dug trenches and constructed Nissen huts. The work was corporeal and mindless. Heinrich was impressed that, to their credit, the professionals and academics, unused as they were to hard work and a lack of intellectual stimulation, carried out their tasks dutifully and without complaint. Heinrich was happy to get back to physical exercise, his muscles still toned from his months as a fisherman, but the monotony of the work combined with the endless dust, grime, mud and damp were beginning to take their toll on his spirit.

Just when he thought he was reaching breaking point, the rumour factory began to buzz with reports that special units of alien soldiers were being organised. Mysterious figures from Military

Intelligence were seeking fluent German speakers for secret missions. Hushed whispers intoned words like *elite, commando, special duties. Here's my chance,* thought Heinrich, and he wasted no time in approaching his commanding officer and putting his name forward for consideration.

Before he knew it, Heinrich had in his hand a train ticket and directions to a meeting at a London hotel. He enjoyed the ride through the English countryside, but as the train passed through more heavily urban areas on its approach to its destination, Heinrich was dismayed at the gruesome evidence of German bombing – piles of rubble where buildings once stood, while those that had withstood attack boasted broken windows and facades heavily pockmarked by shrapnel. When he exited the station, he was surprised and pleased to see that it appeared to be business as usual in the city centre. The main thoroughfare was bustling with pedestrians and traffic, the famous red double-decker buses were running along, and while some of the stores were boarded up, others appeared to be doing lively trade. Feeling almost like a free man, he strode along with a spring in his step until he reached the hotel.

Having expected some backstreet hole-in-the-wall establishment he now stood transfixed in wonder in front of a majestic, imposing redbrick eight-story edifice which occupied an entire block. It was built in the Gothic style with mock parapets, conical towers, pointed arches, and deeply pitched rooves lined with dormers. The building was topped by an impressive clock tower and Union Jacks which flapped proudly in the wind at each corner of the roof.

Heinrich walked through the arched entranceway into the hotel's interior where he found himself in a glazed courtyard beneath a magnificent glass-domed atrium around which the hotel was built. This must have been spectacular in its day, he imagined. On closer inspection, he discerned an aura of disrepair and neglect. The only patrons appeared to be military personnel. He presented himself at the reception desk and was escorted along a corridor to a room where he was instructed to wait. After a few minutes, a tall senior officer entered. Heinrich stood and saluted.

"As you were, Private Graber. I am Major Sutherland. It's my job to ascertain your suitability for more active duty than the Pioneer Corps."

He browsed through Heinrich's file and asked several questions, verifying facts and checking details about his Pioneer Corps service. Sitting across from his interviewer, Heinrich could tell that the meeting was not going well.

"We are in the process of forming a number of groups for special missions both in front of and behind enemy lines. I should warn you that the preparation will be grueling. You are a little older than the recruits we are seeking, and from what I can tell from this report, you didn't exactly excel in basic training. Our missions are top secret and extremely dangerous, so we can only afford to take the best and most promising candidates. I feel, Private Graber, that you do not fit the bill."

"I would ask that you do not underestimate me," Heinrich insisted.

Sutherland looked again at Heinrich's file. "It says here that you were a businessman and that you had to flee Germany because you got into some trouble with the local Gestapo. You managed to escape by ship which sank, and you were picked up on the cusp of death by a fisherman. None of this really qualifies you for what we have in mind. Do you have anything to add which might convince me otherwise?"

Heinrich weighed his options. If he stuck to his story, then it was obvious he would be disqualified. To come clean and tell the truth was a gamble. Would he revert to enemy alien status? What was the worst that could happen? They could send him back to the monotony of the internment camp, which may even be preferable to returning to his mindless duties in the Pioneer Corps. Or was there a chance that his military history might persuade them to give him an opportunity to prove himself? Either way, he had nothing to lose.

"Sir, I'm afraid that I have not been totally honest with regard to my background before I came to Britain."

Sutherland cocked an eyebrow. "Is that so?"

"I was Major Graber, an officer in the Wehrmacht." From Sutherland's expression, Heinrich could tell that he had caught his interviewer's attention.

"My two older brothers fought in the last war and were decorated with the Iron Cross posthumously for their courage. I admired them greatly, and when I turned eighteen I decided to follow in their footsteps. At that time, there were no restrictions regarding recruitment of Jews into the military. I was an exemplary soldier and made my way quite quickly up through the ranks. And then Hitler rose to power. I became more and more disillusioned as the Führer's plans for aggressive action began to reveal themselves, and I began to discern anti-Semitic sentiment among newer recruits – and even among those with whom I had served for many years. I watched in horror as the racist laws and government sponsored thugs made life for German Jews unbearable. And then it was my turn. One night, I was set upon by a number of my fellow officers. I was beaten and stabbed and left for dead. Bravely aided by a kind and concerned person to whom I owe my life, with the last vestiges of my strength and willpower I managed to get to my brother's apartment. He is the businessman in the family, and he was the one who managed to smuggle me onto a ship and out of the country."

Heinrich waited for a reaction. A few moments passed and the Major leant back in his chair.

"Well, that's some story, Private Graber. I can understand your reluctance to share it before now. Let me pick up on a few points. You say that you were a commissioned officer, a Major?"

"Yes, Sir."

"How did you become aware of Hitler's intentions?"

"We were sent on a hugely increased number of maneuvers, many of which included all branches of the military – ground forces, navy, and Luftwaffe. We learned new strategies and tactics, combined battle plans and offensives. There was nothing defensive about it. It was obvious that an attack was in the making. I had always said that I would defend Germany in the face of aggression, but I was not prepared to participate in unprovoked hostility."

"Thank you for your honesty, Private Graber. Of course, this does raise questions regarding loyalty and security risk."

"That's precisely why I have kept it to myself until now. But I can assure you, Sir, my loyalty is undivided."

Sutherland was silently thoughtful for a few minutes.

"Go out and get yourself some lunch. I will bring your case to my colleagues. Report back to me at sixteen hundred hours."

Heinrich stood and saluted. As he exited the hotel, he breathed a sigh of relief. Keeping up the pretense about his past had not been easy, and now he had finally shed the lie which had weighed heavily on him since his arrival in Britain. He might not get a special mission, but if Sutherland let him out to wander the streets of London freely, he obviously did not think Heinrich posed a security threat.

Heinrich returned to the hotel well before the appointed time. When he was summoned into the room, he was surprised to see a Colonel sitting behind the desk. Major Sutherland introduced him and then left the room.

"So, Private, or should I say, Major Graber, it seems that you are not exactly what you appear to be." Heinrich started to feel hot under the collar. Was this to be an interrogation? It was hard to gauge whether the Colonel's tone was hostile, and he was very aware of the handgun lying on the table within the officer's easy reach.

The Colonel leafed through Heinrich's file to which Major Sutherland had added his notes made during the first interview.

"Not an innocent businessman hounded by the Nazis but a commissioned officer in the *Wehrmacht*?"

"Correct, Sir. But to the Nazis, a Jew is a Jew no matter his profession or rank."

"And where were you stationed?"

"In various locations throughout Germany, but for the last three years before I escaped I was billeted in my home town of Breslau in Upper Silesia."

"I understand from my colleague that you participated in numerous maneuvers and training exercises. Is that correct?"

"Yes, Sir." Heinrich nodded his affirmation.

"So it is safe for me to assume that you have intimate knowledge of Hitler's military strategies and battle plans and that you are fluent in technical military jargon?"

"To the very smallest detail, Sir. I doubt whether you will find anyone more knowledgeable than me among your candidates."

"And you can differentiate between different ranks and regiments?"

"Of course."

"How about understanding different German dialects?"

"I served under, alongside, and above soldiers from all over the country and can tell which region someone comes from by his speech."

Heinrich wondered where all this questioning was leading.

"Right then, Private Graber. I believe that you are the perfect candidate for a special mission under my command in the Intelligence Corps. But before I tell you any more, you must sign the Official Secrets Act. If you agree to sign, from this moment on everything you hear, read, or see must be kept secret. Breaking the act can be punishable by death. No one will know where you are and you must never discuss your work with anyone."

"Does this mean that I will finally be seeing action?"

"You won't be leaving British soil, if that's what you are asking, but what you are about to do is infinitely more important than firing a rifle or driving a tank."

Heinrich was disappointed but at the same time intrigued. What could this mission possibly entail? How did his background qualify him for the task? He would not see combat, but the Colonel had insisted that his job would be equally, if not more, important in the long run.

He picked up the proffered pen. "Where do I sign?"

"Just one more thing, Private Graber. We need you to anglicize your name. For your own safety and for ours."

Heinrich thought for a few moments and then signed on the dotted line. The Colonel looked at his signature and then shook his hand.

"Welcome aboard, Sergeant Henry Grant."

CHAPTER THIRTY

Heinrich was surprised by the shortness of the train journey to his new destination. He had been briefed on the mission without being given too many specifics, and he had assumed that such a clandestine operation would have been conducted much further away from London and other major cities which were still the targets of German bombing raids. He was met at the station and driven a couple of miles into an area of parkland whose loveliness took his breath away. He became even more confused as the car turned through a walled gateway into an avenue of lime trees, which opened out to a sweeping driveway bordered by carpets of yellow and white daffodils. The car continued on its way towards a magnificent stately home which presided over the surrounding countryside like an estate in a Jane Austen novel.

Before reaching the main entrance of the huge redbrick mansion, the driver swung around to the side of the building and pulled up at a discreet door. Heinrich was ushered inside and shown into a small room. He saluted the officer seated behind the desk.

"Sergeant Heinrich, er, I mean Henry Grant reporting for duty, Sir."

"At ease, Sergeant. Welcome to our little operation."

"I am confused, Sir. I was told that I would be coming to a prisoner-of-war camp. This bears no resemblance to any German *Stalag*."

"Don't worry, Sergeant Grant. All will be revealed."

As if on cue, the door opened and another soldier entered the room and saluted.

"Right on time, Sergeant Spencer. This is Sergeant Henry Grant. Show him around and bring him up to speed on his duties. Dismissed."

"Bring your things and I will show you your room."

Heinrich was surprised by Spencer's German accent.

"*Sind Sie aus Deutschland?*"

"Yes, I was born in Berlin. But they prefer that we stick to English here and use our new names. You can call me Mark."

"I assume that is your anglicized name. How did you come up with it?"

"I was a bit early for my interview so I went into a store to kill some time – Marks and Spencer. My given name is Marcus so it was the first thing that came in to my head when they told me to pick a name. What about you?"

"I just wanted to keep my initials. I chose the two best-looking film stars I could think of – Henry as in Fonda, and Grant as in Cary."

"I like your modesty," joked Mark. "Shame you don't resemble either of them."

Heinrich dumped his kitbag on the bed he had been assigned and followed Mark out of the room, down two flights of stairs, and along a narrow corridor. Mark opened a door. "This is the M room. M for microphone. You are now officially a secret listener."

Heinrich surveyed the large space. Rows of tables were manned by soldiers wearing headphones. Mark showed Heinrich to an empty table. In front of him was an old-fashioned switchboard complete with numbered sockets and plugs.

"When you plug in to a socket, you will be able to hear the conversations of the cellmates in a particular room. This is recording equipment," Mark said, pointing to a turntable. "If you hear something which you think may be of importance, press this button to start the turntable revolving, and pull this lever down to lower the recording head onto the record. The conversation will be recorded."

"What are the chances of hearing something valuable?" said Heinrich, skeptically.

"All the prisoners here are high-ranking German officers. We even have Generals. The entire compound is bugged. Wherever they are, whether in the dining room, their bedrooms, playing billiards, taking afternoon tea, and even when they are out strolling in the grounds, we can hear what they are talking about."

"Aren't they suspicious? Don't they think they are being bugged?"

"Actually, no. The very opulence of the estate and the VIP treatment they are receiving, which their ridiculous egos assume is justly deserved, lull them into a false sense of security and they don't guard their tongues. They like to boast to one another about their military accomplishments and knowledge, convinced that Hitler will win the war. You would be amazed at some of the intelligence we have picked up."

Heinrich was intrigued and couldn't wait to get started. Mark explained the rest of the procedures and cautioned him not to discuss anything he overheard or any aspect of his work with anyone, not even the other secret listeners.

For the first few days, the conversations on which he eavesdropped were disappointingly banal. But then one afternoon, Heinrich's senses were alerted to a different kind of exchange. One of the prisoners had been taken for interrogation and returned to his room preening with pride that he had not told "the stupid British" anything about Hitler's secret weapons programme. Heinrich's pulse quickened as he overheard the specifics which the prisoner was happy to impart to his cellmate. He entered the prisoner's name, topic of conversation, and time of day into the daily log, and took the recording to an adjoining room for transcription, as he had been instructed. After the silence of the M room, the cacophonous clattering of typewriters was an assault on his ears. He scanned the room, wondering to whom he should give the record. Most of the personnel were men, but several uniformed women manned desks and telephones. His eyes locked on to a stunning redhead whose fingers danced on her keyboard faster than he thought possible. Her perfect face held a look of determined concentration as she listened intently on her headphones to the recording she was transcribing. Then, as if she felt his gaze on her, she looked up directly into his eyes and smiled the most disarming smile. Heinrich was smitten. His mouth was suddenly dry and the stirring in his groin was instantaneous. He hadn't felt so aroused since …

"Do you have something for us, Sergeant?" asked the soldier sitting at the nearest desk, giving a knowing wink. "Name's Gordon, by the way."

Heinrich, embarrassed at having been caught out, gave him the record.

"And you are?"

"Henry Grant," he said, his eyes drawn back to the typist.

"She's a real dish, isn't she?" Gordon whispered. "Don't get your hopes up, mate. Many have tried; all have failed."

Heinrich went back to his station, making a mental note to ask Mark about the regulations regarding fraternization with female personnel.

Over the next few days, Heinrich hoped and prayed that he would hear something significant to record, which would give him an excuse to see her again. He pictured her in his dreams and fantasized about getting her alone. For the first time in years, his erotic reveries were not punctuated by Lily's face. It was time to get on with his life once and for all, and this fiery beauty who had reignited his desire was the woman to help him move on. Finally, one of his "charges" was joined by a new prisoner and they began to exchange confidences, talking about a new rocket programme that could change the direction of the war. Heinrich made the recording, filled in the log, and hurried to the transcription room. This was exciting stuff. He handed over the record while he scanned the room for the redhead, but couldn't see her.

"Off on special leave. Some family crisis," Gordon informed him.

Heinrich was surprised at the depth of his disappointment as he went back to work. How long would she be away? Would she come back at all? Had he imagined the mutual frisson created in that single moment of eye contact? Mark had hinted that female personnel were not off-limits and relationships were unofficially permitted, as long as they were discreet and did not interfere with their duties. He couldn't wait for her to return.

CHAPTER THIRTY-ONE

The endless hours of listening to chatter, much of which was mundane, combined with the lack of fresh air and exercise in the basement, had a soporific effect on Heinrich, and by the end of his shift all he wanted to do was stretch his legs outside in the area permitted to personnel, out of sight of the prisoners. After dinner, he would return to his room for a little privacy and quiet. Occasionally, Mark persuaded him to join the others for a game of cards or chess. The mansion's extensive library was bugged and available only to the prisoners, but Heinrich discovered another stash of books in the listeners' quarters, and he began to catch up on his reading, particularly when he had free time during the day before his turn to do an evening shift.

Two weeks passed by and, following several more deliveries to the transcription room still with no sight of the redhead, he finally found out that she had been granted some compassionate leave because her husband had been declared missing in action. *Husband? Of course there's a husband*, he berated himself. *I might have guessed that a woman as perfect as her wouldn't be unattached.*

"Come on, Henry," said Mark one evening. "It's our turn for a well-deserved night off and a few of us are going to the pub for a drink. It's about time we had some R and R. It's a nice place and sometimes there's even a singer. And some pretty faces."

The Rose and Crown was a short drive away. Situated down a country lane, the two-story building, which according to a plaque on the wall dated back to the eighteenth century, was warm and welcoming. It was bursting with traditional character; the ceilings were low, the brickwork exposed, and the whole place appeared to be held up by gnarled timber beams and supports. Warmth emanated from several crackling fireplaces and a winding wooden staircase led up to a mezzanine and a couple of bedrooms. Two friendly barmaids manned the long wooden bar, which had a red luster from many decades of polishing, and they dispensed beer from big white pump handles. A group of men at one end were enjoying a game of darts. Now an experienced listener, Heinrich's ears were automatically attuned to several conversations among the locals.

"Imagine having to pay five and thruppence for a hundredweight of coal. It's outrageous," said an elderly woman.

"It's because they're sending it all to Italy," explained her male companion.

Others were complaining about food shortages: "I did used to like my cuppa tea regular, but now we have to manage with one cup a day, like. Well, what can you do when you only get half a pound a month?"

Mark pulled him over to join a group at the bar. "Now, now, Henry. This is supposed to be a night off. Give your ears a rest. What are you drinking?"

Heinrich began to feel more relaxed once he had downed a couple of pints. It occurred to him that his fellow soldiers must come here regularly, since no one seemed to make any fuss about the ones with German accents. The British uniform was enough to grant them admission into the community, and if any locals wondered what they were doing in this part of the country, no one even considered asking.

"I thought some of our female soldiers were coming to the pub tonight. Where have they got to?" said Heinrich as he took a swig of his third beer.

"They usually prefer the lounge bar over there," said Mark. "It's quieter and has tables and chairs."

After they had been in the pub for about an hour, Heinrich could hear music emanating from the lounge bar, and he saw several customers were making their way in that direction. A pianist had launched into some popular tunes and invited his audience to join in the singalong. Heinrich made his way in the direction of the music and recognised one or two women from the transcription room. There were also several unfamiliar ones who were giving him appreciative looks. He approached one of the tables.

"May I, ladies?" he asked and sat down without waiting for a reply. They exchanged names and a few pleasantries, but then Heinrich wondered what they could talk about, given the secrecy of their work and the prohibition on discussing any of it. He offered to refill their drinks to kill some time while he thought up some topics of conversation. As he returned to the table, a side door, which led to the toilets, opened and in walked the redhead. He almost dropped the glasses he was holding.

"This is Celia," one of the girls accepting her drink introduced them. "Celia meet Henry."

"It's a pleasure," Celia said, once again looking directly into his eyes. Her voice was deep and husky, making simple words sound like a seduction. Could everyone around them sense the magnetic attraction between them?

"I was sorry to hear about your husband," offered Heinrich, trying to break the spell. "Has there been any news?"

"No, nothing yet," she replied, her face betraying no emotion as she looked him straight in the eyes.

The pianist began to play "I've Got You Under My Skin", and the girls joined in.

Celia stood up. "I need some air."

"I need another drink," Heinrich told the girls and made his way back to the bar. Checking that no one was watching him, he slipped outside and made his way to the pub's back garden. Orphaned tables and chairs, unused in the winter months, were propped up on the pub's back wall. Just beyond them, he could make out a spiral of cigarette smoke. And there she was, waiting for him. For several moments he just stood still and looked at her. Then he leaned towards her, touching his lips to hers tentatively. She did not resist. He took her face in his hands and pulled her to him a little more forcefully. She pulled his finger into her mouth and sucked on it greedily till a groan welled up from deep in his throat.

Heinrich dropped his pants and lifted her up, shocked and thrilled to discover that she wore no underwear under her uniform skirt. Had she planned this? She slid onto him easily and they rocked in unison against the wall. His lips found hers once more and he explored her mouth. Now it was her turn to groan with pleasure. They were panting heavily and their hot breath became a mist around them as it mingled with the cold night air. They were both racing now towards the climax which would slake their thirst. Celia threw her head back and gasped as she orgasmed. When she kissed Heinrich with a tenderness that belied the savageness of what had gone before, Heinrich knew she could feel the tears coursing down his cheeks.

"That was wonderful," he told her, stroking her hair.

A snapshot of Lily had flashed fleetingly before his eyes but was now banished forever.

CHAPTER THIRTY-TWO

Although she had been living at Sally's for four years Lily had seen little of the surrounding area. Sally was always too busy with the guesthouse, and on the rare occasion that they went on an outing, they usually stayed fairly close to home. Budget, time limits, and lack of transportation more often than not determined the itinerary. That started to change once Lily and Hughie became an item. Hughie arrived one afternoon soon after their intimate picnic brandishing a small booklet entitled *Furlough in Bournemouth*. It was published by the American Red Cross especially for wounded army personnel recuperating in the town, which had become a centre for rest and recreation for American Forces.

"It says here that Lulworth Cove, Corfe Castle, and the Isle of Wight are must-sees," read Hughie. "Who wants to join me?"

Lily was touched by his generosity towards Sally and the children. Of late, the atmosphere at The Waves had become strained. Rob had received his call-up papers and any day would be leaving. Since finishing school, he had been working as an apprentice car mechanic and would be joining the Royal Engineers. Sally put on a brave face but underneath Lily knew she was a nervous wreck. Gracie had turned sixteen and, as expected, had blossomed into a lovely young woman, but the characteristic rebelliousness and moodiness of almost-adulthood was exacerbated by the constraints of war, and she often tried Sally's patience. The eruption of a pimple or a broken fingernail could easily trigger an outburst and Rob's teasing just stoked the fires.

Lily knew Hughie would rather take her out alone and she admired his sensitivity to their feelings. It was also a way for him to show his gratitude to Sally for the open hospitality she offered him.

"I don't know where they got their information," said Sally. "But I'm pretty sure the Isle of Wight must be out of bounds to visitors. It's been bombed a lot and it's very close to France, which is occupied by the Nazis, if you recall. Rumour has it that Lulworth is being used for army training."

"Corfe Castle it is then," said Hughie refusing to take no for an answer. "Next Saturday if the weather is okay."

Hughie pulled up outside the guesthouse the following weekend and announced his arrival with several blasts of a horn. Gracie ran out, excited to see the army jeep with Hughie at the wheel. Lily knew this would really be something to brag about to Gracie's school friends; they all had crushes on the town's servicemen, especially the Americans. The more brassy girls flaunted themselves and flirted shamelessly, and some boasted about what they got up to. Gracie didn't believe half of it, she told Lily, but the other half, which was very scandalous, might actually be true. Sally had given her a good talking to about dallying with men in uniform.

Lily and Sally followed Gracie outside and Rob brought up the rear. The forecast was warm and dry, but knowing the unpredictability of the British weather, Sally looked a bit skeptical when she saw the open vehicle. It was late September after all.

"It'll be a bit of a squeeze, I'm afraid," Hughie apologised, and, registering the expression on Sally's face, he added, "Don't worry. If the weather changes we can put the top up."

They spent a few minutes swapping positions, Rob's long legs being the major problem, until they found the most comfortable option, with Rob next to Hughie in the front and the ladies in the back. Driving out of town in the direction of Poole, they reached the road which skirted the harbour and led to the narrow spit of land at Sandbanks, where it ended at the chain ferry, which would take them across the harbour entrance towards Studland and the Purbeck Hills. There were hardly any vehicles queueing for the ferry because petrol rationing limited lengthy jaunts into the countryside, but several cyclists and a number of foot passengers, many with dogs, waited ahead of them, probably out for a day's rambling or bird watching. As the jeep made its way up the ramp onto the ferry, Lily's pulse began to race and her hands trembled. She had overcome her fear of being in proximity to the sea, but she hadn't been on the water since her near-drowning, and the panic attack threatened to overwhelm her.

Sally saw the whitening of her knuckles as she gripped the side of the jeep and immediately understood her plight. "Deep breaths, Lily," she whispered in her ear. "There's nothing to be afraid of."

Hughie and the children jumped out of the jeep to stand at the side of the ferry and get a better view of Poole Harbour on the starboard side and the open sea to the left. Lily held tightly to her seat as the ferry began to pull away. The enormous serpentine chain chirred and complained as it coaxed the ferry across the short distance to the dock on the other side. The journey took just a few minutes, but to Lily it felt like a lifetime.

"Are you okay?" asked Hughie with a frown when he started the engine and moved the jeep down the ramp and onto dry land.

"I'll be fine," replied Lily as relief washed over her and her heart returned to its normal rhythm. "Not mad about the motion of the water," she explained.

"Why didn't you say so?" he said and patted her hand. "We'll take the longer route home over dry land."

They continued onwards marveling at the picturesque countryside until they reached the quaint village of Corfe Castle, named for the majestic ruins which stood guard atop a high mound overlooking the surrounding area. The village comprised just two streets, East and West, which connected at the village Square. The Square was bordered by a cluster of stone houses with grey slate roofs, and at its centre stood a tall monument commemorating Queen Victoria's Diamond Jubilee of 1897. Hughie parked the jeep outside the Greyhound Inn.

"Race you to the top," Rob challenged Gracie and they took off up the hill. The adults followed at a more leisurely pace. By the time they caught up, Gracie was waving at them as she leaned out from one of the castle's ruined towers. Rob shouted up at her, "Rapunzel, Rapunzel, let down your hair," and they giggled helplessly. Lily stopped in her tracks. It was as if time had sped backwards and she was with the Müller children on holiday at Hirschberg.

Did I really believe that all love stories have a happy ending? How stupid and naïve was that? She gave a long sigh.

Hughie took her hand. "You look like you've seen a ghost."

"Just reminiscing on times gone by."

"This view is just too darn marvelous," he enthused. He drew her behind a crumbled stone wall out of sight and kissed her deeply. "And very romantic. We must come back here alone some time."

They were all hungry, so they made their way down the hill back to the Greyhound Inn, an old rustic pub. The flagstone floor, exposed ceiling beams and rubble stone walls attested to its age. Hughie ordered a beer for himself and for Rob, after asking for Sally's approval, and the girls had soft drinks. Sally passed round sandwiches she had brought from home. "With rationing, you never know what's going to be available when you go out," she explained.

The pub was cosy with a congenial atmosphere. Lily could sense Sally starting to relax. She squeezed Hughie's arm. "This has been a really good idea. Thank you," she whispered to him.

By the time they were ready to leave, the air had turned a little chillier, so Rob helped Hughie open up the jeep's folded roof, which did little to protect them from the elements. The girls huddled together for warmth in the back while the men seemed unaffected by the cold wind. As promised, they drove home overland via Wareham and Lytchett Minster, and less than an hour later they were back at The Waves. Rob and Gracie dashed inside to warm up, shouting their thanks as they ran.

"Thank you for a wonderful day," Sally said and hugged Hughie. "It was just what the doctor ordered. Come inside and warm up over a plate of hot soup."

Hughie waited until Sally and the children were safely inside before pulling Lily into his arms. He knew it was important for her to exhibit some semblance of propriety, especially in front of the children, and he kept physical contact to a minimum in the guesthouse. Lily still shared a bedroom with Sally, and she had made it clear to him that it was strictly out of bounds for any hanky-panky – another English expression that she found hilarious. She hadn't divulged to him that a week earlier she had left work in the middle of the day feeling off colour, and had arrived home unexpectedly to find Sally and one of the Americans *in flagrante* in said bedroom. Sally must have known that Lily's relationship with Hughie would have progressed to lovemaking, but she never made any judgmental remarks, only telling her *to be careful*. Lily had repaid the thoughtfulness by smiling at the surprised couple, closing the bedroom door, and going instead to Gracie's room for a lie down. Secretly she was delighted that Sally was letting her hair down and having a romance of her own. It made her feel less guilty about her relationship with Hughie and more hopeful about Sally's future when Rob left for military duty.

CHAPTER THIRTY-THREE

Lily had made a new friend. Her name was Millie Court, and she was a member of a theatrical troupe who toured the country bringing London's West End to the provinces. Lily and Hughie first saw her in a production of *Full Swing*, a light-hearted musical comedy staged at the Boscombe Hippodrome. A couple of months later, Hughie bought tickets for *No, No Nanette* at the Pavilion, and in this production Millie was playing one of the leading characters.

"She's very talented, isn't she, Hughie?"

"She sure is, and she can really hold a tune. With those looks, I reckon if she gets a break she could be a star."

Whenever they were appearing in the Bournemouth area, the cast and crew stayed at the Metropole. Lily had seen them coming and going quite often while she waited in the lobby for Hughie who was billeted at the hotel, or when they were eating in the hotel's restaurant.

A few days before Christmas, the company came back to town to perform the pantomime *Babes in the Wood*. This year, the holiday atmosphere in Bournemouth was more palpable than it had been during the previous three wartime Christmases. People's spirits had been lifted by the Allied victory over the Germans at El Alamein, which was still fresh in their memory, and by recent news of heavy German losses at Stalingrad. There was a feeling that this Christmas was the beginning of more peaceful days ahead and that the end of the war might come soon.

One morning during her tea break, Lily bumped into Millie in Beales. Lily was last-minute present-hunting for Hughie. She had no idea what to give him and hoped to get inspiration by browsing in the men's gifts department. As if it had been rehearsed, Lily and Millie simultaneously pointed at the same pair of leather gloves and asked the salesman in unison, "May I see those ones please?"

They turned to look at each other and burst out laughing.

"You're Millie Court, aren't you? I'm a big fan," Lily blurted out and then blushed in embarrassment. "Sorry, I feel like an idiot. You must get that all the time."

"Not at all. I'm flattered you even recognise me. I'm not exactly Vivien Leigh, after all."

The gloves were forgotten.

"Would you like to join me for a cup of tea?" Millie asked.

"I'd love to, but I have to get back to work. Perhaps later?"

"Sorry, I have an afternoon matinee and then the evening performance. Do you have any free time tomorrow?"

"I finish work at five-thirty and I don't have any plans."

"Perfect. There's no matinee tomorrow, so I'm free till about seven. I'll meet you at the front entrance of the store."

They said their goodbyes and Lily hurried back to the sewing room.

"What's that big smile about then?" asked Elsie.

"Nothing special," said Lily. She had no intention of sharing Millie Court with any of her workmates. She respected Millie's privacy as well as her own, and wanted at all costs to avoid their predictable incessant interrogation for gossip and tidbits.

Lily did however share the news of her meeting with Sally when she got home that evening.

"She's very beautiful in an exotic sort of way and not at all standoffish."

"Well, invite her round for tea sometime. I'm sure Gracie would be head over heels at having a celebrity in the house. And maybe I could get her to autograph a photo to send to Rob with my next letter."

The next day, Millie was waiting for Lily as arranged. She linked her arm through Lily's, leading her towards the Square. "Let's go to the restaurant in Bobby's. I'm sure we can find a quiet table away from prying eyes."

When they were seated and their tea ordered Millie asked Lily to tell her about herself.

"I detect the hint of an accent. Are you a refugee?"

Lily reeled off her well-rehearsed story, which she had repeated so many times that it almost didn't feel like a lie any more.

"And do you enjoy your job at Beales?"

"I was very lucky to get it, but it is a little frustrating just doing alterations. My dream is to work in exclusive fashion. I hope when the war is over to find work in an haute couture house and from there develop my own business with my own designs."

"Big plans indeed. Have you ever thought about costume design for theatre, or better still, films?"

"Not really. Although when I'm watching a film I tend to be quite critical about what the actors are wearing. I sometimes drive my boyfriend, Hughie, mad with all my comments."

"You have a boyfriend? Lucky girl."

"He's with the Canadian Air Force."

"Serious?"

"I don't know yet." Lily, as always, was keeping her cards close to her chest.

Millie looked at her watch. "This has been really lovely, Lily. I hope we have another chance to get together before I move on."

"I know you don't have a performance on Sunday. Would you like to come to The Waves for lunch? Hughie is coming as well. I know Sally will be pleased."

"I'd love to," Millie said with a smile. "It would be so nice to eat a home cooked meal for a change. Some people think that all this moving around from hotel to hotel and eating out is a glamorous life, but I am a homebody by nature and get quite fed up with it all. But I am always happy to come back to Bournemouth. It's such a friendly town and feels almost like home."

"Sally, you've really pulled out all the stops," said Lily the following Sunday, admiring the spread that Sally was preparing to put out on the table. Gracie was fussing about checking the decorations and place settings, clearly beside herself with excitement at meeting Millie face to face. When Gracie heard the knock, she ran to open the front door.

"Look who I found standing on the doorstep," joked Hughie as he escorted Millie inside. He seemed a little awestruck, too.

"So kind of you to invite me, Sally," said Millie. "And you must be Gracie." She offered her hand, which Gracie shook with great enthusiasm.

"We're delighted you could come," said Sally, showing her guest into the dining room.

"Doesn't this look festive! You've done a great job under the present circumstances."

"It must be very hard for you, Millie, being away from your family at Christmas time. I know it is for me," offered Hughie.

"My family isn't really into Christmas," she said, taking off her coat and depositing it into Gracie's outstretched arms, before accepting the chair proffered by Sally. "So none of us minds that it's a busy season for me with pantomimes and the like. I haven't spent the festive season at home for several years. Tell me, Sally, how do you manage to entertain guests with all the rationing and shortages?"

"Lucky for us, we are quite self-sufficient with our garden produce and the little extra we receive from the military, but all the same, I can only serve simple fare, today starting with homegrown carrot soup."

"I have a surprise," announced Hughie, unpacking the bag he had brought with him and putting six glass bottles of Coca-Cola on the table. "I managed to cadge these from the American boys. Apparently it's included in their army rations."

"Well this is a real treat. Thank you, Hughie," said Sally. "I'll get an opener."

Lily was about to say that it was a very popular drink in Germany and that she really liked it, but checked herself in time. Hughie and Millie believed she was from Switzerland and she had no idea of Coca-Cola's popularity there. Instead, she steered away from the subject by complimenting Sally on the main course of roast chicken with parsley and celery stuffing and baked potatoes.

"Would anyone care for tea or some ersatz coffee I managed to get my hands on with their date pudding?" asked Sally, clearing the plates while Gracie brought the dessert to the table.

Millie patiently answered all Gracie's questions about the theatre, and when it was time to leave, she gave her two complimentary tickets to the pantomime. "Feel free to bring a friend and you can come backstage afterwards if you like."

"Like? Of course I'd like! Thank you so much."

"That's very kind of you, Millie," said Sally.

"Not at all. I've had a lovely afternoon. The food and the company were wonderful. Thank you for including me."

"Let me escort you back to the Metropole," Hughie offered.

"That would be great, as long as it doesn't interfere with any plans you had with Lily."

"It's fine by me," Lily insisted. "I'd feel happier if you weren't out alone in the dark."

They hugged goodbye and Millie promised to stay in touch.

"I'll see you all next time I'm in town."

CHAPTER THIRTY-FOUR

1943–1944

It was a glorious spring day. Lily gazed out of the hotel window at the sparkling sea and the waves lapping gently on the golden sand. The promenade was already busy on this Sunday morning in May. Almost four years of war had not managed to drive Bournemouth into despair despite the bombings, forty-seven in total according to the newspapers, which had cost civilian lives and destroyed or damaged homes and businesses. They considered themselves lucky in comparison to other cities across the country, particularly London.

She turned back to the bed where Hughie slept, the sunlight catching his blond hair. This was not the first time she had spent the night in his hotel room. She wondered how on this occasion she would get past the concierge unseen on her way out. He was probably used to that kind of thing and turned a blind eye, but she always felt embarrassed at the thought of his judgmental scrutiny.

Hughie must have sensed Lily watching him, because he opened his eyes and smiled his lopsided grin.

"Good morning," she said and kissed him.

"I'm the luckiest guy who ever lived," he said with a sigh, "waking up to the kiss of the most beautiful woman in the world." He pulled her towards him, opening her robe so that he could admire her naked body. Hughie had brought her to pinnacles of passion she hadn't imagined possible and her lack of inhibition with him never ceased to amaze her. She lay down beside him and raised her arms above her head, inviting him to take possession of her again.

Sometime later, Lily slipped out of bed and began to get ready for the day ahead. Millie was back in Bournemouth and had arranged to meet her and Sally in the Gardens in the town centre at lunchtime.

Hughie would catch up with them later on.

"Lily, before you leave, I have something for you," Hughie said, his voice serious.

Lily watched as he went over to the bureau and opened the top drawer, slowly withdrawing a small box. Her heart lurched. *Please don't let this be a proposal*, she willed silently. She was very fond of Hughie. He was kind and attentive and she couldn't deny that the sex was fantastic. But she didn't love him. She didn't yearn for him when they weren't together; she didn't feel the flutter of anticipation when she caught sight of him in the distance; he wasn't the first thing she thought of when she woke up, or the last thing on her mind before she fell asleep. She didn't possess the depth of feeling for him that she had had for Heinrich, and although she had accepted that Heinrich was lost to her forever, she still hoped to find someone to love as much as she had loved him. So she didn't want Hughie to propose. She didn't want the commitment of being *"my girl waiting for me back home"* when Hughie was inevitably and unavoidably sent into combat. The future was too uncertain and his return not guaranteed. Neither was she ready to uproot to some backwater in rural Canada far from the centres of fashion and *haute couture* which would once again be her focus when this madness was over. Her fingers trembled as she opened the box. On the satin interior lay a pair of crystal earrings.

"I saw these and thought they would look real good with your flower brooch."

It was as if an arrow pierced her heart, and it was not from Cupid's bow. Heinrich, the restaurant, the intimacy of that magical New Year's Eve when he had given her the treasured brooch – it all came flooding back. The blood drained from her face.

"Lily, darling, are you alright?" Hughie said, stroking her cheek.

"Yes, I'm fine. Thank you so much," Lily said, forcing a smile. "These are beautiful. I was just jolted by a memory from the past which unsettled me. I'm sorry. Let me try them on."

They really were lovely and Hughie was so thoughtful. She chastised herself for her reaction and threw her arms around him.

"I really do love them and I will wear them with the brooch next time we go dancing." She planted a kiss on his lips hoping she had convinced him. "Now I must go or I'll be late. We'll see you later."

As she exited the hotel, Lily noticed that the dining room was filling up with people waiting to enjoy a Sunday roast. The aroma filtering out of the kitchens made her mouth water and her stomach rumble. Outside it was a picture-perfect day, warm and lazy. She was running late and would have to walk briskly. It would take at least a quarter of an hour at a fast pace down the Old Christchurch Road to reach the Gardens. By the time she reached the Square, she was quite out of breath having had to dodge hundreds of men and women who packed the streets. The lawns in the Gardens were jammed with playing children, soldiers and airmen, civilians and their wives, strolling about or lying on the grass and basking in the sun under the clear blue sky. How would she find Millie and Sally amid the crowds? She scanned the area several times and finally caught sight of Millie jumping up and down and waving her arms to attract her attention.

Lily grinned and began to push her way towards her two dearest friends. Suddenly, the hubbub of the Gardens was replaced by a low-pitched hum from over the East Cliff, followed by the roar of twenty German bombers bearing down on the centre of town, so low that the pilots' faces were clearly visible. There had been no warning, no sirens, no chance to run for safety. The marauders scattered their bombs across the town and strafed the Gardens with machine gun fire. The planes banked and turned, lining up for a second assault as they headed back out to sea, leaving a scene of intense devastation in their wake. The brutal attack was all over in sixty seconds.

As the sounds of the aircraft faded in the distance, they were replaced by an unnatural silence. The sky darkened with thick black smoke rising up from Bobby's Department Store which had been hit by bombs and gunfire, and spreading out over the surrounding area. And then the silence was shattered by the pandemonium of screaming, wailing and shouting. The Gardens, which a few minutes previously had been the scene of people enjoying life, were now a tableau of death and destruction.

Lily slowly regained consciousness, but she was pinned down and unable to move. She brushed away the dust from her eyes, alarmed to find her hand wet and sticky from a trickle of blood sliding down the side of her face. She probed around for the source of the bleeding until her fingers found the shard of broken glass embedded in the hairline above her left eye. Panic set in. She must find Sally and Millie. She pushed the heavy weight off her and tried to get up. Her legs were unsteady and her dress was covered in blood. She could hear screaming. It seemed to be coming from inside her. The body which had trapped her belonged to an airman. One of his legs was missing and his eyes stared at her glassily from a face half blown off. She vomited violently.

For a moment, she was back in the lifeboat watching dead and injured bodies floating past her in the water. She spun around in a state of rising panic. Looking across the Square, she saw maimed buses, windows blown out, and metal mangled. Behind her, Bobby's frontage was shattered; perhaps that was the source of the glass in her bleeding head. The rest of the blood splattered on her belonged to the airman. Where were her friends?

The unharmed and lightly injured were getting to their feet, looking around for their companions. Others were trying to help the wounded. Mothers were screaming for their children, hugging them tightly when they located them, some alive, others not. The noise was augmented by the sound of car horns and ambulance sirens as the casualties began to be evacuated to Victoria Hospital.

This is almost like a scene from a film I've seen, Lily thought. At last, she caught sight of Millie and Sally picking their way through the bodies as if through a minefield, supporting each other as they made their way towards her.

"Thank God we're all in one piece," said Sally as the three women huddled together and wept.

CHAPTER THIRTY-FIVE

Lily and Millie had said goodbye to Sally, who had rushed to The Waves to check on Gracie, and made their way back up the Old Christchurch Road towards the Metropole. The street was littered with broken glass and the contents of window displays. They were horrified to see that in the midst of all the bloodshed and tragedy, a few people were looting the shops. As Beales came into view, Lily stopped dead in her tracks. Firemen were battling a fierce fire consuming the ruins of the gutted department store. Grief tore through her. "My beautiful store. My work," she cried.

"There's nothing you can do here," said Millie, dragging her stunned friend away.

They continued their climb uphill towards the hotel, but their progress was slow, hindered by debris and rescue teams. As they neared their destination, they saw a pall of black smoke and ash rising in the air, and their nostrils were assaulted by clouds of dust and the smells of explosion and destruction. The Metropole had taken a direct hit and looked as if it had been sliced in two.

The scene was shocking. People were running in and out of the hotel, ferrying out the dead and the wounded. Others were giving first aid to those whose injuries did not require immediate hospital treatment. Those who did were being loaded into ambulances and cars. Firemen on turntable ladders were evacuating those trapped on the upper floors. Canadian airmen desperately clawed at the piles of bricks and rubble in an attempt to rescue their friends who had been drinking in the hotel's bar only minutes before the attack. Bodies clothed in uniform lay side by side with well-dressed men and women who had been dining in the restaurant. Lily began to scream. "Has anyone seen Hughie? Hughie Gardner?" No one paid attention to her cries. They were too busy with their gruesome task. She looked up at the grotesque gaping hole where only a few hours earlier she had stood by the window enjoying the view, and where she and Hughie had lain in bed.

An airman approached her. "Lily, isn't it?"

She nodded.

"Hughie's girlfriend?" he confirmed.

"Yes. Where is he? Is he ... He's not?"

"He's been injured pretty badly. They've taken him to Victoria Hospital."

"Thank you," Lily said and squeezed his arm.

She found Millie with the troupe's distraught but unharmed director who was trying to account for the cast and crew.

"Hughie's been injured. They've taken him to hospital. I'm going there now. You stay here and find your friends. I'll be all right. We'll catch up later."

Before Millie could protest, Lily was running in the direction of an ambulance to hitch a ride.

"Glass in my head," she said and pointed to the dried blood on her temple to convince the driver to take her.

The short journey to Westbourne seemed interminable to Lily. She sat in the back watching over a casualty lying semi-conscious on a stretcher, blood seeping through the makeshift dressing on his torso. He groaned in pain with every bend and bump in the road, the bouncing amplified by the speed of the ambulance.

The entrance to the hospital was chaotic, with ambulances and all manner of vehicles queueing to offload their wounded. Beyond the open doors, Lily could hear the roars of pain coming from the emergency room and she hesitated in fear before entering. Inside, desperate doctors and nurses attended one victim after another, but the task was mammoth and the resources limited. All the beds and stretchers were occupied and some poor souls were lying on the floor with missing limbs and gaping wounds, agony etched on their faces. There was blood all over the place, giving off a metallic odour which made Lily want to retch. People were crying for help and for something to kill the pain. Others were shouting out the names of relatives in the hope of locating them. Lily noticed a young boy of about eleven or twelve strapped onto a stretcher. His hair was burnt and standing on end, and he was deathly white. He stared at Lily with huge, frightened eyes. Lily forced herself to look away. She made her way to the reception desk and asked for Hughie. The receptionist rifled through a sheaf of papers where names had been scribbled hastily in one column and their status in another: dead on arrival, fatal injuries, treated on site, treated and released, in surgery. She scrolled down the list until she reached Hughie's name.

"He's in theatre, Miss. It could take a long time and you won't be able to see him today. I advise you to go home and come back in the morning. I'm sorry I don't have any more information."

Back now from her return visit to the hospital, Lily gratefully accepted the tea Sally pushed in front of her.

Lily dropped her bag and sat down at the kitchen table.

"The hospital was quieter and more organized this morning. They seem to have everything under control. Hughie came through surgery which was long and complicated. They only let me stay a few minutes so as not to tire him. His head is bandaged." Lily's voice faltered. "He has lost one eye and the other is scratched but will heal with time. They removed shrapnel from his chest which, by some miracle, didn't cause any serious injury. He is very weak, in and out of consciousness, but he knew I was there."

"I'm so sorry." Sally hugged her. "At least he is alive. According to today's paper, at least one hundred and thirty people are known to have died, although we may never know the exact total, and hundreds more are maimed for life."

"Hughie is going to be one of those unfortunates," Lily sobbed.

For the next few days Lily's only outing was to the hospital. There was nothing she could do except sit by Hughie's bedside and stroke his hand. When he was conscious, she endeavoured to make conversation, but it was all meaningless chatter and he didn't have the strength to talk. Much of the time he slept. After a couple of days, Sally joined her with Gracie, who insisted on visiting even though Lily tried to persuade her otherwise. Hughie was not a pretty sight and she didn't want the young girl to be traumatized. To her credit, Gracie smiled and remained quite calm until they left the hospital, and then she ran into her mother's arms, tears pouring down her face. On the fourth day, Millie was at Hughie's bedside when Lily arrived.

They chatted a little as Hughie slept.

"What's been happening at the theatre?" Lily asked her friend.

"The Pavilion wasn't hit. I don't know how the bloody Germans managed to miss it, but thank goodness they did. But we had to cancel the rest of our performances. Nobody was in the mood for it anyway, neither the cast nor the audience. And what with the injuries, well, you can imagine."

"I'm so sorry, Millie."

Hughie was still asleep, so Millie suggested they grab a tea somewhere. She was very concerned about Lily's gaunt appearance, she told her friend, and the effect Hughie's injuries were having on her.

"What are your plans now, Lily?" she asked as they sat down at the tea shop.

"I don't really know."

"What about Hughie?"

"He won't be able to fly any more, even after his injuries have healed, however long that might take. As soon as he is well enough to travel, he will be taken home to Canada."

"And will you go with him?"

"No," Lily said, looking down at the table. "I feel guilty, but it's not an option for me. Am I a terrible person to be thankful that he never asked me to marry him, because that would have put me in an awful position? If he had I would have refused him anyway. I'm not in love with him."

"You're not terrible," said Millie, taking her friend's hand. "Look at me, Lily. You are making the right decision. Better not to go at all than to go for the wrong reasons. You would both be miserable. So, what now?"

"Well, my job at Beales has gone. The management have been very good about it and given me and the other girls a small bonus to tide us over. They have also offered to write me a letter of recommendation, but I'm not very optimistic about finding another job in Bournemouth or nearby. Maybe I should try the stores in London."

"You'd consider leaving here, then?"

"I would miss Sally, of course, but without employment, I won't be able to pay my way and she has already shown me more goodwill than I thought possible."

"Well," said Millie said with a smile, "I have a proposition for you. As you know, Kate, our wardrobe mistress, was badly hurt in the bombing, and the costumes which were in her room at the Metropole were destroyed or are in need of major repair and remodeling. How would you like the job?"

"Me?"

"Well, you are the most talented seamstress I know, so of course you." Millie's eyes sparkled. "It would mean traveling with the company all round England."

"That sounds wonderful," said Lily, feeling the seed of excitement sprouting inside her. "I will have to discuss it with Sally. When do you need my answer?"

"We will be leaving at the end of next week for Bath, our next booking. Luckily some of the costumes were left in the theatre, along with Kate's sewing machine and accessories, and we can use them for now. But you would have to get started on the rest as soon as possible."

Lily didn't really need to think twice about the offer, but she wanted Sally's seal of approval. After all, she owed her everything and she didn't want to leave if it meant letting her down.

Lily made her way slowly back to The Waves mulling over Millie's proposition and wondering how to break the news to Sally. When she arrived home, she found Sally and Gracie in the garden collecting vegetables for the evening meal. How she loved watching them work together in cheerful companionship. It brought back memories of her sewing lessons with her mother. She missed her mother and those happier times so very much, and she knew she would miss Sally and Gracie terribly when she left. When they came back into the kitchen, Lily told them the details of her conversation with Millie.

"So what do you think of Millie's proposition, Sally?" Lily asked her friend.

"You know you are welcome to stay here as long as you like, Lily, with or without a job. But I think this could be a great opportunity for you. A clean slate. If it doesn't work out your bed will always be here for you."

Gracie was tearful. "Everyone's leaving. First Rob, Hughie will be gone soon, and now you."

Lily hugged the young girl who had been her savior when Sally had first brought her home.

"I'll miss you like mad but I'll keep in touch and visit whenever I can," she promised.

The following morning, Lily made her final visit to the hospital. She stood at the entrance to the ward, summoning up the courage she would need to tell Hughie of her decision to join the theatre group. He was awake and some of the colour had returned to the parts of his face which were visible. His eyes were still bandaged.

"Lily."

"Hughie." They both spoke at once.

"You go first, Hughie."

"The doctors tell me that I will be able to go home next week."

Lily dreaded what was coming next.

"You must know that I love you, Lily. After this damn war is over, I had hoped to ask you to be my wife."

Lily kept silent. He felt for her hand and squeezed it.

"The situation has changed, and I'm happy that I didn't jump the gun and propose during these uncertain times. We are not engaged and I am no longer the man I was. You mustn't feel under any obligation to me. You have your whole life ahead of you and I pray you get to fulfill your dreams. It's best if we part ways now."

Tears poured down Lily's face. How brave Hughie was, and how generous of spirit. *He could have used emotional blackmail to tie me to him,* she thought. *But he loves me enough to release me from any sense of commitment and let me go.*

"I will think of you when I'm back in Moose Jaw, and I look forward to reading in the newspaper about the famous fashion designer I had the pleasure of knowing when I was stationed in Bournemouth."

"I will always treasure the time we had together, Hughie. The past couple of years have been the happiest in my life," Lily lied. "I know you are strong enough to overcome your injuries and I'm sure you'll find the right girl for you back home."

She leaned over the bed to give him a final embrace and a goodbye kiss.

CHAPTER THIRTY-SIX

Following their passionate encounter outside the Rose and Crown, Heinrich and Celia had reentered the pub separately wanting to avert suspicion, studiously keeping their distance until it was time to leave. For days, they had no opportunity to meet in private. Whenever Heinrich brought a recording to the transcription room, he avoided catching her eye, determinedly suppressing the urge to leap across the tables into her arms. Now, finally, they had managed a clandestine meeting in Celia's room, her roommate away on leave for a few days. This time, their lovemaking was less wantonly urgent and they luxuriated in exploring each other's bodies unhurriedly.

"So, how did you end up here in special ops?" inquired Heinrich, now sated, running his fingers through her glorious red curls.

"My family's quite well off and I grew up with a German nanny, so I'm bilingual," Celia explained. "And then I studied German in school to bring my grammar up to par with my conversational skills. I joined the Auxiliary Territorial Service after hearing the Princess Royal's impassioned broadcast, 'Your King and country need you – join the ATS.'" Celia smiled at the recollection. "The Army sent me for three weeks' basic training and then on to London to be trained as a teleprinter operator. When my German fluency was discovered, I was summoned for an interview and sent here."

"Have you ever been to Germany?"

"I took part in a student exchange programme and went to spend time with a family in a small town on the outskirts of Göttingen. The timing was unfortunate, as the winds of war were already blowing. My short stay was a happy one, but several things struck me as sinister. Firstly, on my arrival in Germany, the customs officer confiscated my English newspaper, which struck me as very odd. A couple of weeks into the visit, the family took me to a swimming pool. Fixed to the entrance gate was a sign

'*Juden sind unerwünscht*'. I asked my host why the Jews were not wanted, but he just coughed nervously and avoided giving me an answer. I didn't see any evidence of a military build-up, but the people I was staying with bundled me home in a hurry, because the news implied that the situation was getting serious and they were afraid for my safety."

Celia traced her finger over Heinrich's scar. "What's your story, Henry?"

"I come from Breslau in Upper Silesia," Heinrich began. "I hero-worshipped my two older brothers who were decorated in the last war, and I followed them into the military. Until I left Germany I was an officer in the Wehrmacht."

He described his growing disillusionment with Hitler and the Nazis, and the persecution of the Jews and others not considered Aryans. "In truth I never felt particularly Jewish until then."

He trembled as he recalled the night of the brutal attack and his escape.

"I can't remember too many details of the sinking ship, but I can still feel the numbing chill of the freezing water in my bones. God must have been watching over me because my rescue was indeed miraculous. As far as I know, no one else survived."

He knew his face betrayed the depth of his trauma and it took several minutes for him to regain his composure. He made no mention of Lily; he wasn't ready yet. He wasn't sure if he ever would be.

Celia held him close, perhaps sensing there was more to this story than he was willing to divulge. "What has happened to your brother and his family?"

"I have no idea. I wrote to him a number of times before war was declared but received no reply. I can only pray that he got his family out of Germany in time."

Heinrich and Celia soon discovered that privacy was a rare luxury and personal lives suffered the most. They snatched every opportunity to be together, taking advantage of empty rooms and secluded corners of the grounds. The furtive sneaking around and clandestine trysts added a thrilling undercurrent of illicitness and excitement to their coupling. Try as they might to keep their liaison a secret, the rumour mill was hard at work, spreading any gossip that would add a little spice to the mundane day-to-day routine. They were by no means the only couple who found themselves the subject of speculation and chitchat.

"Gotta hand it to you, mate," said Gordon, the next time Heinrich handed over a recording. "I don't know what your secret charm is, but she's never given anyone else the time of day. You lucky sod!"

Heinrich certainly did consider himself lucky. Celia was beautiful, sensual, and intelligent. Instinctively, he touched the breast pocket of his uniform where he kept Lily's photograph. *I hope you understand and forgive me, my love. I just couldn't go on any longer without some physical comfort and affection.* He held no illusions about his affair with Celia. For the time being, they fulfilled each other's needs. The only difference between them was that she had not given up hope of seeing her husband return safe and sound from the war.

Weeks passed in repetitive routine. Heinrich's twelve-hour shifts did not always coincide with Celia's, and there were successions of days when he had nothing important to record and take to the transcription room. Several days or more could go by without them having any contact at all. It was frustrating, but they never lost sight of the fact that the work they were doing was of vital importance to the war effort and superseded any inconvenience in their personal lives.

One evening in October, Heinrich sat down at his post and adjusted his earphones. The prisoners, who were allowed to listen to the BBC news in German, would have heard the reports about mass executions in Poland, and he wondered what his two Generals would have to say about it. They were having a wager about how many millions of Jews, men, women, and children had been slaughtered under the Führer's directive. One boasted of his involvement, while another admitted to turning a blind eye. Heinrich couldn't believe what he was hearing. Nausea, revulsion, and fury bubbled up inside him as he listened to this casual confession of collabouration and culpability. These were the sort of men he would have been serving under had circumstances been different. And officers like his nemesis, Lieutenant Bauer, would undoubtedly have been more than willing to carry out such nefarious orders.

As he listened to the catalogue of despicable stories the two men were exchanging – of shootings, mobile gas trucks, and mass graves – tears began to run down Heinrich's cheeks. He wept for the Germany of the past, whose illustrious history was now tainted forever, and for the Germany of the future, which would have to bear responsibility for the inhumanity and destruction perpetrated by and upon its people and those of its neighbors; he wept for the atrocities visited upon innocents, which his former countrymen would have to answer for when the Allies were victorious. At that moment, it was inconceivable to Heinrich that such evil could triumph over good or that the Nazis would succeed in crushing the British fighting spirit and stiff upper lip, which he had derided at first but had come to admire and applaud. Finally, he wept for his brother's family and gave a silent prayer that they had been spared the horrors he was hearing about.

When the Generals' conversation came to an end, Heinrich stopped the recording and heaved himself out of his chair. He slowly scanned the room and saw his own emotions reflected on the faces of some of his colleagues, the majority of whom were Jews who had left family behind in Europe. Had they also overheard similar accounts? They would not be able to discuss what they had heard, or share their fears, and yet somehow the collective silence offered mutual solace and support.

Celia looked up from her desk when Heinrich entered the transcription room with his recording. She was taken aback by the ravaged expression on his face. He looked as if he had been crying. Of course he would not verbally share the secrets he overheard, but she would know soon enough when she transcribed and translated it. She set aside the material she had been working on, replacing it with Heinrich's, and she began to type. *You smug murderous bastards*, she cursed, punching the keys with uncharacteristic ferocity and cringing as the words took shape on the page before her, eliciting questioning looks from her colleagues. *They'll pay for this.*

When her shift ended, she searched for Heinrich and found him sitting at the small table in his room, rocking back and forth on his chair and pounding the wooden surface with clenched fists.

"Shush now. That's enough," she soothed him, taking hold of his hands and leading him to the bed. Their lovemaking was almost desperate in its intensity, as if the pleasures of the flesh could vitiate the insanity of war.

The following week Heinrich was told to report to the Commanding Officer.

"You have a week's furlough, Sergeant Grant. Use it well and be back here refreshed and rested next Monday. And remember, no one must get any inkling about where you are serving or what you are doing."

Heinrich hadn't asked for leave and wondered whether it was a reward or a punishment. Perhaps his affair with Celia had landed him in trouble.

"Don't worry. You're not special, Henry. The CO gives us all a short period of much needed time off to clear our heads," Mark explained. "This week it's your turn."

Heinrich considered his options. He wasn't happy about leaving Celia, but a few days in Lowestoft's fresh sea air with perhaps some fishing might be, as Mrs McFee would say, just what the doctor ordered.

CHAPTER THIRTY-SEVEN

The last few weeks on the road with the touring theatre group had been exhilarating. Admittedly, the accommodation wasn't always as splendid as the Metropole, but it was generally clean and tidy. Lily had spent the first few days of her new position repairing damaged costumes and taking inventory of the ones which had been safely stored at the Pavilion, so that the company's wardrobe was more or less complete in time for their departure from Bournemouth. They had played to full houses in Bath, Bristol, Birmingham, Manchester, Nottingham, and Leicester. Lily loved the excitement of seeing new places and people, and of becoming part of this theatrical family. There was a camaraderie among its members, bereft of petty jealousies or intrigues, and they had welcomed her immediately into their ranks.

And then came one surprising night in Peterborough. Lily was in Millie's dressing room, waiting for her friend to finish removing her stage makeup, when there was a knock at the door. One of the stagehands poked his nose around the door. "You seem to have an admirer, Millie. May I let him in?"

"Does he look respectable?" she asked, surprised.

"Very".

"All right then. Give me a couple of minutes. You stay here with me, Lily. You can be my chaperone."

When there was a second knock, Millie called, "Come in."

A smartly dressed middle-aged gentleman entered the room and presented Millie with a small bouquet of flowers. He removed his hat and introduced himself.

"My name is Alfred Stevens, Miss Court. I don't know whether that name means anything to you."

"I'm afraid not," Millie replied.

"I am a film producer and director at Excelsior Studios. I have been following your career and seen several of your performances. You are indeed not only beautiful but also a very talented actress. I have a proposition for you."

"Now wait a minute, Mr Stevens," said Millie, straightening her shoulders. "Just what are you suggesting?"

"No, no, nothing like that, I assure you," he continued. "Excelsior Studios has just embarked on a new project; we are filming an historical romance. I would like to offer you a role. Not the main character, obviously, but a part which will get you noticed and pave the way for more roles in the future."

Lily watched as Millie was stunned into silence. Lily knew her friend would be suspicious that, despite his insistence to the contrary, Mr Stevens's motives might not be as above board as he would like her to believe.

"Well, I don't know what to say," said Millie finally. "This is so unexpected and, frankly, quite unbelievable."

"You don't have to answer right away. Here is my card. If you think you would be interested to talk about this further, give me a call. I do hope you will consider the offer favorably. Cinema is the theatre of the future, with audiences in the thousands, no millions. I could make you a star and a household name."

After he left, the two women squealed with excitement.

"Can this be real?" Millie asked Lily.

"It seems so. But I think you should do some investigating to find out more about Mr Stevens and Excelsior Studios. Let's see if the director or actors have heard of him. But if he is who he says he is and the offer is genuine, this could be an amazing opportunity for you."

"I can't believe it," exclaimed the director when Millie and Lily went to tell him the news. "Alfred Stevens has been to see our performances? The Alfred Stevens?"

"So he is who he says he is?" Millie asked.

"He is a well-respected producer and director with a number

of box office successes. Historical romance is not his usual genre. Most of his recent films have been thrillers or war-related. He must be very impressed with you, Millie, if he is taking a chance on an unknown for his new production."

Not wanting to appear too eager, Millie waited several days before she called the number on the business card. Stevens returned to Peterborough to discuss the terms and conditions of his offer.

"I have one additional condition, which is not negotiable," said Millie, trying to sound more confident than she felt.

"And what might that be?"

"My dresser, Lily, must be included in the deal."

"But we already have a perfectly good wardrobe mistress, Rose Bartlett."

"I must insist," she stood her ground.

Stevens was silent for a few moments. Millie's heart was thumping. How did she have the nerve to make such a demand and not be intimidated into giving in?

He smiled at her. "Oh well, a Rose by any other name ... is a Lily, I suppose."

They shook hands. Millie thought she might faint from relief. She couldn't wait to tell Lily.

"I will send a car to collect you immediately after your final performance in Lowestoft. I'm taking a chance on you, Miss Court. I hope you won't let me down."

CHAPTER THIRTY-EIGHT

As the train pulled out of the station on its journey back towards London, Heinrich reflected on his short stay in Lowestoft. In the few years since he had been taken away for internment, the town had suffered quite a beating, with frequent bombing raids targeting the naval base and engineering works. The fishing industry was all but non-existent; the North Sea was almost entirely closed to commercial fishing because of the dangers of enemy mines and submarines as well as aerial attacks. Many fishermen had been called up and most fishing vessels had been requisitioned for war service as minesweepers.

"Come in, come in," Mrs McFee had welcomed him warmly when he knocked on her door. "Don't you look just grand in your uniform! McFee isn't here yet. He's moved north to Scotland for the fishing, but when he heard you were coming to visit he made plans to travel down to see you."

"You didn't go with him?"

"I'm too set in my ways to up sticks and relocate to who knows where. I prefer familiar surroundings and the company of friends in these terrible times."

"Has it been very hard?" asked Heinrich.

"Well, we seem to be a prime target for the *Luftwaffe* and there has been a lot of naval activity too. Because the town was designated as a risk area for bombing, or even invasion, about three thousand local children were evacuated to Derbyshire and Nottinghamshire. The evacuation reminded me of those poor Jewish children who came through *Lowestoft* on the *Kindertransport*. The town seems very solemn without the noise and laughter. Bit like the story of the Pied Piper of Hamelin. But at least they are out of harm's way."

"Aren't you lonely without McFee?" said Heinrich.

"No time for that. Since he left, a whole stream of soldiers and sailors have been billeted here. The house hasn't been empty for a minute. I'm glad I've got the chance to do something for the war effort, however small. But don't worry. Your old room is waiting for you."

McFee arrived early the next morning just as Heinrich and Hilda sat down for breakfast. He greeted Heinrich with a great hug. "Bin promoted to Sergeant, have ye? What have ye bin doing to earn yer stripes?"

Heinrich told them about various jobs he had done in the Pioneer Corps where, as far as McFee knew, he still served, embellished with stories he had heard from other soldiers to account for the time since he had joined the Intelligence Corps.

"By the way, I go by the name of Henry now. Saves a lot of explanation. I'm sorry to hear about the fishing, McFee. I was looking forward to some time at sea with you."

"Well, unless ye want to try youse hand at minesweeping, Ah'm afraid that pleasure will have to wait until this damn war is over."

"I'll hold you to that," said Heinrich.

"I have tickets for a comedy at the theatre," announced Hilda. It's being put on by a company of actors who have been touring the country. They've just finished a couple of weeks in Peterborough and the reviews are very good. It stars Millie Court who is an up-and-coming young actress, according to the publicity flier, and quite beautiful. The cast and crew suffered some casualties during the awful bombing raid in Bournemouth last May, and a local Lowestoft lad I know, Colin Forth, who until then was an understudy and general stagehand, took over the role of one of the lead players. It's the last performance of the season and he has invited me to come backstage after the show and meet the cast. Will you come with me, Heinrich? I mean, Henry." She smiled. "McFee's not one for the theatre."

Heinrich couldn't remember the last time he had been to the theatre, or even to a film, for that matter. He had forgotten how much he enjoyed the arts, of which there had been no shortage in

Breslau. The last time he'd gone to a concert was with Lily, when he had taken her in a rowboat to Malt Island. How he had delighted in watching the look of sheer pleasure on her face as he introduced her to unfamiliar experiences. It seemed like another lifetime. No, it *was* another lifetime.

"I'd be delighted to accompany you, Mrs McFee."

Heinrich was amazed to see that the theatre was still standing. The surrounding area was littered with mounds of rubble and very few of the buildings remained undamaged.

"How have they managed to keep the theatre open when the risk of attack is so great?" he asked Mrs McFee.

"People need some recreation to keep them sane. The very fact that it is still in one piece when everything around it has been demolished makes it seem invincible, a sort of Lowestoft talisman. There is a big shelter under the building just in case," she laughed.

The inside of the theatre was in need of refurbishment. It was obvious that no money had been invested in it for some time. The carpets were threadbare and the seats worn. The curtains at the side of the stage were faded and some of the chandeliers were shattered or missing, rattled by the barrage suffered outside.

The lights in the auditorium dimmed and the stage lit up to reveal the players. Heinrich was struck by the beauty of the lead actress and he settled down to enjoy himself. Even if the play was lousy, he was happy to feast his eyes on her for an hour or two. After two acts, a short interval was announced, and Mrs McFee unwrapped the sandwiches she had brought with her. As she passed one over to Heinrich, his eyes strayed to the wings at one side of the stage. Just behind the curtain, the lead was talking to another woman who half-turned momentarily, and Heinrich was so shocked that he dropped the sandwich. Apologising to Mrs McFee, he bent down to retrieve it, but when he looked back towards the wings, the women were no longer standing there.

"Are you all right, Heinrich? You look like you've seen a ghost."

"I'm fine. It's nothing. My imagination running away with me."

An unsettling sensation caused his pulse to race and his hands to sweat. He knew it wasn't possible – she must be a *doppelgänger*, or else his eyes were playing tricks on him. He could hardly concentrate on the second half of the performance and was relieved when the cast came forward to take their bow. They received a standing ovation and returned to the stage for a second curtain call together with some of the backstage crew.

"Come on, let's go and find Colin," said Mrs McFee dragging Heinrich by the sleeve and slowly pushing their way towards the steps leading up to the stage. She didn't want to miss her introduction to the players.

"How did you enjoy the performance, Hilda?" asked Colin, visibly excited by his role and the audience's approval.

"Very much, didn't we Hein— er, Henry?"

"Yes, indeed," he replied vaguely, his eyes scanning the stage and the wings.

"I think he's taken a shine to Millie Court," Mrs McFee whispered to Colin. "She is rather beautiful."

"Yes, and a talented actress," Colin agreed.

"So, can we meet some people then?"

"Sure thing."

Colin led them backstage towards the dressing rooms, filling them in on the names of some of the other actors. He raised his fist to knock on Millie's dressing room door.

"Sorry, Colin, she's already left for London," a passing stagehand informed him. "A car was waiting for her right after the first curtain call."

Mrs McFee's disappointment was evident but cut short by the unmistakable pitiful wail of air raid sirens.

"Everyone to the shelter," called the director. Heinrich took Mrs McFee's arm and followed the others. The shelter was very crowded; other members of the audience who had not yet left the premises were streaming in, as well as passersby who did not have a nearby shelter to run to. Heinrich searched the faces one by one, but the light was dim and no one looked like the woman in the wings who bore such a strong resemblance to Lily. A flash from someone's torch glinted briefly on the hair of a woman whose back was turned to him. He caught his breath. The titian curls resting softly on her shoulders were exactly like Lily's. He pushed his way towards her, jostling people in his way. She slowly turned to face him and smiled. He froze. The woman must be at least fifty, Heinrich calculated. The hair colour was no doubt from a bottle. He coughed and turned, making his way back to Mrs McFee. He chided himself. Of course it wasn't Lily. How could it be? Was his imagination now causing hallucinations?

Finally, the All Clear sounded. They left the theatre and started to walk home.

"You're very quiet," Mrs McFee remarked.

"Sorry. It's nothing. A woman behind the scenes reminded me of my lost Lily, that's all."

She squeezed his arm. "Have you not found a new lady friend?"

"Well, there is someone, but I'm not sure how serious it is."

"Give it time, love. Everything is uncertain while the war is on. If she isn't the one, I'm sure the girl of your dreams will come along sooner or later."

Mrs McFee's words echoed in his ears as Heinrich made his way back from the train station to the estate and the M room. He wondered if Celia had missed him as much as he had missed her. He went straight back to work and several days passed before he recorded something of importance. His heart beat wildly in anticipation of seeing her again.

"Back from your R&R, Henry?" asked Gordon. Heinrich didn't reply as his eyes settled on Celia's empty desk.

"She's gone, I'm afraid, mate. Her husband was found and

brought home in a pretty bad state. She's been granted unlimited leave so that she can nurse him."

CHAPTER THIRTY-NINE

1944–1945

It had all happened so quickly. One minute, Millie was taking her bow, and the next minute they were being whisked away in a posh car towards London. During the interval, Millie had told Lily to finish getting all their belongings ready as they would have to leave immediately after the performance. While they were talking in the wings, Lily had had the strangest feeling that someone was watching her. She had turned slightly and scanned the audience, catching sight of a soldier who looked alarmingly familiar. She wanted to look more closely, but he bent down to pick something up from the floor, and before he reappeared, Millie was hurrying her towards the dressing rooms.

Her fingers trembled as she put the last few things into their suitcases. The soldier's striking resemblance to Heinrich had completely unnerved her. She breathed deeply in an attempt to calm her racing heart. *Stupid girl, letting your imagination run away with you*, she scolded herself. *What, you believe in ghosts now, or resurrection?* She forced herself to turn her attention back to the task in hand.

Life at Excelsior Studios was nothing like the touring company. There was a an excitement mingled with stress and fatigue. Words such as "deadline", "disaster" and "dreadful" reverberated around the set when the actors didn't perform to the director's satisfaction, and there was always someone who was boiling with anger or crying in frustration. Lily wasn't really allowed on the set and, far from being disappointed, she was relieved to be away from the firing line. Petty jealousies were rife, and Lily was careful to tread warily in her interactions with other studio staff and crew until she could fathom out who played for which team.

Rose Bartlett had clearly not taken too kindly to Stevens's

foisting a new seamstress upon her, especially one who was so close to his protégée, Millie Court.

At first, she just gave Lily menial tasks like rolling fabrics, sharpening pencils, and passing pins to other seamstresses. Lily didn't complain and she was never idle. When work was slack, she sat at a table and sketched some designs or practiced embroidery. She even reworked some costumes which had been discarded as unsuitable.

Rose begrudgingly could not help but notice the quality of Lily's workmanship and, swallowing her pride, she began to allow her to work on the costumes of lesser actors and the extras. By the time production began on the third film, with Millie finally in the starring role, Rose was incorporating some of Lily's original designs and creative touches into the costumes. The competitive atmosphere of the studio made Lily anxious that jealousy and rivalry would ruin her friendly relations with the other seamstresses. Luckily, her amenable and modest disposition had earned her the goodwill of most of her fellow employees. Unfortunately, her minor successes also attracted unwanted attention.

On her way out of the workroom one evening, she was accosted by a junior studio executive. He leaned casually on the door frame, barring her exit. Lily had noticed him on several occasions, hanging around the studio making suggestive remarks to some of the girls and actually touching some of them inappropriately. Most were afraid to dismiss his overtures for fear of repercussions and they cringed without actively rebuffing his advances. A few even played along with him in the hope of advancing their careers.

"Good evening, Lily. Working late?"

"Please let me pass."

"You know you are much too beautiful to be working behind the scenes. You should be a film star."

She tried to push her way past him.

"I can make it happen. All you have to do is be nice to me."

"Let me pass," she repeated, desperate to escape.

"That's not very friendly now, is it?" He grabbed her arm and, groping her bottom, pulled her towards him.

The face in front of her morphed into the face of Lieutenant Bauer.

"Get off me," she growled and, using all the force she could muster, she kneed him in the groin, watching with satisfaction as he crumpled to the floor in pain clutching his genitals. "Don't you ever come near me again, you filthy animal."

She ran out of the building, tears streaming down her face. *What have I done? This could cost me my job*, she admonished herself. She stopped to catch her breath. Slowly the tears were replaced by a smile as her distress gave way to a wonderful feeling of exhilaration and empowerment. She had defended herself. She was not a victim. The Bauers of this world would never threaten her again.

Because of the altercation, Lily was running late for her dinner with Millie. They had discovered a cozy café not far from the studio, for some reason not popular with their colleagues, where they liked to catch up with each other on the day's events. Millie was already seated when Lily arrived, flushed and out of breath. Once she was calm, she recounted to Millie what had happened.

"I can't believe I actually did that," Lily admitted.

"Good for you is all I can say. It's about time that fleabag got his comeuppance."

"But what about my future at the studio?"

"Lily, you really don't need the studio, you know. You'll never realise your true potential under someone like Rose Bartlett. Do you really want to remain a backroom seamstress all your life? The dresses you have designed and made for me for all those detestable parties I have to attend have caught the attention of rich wives, society ladies, and established stars of the silver screen. I am always being asked who my dressmaker is. You should be making gowns for discerning clients who appreciate your talent and worth. I think it's time for you to set up your own fashion house."

"You're crazy, Millie. That would cost a fortune. The dresses I design for you are paid for by the studio. I have saved quite a bit, but nowhere near enough to launch my own business."

"I would be happy to lend you some money."

"Oh no, Millie, I couldn't risk it. What if I failed and couldn't pay you back?"

"Lily, for almost two years we have been working hard at the studio, each of us honing our different skills, while we prayed for the war to be over and for life to return to normal. My career, for the time being, is tied up with the studio, but yours isn't. Now that hostilities in Europe are finally over and there is optimism in the air, this is the perfect time to seize an opportunity. It's almost party season and people are dying to break out from the austerity of the war years. The society women I have mixed with will be racing to show off fashion's newest creations and outdo one another."

"But why would they choose an unknown designer like me?"

"You may be unknown, but your designs aren't," insisted Millie.

"Let's start by getting you a few commissions. Until now I have not given away the name of my *secret couturiere*, but the next time I'm asked, I am going to send business your way. I will invest a small sum to cover some of your initial costs, and you must take down-payments from the clients for the purchase of fabrics and accessories. And, of course, you must charge an exorbitant fee for your work and the exclusivity of your designs. I promise you they will be lining up at your door."

Lily was thoughtful for a while, going over the possibilities in her head. It was a tempting idea, to be sure.

"Do you really believe I could make a go of it?"

"I'm absolutely certain. And I will be the proudest person in the world when you are famous."

"You're going to be the famous one, not me," Lily laughed.

Lily arrived for work at the studio the following morning. As soon as she took off her coat, Rose Bartlett told her she was to report to the office of Mr Gavin, one of the senior executives.

"I hope you haven't done anything stupid," said Rose, sounding genuinely concerned.

Mr Gavin's secretary showed her into the office.

"Good morning, Lily. Take a seat over there on the couch. Make yourself comfortable. There's nothing to be alarmed about."

Lily sat down. Having made her decision to quit the studio, she didn't feel in the least bit intimidated. She decided to wait and see what Mr Gavin wanted.

"I hear you had a small misunderstanding with Elliot last night."

"I would hardly call it a misunderstanding," said Lily. What had Elliot told him?

"If you had your sights set on an audition, you should have come directly to me and not wasted your time with small fry like Elliot."

Was he suggesting that she had come on to Elliot and not the other way around? Was Elliot trying to protect himself in case she complained? What would be the point? His sort of behavior was commonplace in the industry and the big wigs always took the man's side if a woman had the guts to complain, which rarely happened.

"Audition? For what exactly?"

Mr Gavin crossed over to the couch and sat down next to her. "I must say his description of you doesn't do you justice. We could certainly find a role for you."

"I have no interest in acting." Lily could see where this was going. "If you think you stand more of a chance with me than Elliot, you are mistaken. Keep your lecherous thoughts to yourself. I quit."

With that, she stood and walked out of his office head held high, registering the look of astonishment on the secretary's face as she passed her desk.

She returned to the sewing room to collect her things.

"You were fired?" asked Rose.

"No, I quit."

"Well, I hope you know what you're doing. Despite our shaky beginning, I'm sorry to lose you. You are very talented."

Lily was worried she'd made a terrible mistake leaving the studio before she had made a concrete plan for her future. Now she would have to wait and see whether Millie's predictions proved reliable. As it turned out, she needn't have worried. When her friend made her entrance into the hotel ballroom a couple of weeks later, all heads were turned and there was an almost audible gasp. Lily had created an egg shell blue, silk chiffon body-skimming sheath, cinched at the waist with a bead-encrusted belt. The delicate georgette bodice was a modest contrast to the sensuality of the skirt, and to the stunning draped cowl back which oozed Hollywood glamour. Lily still idolized Schiaparelli and was influenced by her designs, which encouraged women to display their curves. The overall look was a sophisticated elegance which accentuated Millie's natural poise and beauty. Millie allowed her inquisitors a few minutes of frustrated begging before she reluctantly capitulated and surrendered Lily's details.

Her ploy was a great success. Almost immediately, the first orders trickled in and the House of Lily G was launched. The choice of using the initial of Heinrich's surname had come to her spontaneously when she was deciding on the name for her new business. Had it not been for the fateful shipwreck, Graber would have been her surname. It was not the only reason, though. He had been the first person to believe in her talent, giving her encouragement and her first sketchbook and pencils. This was a way to honour his memory.

CHAPTER FORTY

Dear Lily,
Life in Bournemouth is beginning to get back to normal after all the celebrations to mark the end of the war. I still have a hard time convincing myself that it is all over. After the Japanese surrender in August, a huge crowd gathered at the Square and danced to music played by an American orchestra. The following day bands played in the Gardens and the King's speech was broadcast near the Pavilion. Gracie and I went there and joined in community singing around the fountain from which a jet of multi-coloured water shot about twenty feet in the air. Festivities continued for the following two days. The Gardens were floodlit and there were illuminations in the Square. I wish you could have seen it. I hate to think that the picture etched in your memory is of the last view you had of the town centre, on the day of the bombing.

Rob has been demobbed and is back at home safe and sound. He doesn't talk much about his experiences, and, quite frankly, I prefer not to know. He seems healthy, both physically and emotionally, and I'm sure that once he has had time to adjust back to civilian life, all will be well.

The town is flooded with holidaymakers again. The beaches have been cleared, the chines are accessible, and the beach huts have been reinstated. Business is booming and The Waves has a "No Vacancies" sign up all the time. Thank goodness I have Gracie to help me.

All the Canadians have been repatriated. The place isn't quite the same without them. They really became a part of the town. Meanwhile, over the summer there was an influx of American soldiers returning from the battlefields of Europe, given a week's leave to enjoy rest and recreation before being posted elsewhere. They have named Bournemouth "The Miami of Britain".

Speaking of Americans – in my last letter I mentioned the scheme set up to provide hospitality in local homes for the wounded from American hospitals located nearby. A very nice young soldier in the project has been coming to The Waves every weekend for the past few weeks. The driver who transports him is an even nicer man, a local fellow, and I'm happy to report that we have been seeing a lot of each other. He gets on well with Rob and Gracie and I have high hopes for our relationship. I'll keep you posted. What about you? No one interesting in your love life? Can't Millie introduce you to a handsome film star?

I hope you'll have some time off soon to come and visit us.

The kids send their love,
Sally

Lily was delighted to hear from Sally, and especially happy that her friend had some romance in her life. She had been a widow for eighteen years, and although she put on a brave face, Lily was certain that Sally was lonely without a companion. She had had a few flings with Allied servicemen during the war years, but she was definitely in the market for a steady, permanent partner. Lily hoped this new beau was the one. As for her own love life, despite Millie's brave attempts, Lily had not been persuaded to go on any dates, and anyway, she had no spare time. There were not enough hours in the day, and in the evenings she barely had the strength to eat before crawling into bed.

She missed Bournemouth and would love to visit, but now that her new venture was taking off, she couldn't foresee any free time in the near future. Several months passed before she even had time to write back.

Dear Sally,
I'm so sorry I haven't been in touch for a while. Things have been hectic here. The House of Lily G has really taken off. I sometimes wonder if I have bitten off more than I can chew. I have been working round the clock building up a portfolio of designs to show to prospective clients, and when I'm not doing that or sewing I am busy sourcing fabrics and trimmings and other paraphernalia. The number of orders has expanded rapidly and believe it or not I have had to move to larger premises and take on four extra seamstresses. Two of them are German refugees. It seems that a large number of Jewish immigrants have played a vital role in keeping London's garment trade going during the war. I was very lucky to find a girl whose beadwork and embroidery are exceptional, which has relieved me of those time-consuming jobs. You wouldn't believe some of the names, celebrities included, knocking at my door. Millie took me to an event where I was introduced to Norman Hartnell, designer to the Royals. I'm quite star struck! She says she's sure she can get the studio's publicity man to set up some magazine interviews for me, but I'm not ready yet. I prefer to stay out of the limelight for now, happy to leave all that fuss and glamour to her. Whoever thought that we would be friends with a film star?
Anyway, I hope you understand that, regretfully, I have to postpone my visit to Bournemouth until things settle down. I hope you like the enclosed outfit and that it suits you. Please send photos.

Love
Lily

Lily was very disappointed that she couldn't get away for Sally's wedding. She had been so excited when her friend phoned to tell her the news. If she couldn't be there, the least she could do was make her bridal outfit. She opted for a fairly simple but stylish suit which Sally would be able to wear after her Big Day. There was no point in making something extravagant which would sit in Sally's wardrobe gathering moths.

The showrooms and workshops of most of London's couturiers were situated in and around aristocratic Mayfair, a location where rental costs were unaffordable for a newcomer like Lily. She had managed to find a small property in close proximity, but before long the space was too cramped and she worried that it was making a negative impression on her clients.

"I don't know what to do," she confided in Millie one afternoon over tea. "I have to decide whether occupying a second-rate atelier near Worth, Bianca Mosca, and Hartnell for an exorbitant rent is preferable to being a pioneer and relocating to a more remote location. I have seen a lovely bright and airy set of rooms not far from Selfridges which would be perfect and affordable. But will this move, even further away from Mayfair, deter my clientele?"

"I think the quality and exclusivity of your designs and workmanship are what matters to your clients, not your address. You can't work well in unfavorable conditions. You need a space where your customers feel pampered and indulged. That's what will keep them coming back and recommending you to others."

Taking Millie's advice, Lily relocated the House of Lily G. The new premises provided much more workspace with improved lighting for the seamstresses, and she turned one of the rooms into her salon. It wasn't sumptuous like Frau Schwartz's; she couldn't afford such furnishings. Anyway, she was going for a more modern, post-war feel. She created a simple but elegant atmosphere with walls painted in tones of grey with touches of silver woodwork. Adopting Frau Schwartz's attention to detail, she hung framed magazine covers on them. She still dreamed that one day her designs would feature in Vogue or Harper's Bazaar. She made sure that vases of fresh flowers perfumed the room, choosing fragrant lilacs, freesias and, whenever she could find them, lily-of-the-valley, and offered her guests beverages and pastries.

The change in location did not put off her customers. Indeed, many of them remarked on her courage and gumption in taking a step away from "stuffy" Mayfair. It was her natural charm and refreshing amiability, she was told, which drew them to her salon. She showed none of the self-importance and pretension of other designers and she was eager to please them. At the same time, she didn't balk at speaking her mind when a client was insisting on an unsuitable or unflattering colour or concoction. Lily's reputation built up surprisingly quickly.

CHAPTER FORTY-ONE

1946

The war might have been over, but the M room's secret listeners still had a lot of important work to do. With Germany's capitulation, there was an influx of high-ranking officers to be unwittingly debriefed as they chatted to their cellmates in the rooms vacated by repatriated prisoners of war who no longer had useful information to offer. As more and more photographs and films emerged documenting the atrocities in the concentration camps, the secret listeners – many of whom had left family behind in Europe – were forced to eavesdrop on their prisoners' reactions from disbelief to denial to outright pride in the efficiency of Hitler's Final Solution.

"How could such unspeakable acts have been committed by so-called civilised people?" Heinrich asked Mark Spencer one morning. The two had become fast friends during their time together at the estate. He was the only person to whom Heinrich had confided the whole story about Lily, the events leading up to his flight from Germany, and his life since the rescue at sea. "I have been overhearing the most unbelievable horror stories and I can't help wondering if they are describing what happened to my family and friends," admitted Heinrich.

"It's almost impossible to be professional and objective listening to the prisoners' discussions about war crimes," Mark agreed. "I hope they burn in Hell for what they've done."

As the date of their demobilization approached, they began to discuss what they would do in civilian life.

"I'm convinced there will be a housing boom. Think about it," said Mark. "The Blitz bombings and the demolition of slum areas means more houses than ever will be needed. People want to look to a bright future after all the misery of the war years, and what better way to move forward than by owning their own property?

And demobilized servicemen will be looking for new homes. I reckon there will be a lot of development in suburban areas away from city centres. Perhaps even completely new towns. I'm sure there could be an opportunity for us."

"You have a point," said Heinrich. "Let's look into it and see where we can fit in. 'Grant and Spencer Properties' has a nice ring to it."

"Spencer and Grant, if you don't mind," laughed Mark, giving him a punch on the shoulder. "I've been meaning to ask you," said Mark changing the subject. "Do you like opera?"

"That's a complicated question. When I was stationed in Berlin, one of my lady friends, a keen opera fan, took me to a performance of Wagner's *Die Meistersinger* at the *Staatsopera*. The opera itself was enjoyable, but over the next couple of years I came to realise that his music was being used as a vehicle of Nazi propaganda, to propagate German nationalism and anti-Semitism. If I didn't know that he died fifty years before Hitler became Chancellor, I would have thought that the Nazis commissioned his work in the thirties especially for their own sinister purposes. Why do you ask?"

"Sarah has an old school friend who is an up-and-coming opera singer. She has given us tickets to the Sadler's Wells theatre and I thought you might like to join us."

"As long as it's not Wagner, I'd be happy to," said Heinrich with a grin.

"It's Verdi's *Rigoletto*."

"Then count me in. Thanks."

Heinrich hoped this wasn't another attempt to set him up on a blind date. Mark had been seeing his girlfriend, Sarah, for the past few months. They had been introduced by a distant cousin of Mark's and had hit it off immediately. She was second-generation British, her grandparents having fled the Russian pogroms before the turn of the century. Ever since Mark had introduced her to Heinrich, she had gone into matchmaker mode, intent on finding him the perfect partner. Was she at it again? Heinrich's mental picture of an opera singer was a big breasted Amazon and he shuddered at the thought.

As it turned out, this description could not have been less accurate. Sarah pointed out her friend who was in the chorus. It was difficult to make out her facial features under the heavy stage makeup, but she certainly looked slender and feminine beneath her costume.

"We've been invited backstage," said Sarah as they got up from their seats to leave.

Heinrich could vividly recall the last time he had heard those words in Lowestoft.

"Dinah, let me introduce you to Mark's good friend, Henry Grant," said Sarah.

Dinah turned out to be pretty with a lovely smile.

"Pleased to meet you," said Heinrich as he shook her hand, surprised that he actually meant it.

When he asked her out on a date the following week, he discovered that she was a well-educated, pleasant companion with a sense of humour and a clear vision of her career path.

"Now that the war is over, I plan to travel to Italy to the La Scala opera house in Milan. It was damaged by bombing, but is about to be reopened," she confided one evening. "You'll think this sounds crazy, but I dream of breathing the same air as my idols, Toscanini and Renata Tebaldi."

"I don't think it's crazy at all. It's good to have dreams and aspirations," said Heinrich. *If only mine hadn't been destroyed.*

Their relationship remained fairly casual, as they both had busy schedules. They enjoyed the occasional dinner and a film; their common interests of music and books provided neutral topics of conversation, much to Heinrich's relief, since he was prohibited from talking about his military service and he preferred to keep most of his personal pre-England history to himself. So far there hadn't been the opportunity to progress beyond holding hands and goodnight kisses. A long time had elapsed since his intense but short-lived romance with Celia, but he still wasn't eager to rush into anything too serious.

One evening several weeks later, they were double-dating with Mark and Sarah. The foursome was having an early meal at Lyons Corner House before catching the new Millie Court movie which had premiered the previous week.

"Believe it or not, I saw her in a play in Lowestoft during the war when she was an unknown actress performing with a touring theatre company," Heinrich told them. "You could tell she had star quality, though. I think it was right after that that she began her film career." *And what ever happened to the woman who looked so much like Lily?* he wondered to himself.

After his visit to the McFees, Heinrich had considered trying to contact the company to see if he could find out about her, but once he got back to the M room, he immersed himself in work to try to get over Celia's disappearance. He was so busy that there had been no time to play detective. Anyway, Hilda McFee had mentioned that the show was the company's final performance of the season and he had no way of discovering when or where they would be next.

He returned his attention to his friends' conversation.

"They say her wedding is going to be the big event of the year," Sarah was telling Dinah. "There are all sorts of rumours about who's designing her dress, but so far they've managed to keep it a secret."

"Well," said Dinah, "if it's anything like the gowns she's been pictured wearing at galas and parties, it will definitely be stunning."

CHAPTER FORTY-TWO

Millie's wedding was being touted as the event of the season, much to her chagrin. She really was a down-to-earth, feet-on-the-ground sort of girl, not letting stardom go to her head. And she knew how much Reggie disliked all the attention.

"How did you meet him?" Lily had asked her friend a few months ago when Millie told her she was seeing someone.

"My aunt invited me for dinner and he was a guest. A very unsubtle bit of matchmaking if you ask me," Millie laughed. "She got to know him while he was serving at the American Air Force Base nearby, having offered hospitality to any of the servicemen looking for a home cooked meal."

The romance had blossomed into a serious attachment, culminating in a proposal which Millie didn't hesitate to accept. Reggie had made a favorable impression on Lily and she was delighted for her friend.

"How is he going to deal with being a film star's husband?"

"He's a big enough man to handle it, and if it ever does become a problem, I will just give it up. You know me, Lily. It's great and I appreciate all it's given me, but I'm not addicted to the idea of being a star. It's only a job really. I was just as happy in our little theatrical group. Marrying Reggie and having a family means much more to me."

"Will you stay in England or does he have plans to return to the States?"

"We'll stay for now. But as soon as he is out of uniform, things might change. And who knows? Perhaps I'll be offered a film in Hollywood."

The wedding day was now drawing near and Lily had, of course, been asked to design Millie's dress. The final sketches and fabric swatches were ready and Millie had invited her to bring them over to her family's house so that her mother could give the final approval.

Lily got out of the Tube at Hendon Central Station, crossed the busy main road, and walked up Vivian Avenue as per Millie's instructions. One side of the street was lined with small shops with flats above them while several four-story apartment blocks occupied the opposite side. It appeared to be a very pleasant neighbourhood. Lily was suddenly aware of a strong fishy smell. Looking through the window of the shop she was passing, she could see several types of fresh fish lying on beds of crushed ice. She looked up to discover that the proprietor's name was Nat Jacobs Fishmonger. To her amazement, she saw that his name was preceded by a large Star of David and followed by the word "Kosher". She carried on a little further passing a Kosher butcher and a Kosher bakery with similar signage. Her thoughts raced back to prewar Breslau and the ugly Stars of David which had been daubed on Jewish establishments as an act of vandalism and hatred. Here, the Jewish symbols were proudly displayed by the owners with no fear of anti-Semitic defacement.

Her thoughts were interrupted when she came to a grocery store. She looked up to see the name of the establishment and her legs became blocks of cement. She couldn't move. The sign above the shop read *A. Graber Delicatessen*. Graber? Could this be a relative? She peered through the window and, taking a deep breath, she gingerly opened the door causing a bell to tinkle musically.

"Can I help you, Miss?" she was greeted by a red-faced, jolly-looking woman with slightly crossed eyes behind thick spectacles. She smelled of fish and was wiping her hands on a greasy apron. "Excuse me, dearie. I'm in the middle of cleaning herring," she added pointing to a large wooden barrel standing at the back corner of the shop away from the shelves of dry goods and cans. In another corner Lily noticed sacks of rice, grains, lentils and similar.

"Ken I help you mit somesing, Miss?" asked a rather formidable, heavy-set man in his fifties with a receding hairline and Charlie Chaplin moustache. He wore a brown grocer's coat and presided over a large counter offering cheeses, smoked fish, and other delicatessen delights.

"I noticed the name over the shop," began Lily. "Are you Mr Graber?"

"I am. Vy do you esk?" his heavily accented English betraying his Eastern European background.

"Before the war, I was engaged to a man named Graber from Breslau. Perhaps you are related?"

"My family was from Galicia in Poland, not Germany. Although Breslau is now located in Poland. It vas conquered by zee Russians at zee end of zee var. The Poles have renamed it Wroclaw. Anyhow, Graber is quite a common Jewish name."

"Oh," said Lily, disappointment evident on her face.

"I'm sorry I can't be of help. Vat are you doing in Hendon, if you don't mind me esking?"

"I'm on my way to visit my friend Millie Court."

"Ah, zee famous actress. To me she is Malka Courland. Her mother has been shopping here for many years. Give her *a varime grus* from me."

"A what?"

"That's Yiddish for *my best regards.*"

Lily bade farewell to Mr Graber and continued on her walk to Millie's house. She was surprised at the depth of her disappointment that the grocer was not related to Heinrich. It has been silly of her to think it was a possibility and chastised herself for grabbing at straws. Heinrich was gone forever. She was intrigued, however, that the grocer knew Millie by a different name and that her family frequented his business. And what of that message in Yiddish? Could it be that Millie's family was Jewish? Why had she never mentioned it? A flashback to Christmas dinner at Sally's reminded her of Millie's comment that her family did not celebrate the holiday. Why hadn't she mentioned her religion? Like Heinrich, could she have had a reason for hiding it?

Lily rang the front doorbell at Millie's parents' house. Millie opened the door and threw her arms around her friend.

"I'm so pleased you're here. Come and meet the tribe. Mum, Dad, this is the famous Lily!"

"Welcome to our home, Lily. We're delighted to meet you at last." Lily's father shook her hand.

"This is my sister Becky, and the youngest member of the family, Cissie. I'm afraid my brother, Max, is otherwise engaged and couldn't be here."

"It's wonderful to meet you all," said Lily. "I popped into a grocery on the way here and the proprietor, Mr Graber, asked me to convey his best regards to you, Mrs Courland."

"Such a nice man. I've been shopping there for years," said Millie's mother. "And please call me Judith."

"So your name is Malka Courland?"

"Yes," confirmed Millie. "Millie Court is my stage name. Flows off the tongue a bit easier, don't you think?"

"And you're Jewish?" Lily surveyed the living room. A glass cabinet displayed similar items to those she had seen in Martin Graber's apartment that fateful last night in Breslau: a silver Menorah, a pair of silver candlesticks, a silver goblet, and a large decorative plate with Hebrew letters inscribed around the edge. A bookshelf held a selection of Hebrew texts.

"Don't tell me you are going to come out with that well-worn comic remark, *Funny, you don't look Jewish*," laughed her friend.

Lily burst into tears.

"Oh, darling, what's the matter?"

"Millie, I haven't been entirely open with you about my background. Nobody knows except for Sally. It's hard for me to talk about it. But you are my dearest friend. You deserve to know the truth."

"You don't owe me anything, Lily. I respect your privacy. But if you want to tell me, I would like to hear your story."

Lily took a deep breath and began to tell Millie and her family about her life in Breslau and her romance with Heinrich. She faltered when she began to recall the night of the attempted rape. The details were not for the ears of Millie's younger sisters so she spoke only of an attack.

"How awful. How brave of Heinrich to defend you," said Millie.

"He was my knight in shining armour. But the situation in Breslau was getting worse by the day. Nazi thugs were everywhere. My attacker was determined to get his revenge and he must have persuaded some of his fellow officers to murder Heinrich, calling him a filthy Jew."

"Heinrich was Jewish?"

"Yes. I didn't know until that night. He made me take him to his brother's apartment to get help. Looking around this room at your religious artifacts and Hebrew books brought it all back to me. I saw the same things there."

Lily took a sip of the drink Millie's mother placed in front of her. Hands shaking, she described their escape to the ship and the plans for a wedding on deck.

"How romantic," sighed Becky. "Like something from one of your films, sis." Millie saw the expression on Lily's face and elbowed her sister to keep quiet.

"There was terrible fog, the ship hit something, and began to sink. The Captain, Sally's brother, as it turned out, threw me into a lifeboat and I was rescued. He went back to save Heinrich, but it was too late. Now they both lie at the bottom of the sea."

Millie hugged Lily, her own tears mixing with her friend's.

"You poor dear," Judith murmured.

Lily completed the story by explaining how she came to live with Sally in Bournemouth. "The rest you know, Millie."

Lily felt as if she had discarded a very heavy weight. There was something cathartic about verbalizing her story. She felt disencumbered, that a burden had been lifted from her heart.

"Well, that's quite an ordeal you've been through," said Millie's father. "You should feel very proud that you have managed to pick yourself up and make a success of your life after such a traumatic experience."

"I owe a great deal to Sally and Millie."

"I'm really proud of you," said Millie. "I'm so pleased we bumped into each other that day in Beales. I love having you in my life. No amount of help from anyone would have got you where you are today without your amazing talent."

"Well, then," said Lily back in control of her feelings, "what about looking at my designs?"

"We can't wait to see them, can we, girls?"

"I have kept the design demure and traditional," she explained as she laid out her sketches on the dining room table.

"That's just as well, since we will be getting married in the synagogue," said Millie.

"Reggie is okay with that?" Lily asked, surprised.

"Why wouldn't he be?"

"He didn't want a church or registry office?"

"Oh, Lily. Do you really think my aunt would have introduced me to someone who wasn't Jewish?"

Lily blushed with embarrassment. "Well, I've only just found out that *you* are Jewish, so I didn't think any further than that."

They all laughed.

She placed the fabric swatches next to her drawings. "The fitted bodice features layers of finely ruched tulle under floral-inspired rich French lace. The high bateau neckline is trimmed with seed pearls which also decorate the cuffs of long lace sleeves. More tulle embellished with lace and pearl appliqués spills down through the dropped waistline to the full skirt of ivory satin. The veil will fall from a pearl headband to complete the picture."

"It's exquisite," said Millie's mother with tears in her eyes.

"It's magical, Lily. Thank you so much." Millie hugged her friend.

"Please tell me if there's anything you don't like or want to change."

"It's perfect, isn't it, Mum? I wouldn't change a thing."

"Let me measure you, Millie, and I will get to work on it first thing tomorrow. And I'll measure Cissie and Becky while I'm here for their bridesmaids' dresses."

Lily had felt Mr Courland watching her thoughtfully throughout her explanation of her designs. Now, he asked, "Do you know what became of Heinrich's brother and his family?"

"I have no idea."

"There are organizations that are helping people trace missing relatives, like the Red Cross and the Jewish Relief Agency. Perhaps you should contact them and see if they can find out for you."

"Thank you. I certainly will as soon as I have some spare time."

Making her way home from Millie's house, Lily considered Mr Courland's advice. She decided she would contact the agencies and attempt to discover what had become of Martin, Golda, and the children. She owed it to Heinrich to find out. More than that, she herself owed Martin a debt of gratitude for getting her away from Breslau, and, in case he was searching for Heinrich, he needed to know about the tragedy that had befallen his brother.

CHAPTER FORTY-THREE

Heinrich and Mark had been running around all morning and much of the afternoon checking locations, ordinances, and planning requirements for construction projects they were considering. Weary and hungry, they stopped at a pleasant-looking pub for a late lunch and pint of beer. Having discussed the information they had gathered while they ate, Mark steered the conversation in a different direction, broaching a painful subject that, until now, he had been nervous to raise: "Heinrich, have you had any word from your brother's family?" Mark asked.

"Nothing. I've made appointments with the British Red Cross and the Jewish Relief Agency to see if they have information or can try to track them down."

"Some friends of Sarah's parents were involved with the *Kindertransport* program," Mark told him. "If you'd like, she can ask them to make inquiries about your niece and nephews. Perhaps they were brought over here in '38."

"Thanks. I'd really appreciate it. I met a group of those children when I was living in Lowestoft just before war was declared. What a sorrowful sight to see those poor children separated from their parents and everything familiar. How many of them will be lucky enough to be reunited with their families, do you think?"

"Unhappily, very few, if you ask me."

Arriving at the Red Cross offices, Heinrich almost bumped into a girl who was on her way out of the building.

"Excuse me, Miss," he apologised as he held the door open for her before making his way inside.

"How can we help you, Sir?" asked one of the clerks.

"My name is Heinrich Graber. I am trying to trace my brother's family who resided in Breslau. The last time I saw them was in 1938.

The name is Graber Martin or Moshe; his wife's name is Golda, and they had four children."

"That's very interesting. The young lady who just left also inquired about them. Do you know her?"

"No, I don't. Did she give a name?" He was flabbergasted. Who else could be looking for his family?

"I'm afraid not. She said she was asking on behalf of someone else. As I told her, if you come back in a week, we may have some information for you."

"When she returns, please give her my details and please find out for me how I can get in contact with her."

Heinrich left the building, his emotions in turmoil. He looked up and down the street in case the young girl was still nearby. He hadn't really taken notice of her appearance. Could she be one of the girls who had arrived in Lowestoft on the *Kindertransport*? Not possible – they didn't know anything about him or his family. Could it possibly be his niece, Martin's daughter? But surely she would have told the clerk at the Red Cross who she was. So perhaps it was a friend of his niece? He prayed that the clerk would have some information for him when he went back the following week.

Cissie and Becky were at Lily's salon for the final fitting of their bridesmaids' dresses. They had arrived late and Lily's attention to detail had added extra time to what should have been a short session.

"Oh no!" said Lily, looking at the clock. "I completely forgot my appointment at the Red Cross. I can't leave now before I finish these dresses. Cissie, yours is done. Do you think you could do me the biggest favor and go to the appointment for me? It's not far from here. You only need to hand in the names of the people I am trying to trace. You can be back here within half an hour, by which time I'll be finished with Becky."

"Of course I'll go," said Cissie, visibly excited at having been given the responsibility.

As predicted, she was back at the salon in no time at all.

"They told me to come back in a week to see if they had managed to get some information. A handsome man with the most amazing eyes opened the door for me as I was leaving," she added, blushing.

"My Heinrich had beautiful eyes," Lily sighed.

"I'm so sorry if I made you sad," said Cissie.

"Don't be silly. I was just reminiscing. Thank you so much for helping me out. I can't wait to see the two of you walking down the aisle in these dresses."

CHAPTER FORTY-FOUR

To Lily, the ceremony in the synagogue was a beautifully moving combination of joy and solemnity, hope for the future rooted in the foundations of the past. Millie and Reggie had invited only family and close friends to the nuptials followed by a modest reception. Later in the day, there would be a glitzy party which the studio had insisted upon and organized. Nevertheless, members of the press and photographers hovered outside the synagogue where they had been instructed to wait until the ceremony was over.

The male guests filled the pews on the left side of the prayer hall, while the women sat on the right. In the centre, on the raised platform from which the rabbi conducted services on the Sabbath, a wedding canopy, the *chuppah*, had been erected, decorated with fresh flowers. Reggie stood there eagerly awaiting his bride. Becky and Cissie walked towards the *chuppah* in their pale peach knee-length dresses, intimating the imminent arrival of the bride. The room hushed. An organ began to play. The congregation got to their feet.

Millie, stunning in the dress Lily had designed and sewn, flanked by her parents, followed in the wake of her bridesmaids towards her groom. She looked radiant. The guests sat down and the service began. The rabbi intoned several blessings and the bride and groom took sips of wine from a silver goblet.

Reggie placed the ring on Millie's finger declaring, "Behold, you are consecrated to me by this ring according to the ritual of Moses and Israel."

The rabbi set a glass down on the floor. "This glass symbolizes that even the most blessed and happy celebration is tempered by sorrow. In this moment of our joy, let us not forgot the six million who have perished." Reggie raised his foot and smashed the glass. Shouts of *"Mazel tov"* and *"Congratulations"* filled the synagogue.

Sally hugged a tearful Lily at the reception. "That is the most beautiful dress I have ever seen, Lily," she said.

"Well, it was a labour of love, but let's face it, Millie would look gorgeous wearing an old sheet."

Sally, Lily, and the children had had an emotional reunion before the ceremony. Gracie had grown into a beautiful, poised young woman of twenty. For the time being, she was still helping Sally at the guesthouse, but she had set her sights on secretarial training and what she called "a proper job". Rob worked as a mechanic in a garage owned by an old friend of his late father and he was courting a local girl he had known since his schooldays.

"And this is Larry," Sally introduced her husband.

"I'm delighted to meet you at last. I'm so sorry I couldn't make it down to Bournemouth for your wedding, but I promise when all this excitement is over, I will come for a visit. I'm so happy that the outfit I made you was a success, Sally. It looks great on you today, too."

"Well, you don't look too shabby yourself. I love what you've done with your hair and your precious brooch looks a million dollars on the lapel of your jacket."

A good-looking man in uniform approached the group and slipped his arm through Lily's.

"This is Steve, a friend of Reggie's," she introduced her companion.

"Pleased to meet you," said Sally, giving Lily a surreptitious wink. "Are you also in the Air Force?"

"Yes, Ma'am. But not for much longer. I will be returning Stateside in a couple of months," he said.

Rob started asking him questions about his role in the war and Sally steered Lily away.

"Why didn't you let on about your man? How long has this been going on?"

"Just a couple of months. There hasn't been much to tell. You know how busy I've been, so we haven't spent that much time together. Anyway, as he told you, he'll be going back home soon, so I have no intention of letting it get serious."

"Well, I hope you do find someone soon. It's about time, Lily. You deserve to be happy."

The guests moved to the adjacent hall for refreshments. As she helped herself to food from the buffet, Lily noticed the grocer standing to one side.

"Hello, Mr Graber, do you remember me?"

"Ah, yes. Malka's, I mean Millie's, friend. A beautiful vedding dress. You have great talent. I am catering the reception. Did you ever find the family you were looking for?"

"Unfortunately, no. But I am hoping for some information in the near future."

"Vell, I vish you luck. Please come by the shop sometime. I vill make you a nice smoked salmon sandvich."

Lily smiled. "I may take you up on that, thank you."

A few minutes later Millie took her friend by the arm.

"Come on, Lily. Let's get this over with. I have to pose for a few photos and answer the press's questions, and I need you by my side."

The ordeal didn't take too long. Lily tried to smile and look relaxed when Millie introduced her as the designer of her dress. As much as she hated the attention, she knew it would be good for business and that the time had come to step into the limelight. But as soon as Reggie joined Millie for a photograph of the happy couple, Lily slipped away to spend more time with her friends.

CHAPTER FORTY-FIVE

It was a beautiful morning in Margate. Doris breathed in the fresh familiar scent of the sea as she picked up the bottles of milk and the newspaper which had been delivered to her front door. She put the kettle on and set the table for breakfast. Fred followed his nose to the kitchen lured by the smell of bacon and eggs, sat himself down, and helped himself to a slice of toast while he waited. Doris warmed the teapot, spooned in some tea leaves, and left them to brew in boiling water while she finished the frying.

"Anything interesting in the news, luv?" she asked her husband, who had unrolled the newspaper.

"Just the usual. And a load of pictures from some film star's wedding."

"Millie Court. Let's have a look then." She relieved Fred of the newspaper, replacing it with a plate of food.

Her mouth dropped open. "Oh my Lord. Look, Fred. That's the poor girl the lifeboat fished out of the sea all those years back. Do you remember? Look, she's even got on that pretty brooch she was wearing."

"So it is," said Fred. "My, my ... Well, it's lovely to see she's made something of herself."

"Something? She's only gone and designed the wedding dress of the year for a famous film star. It's blooming marvelous."

In Lowestoft, Hilda McFee was clearing away the breakfast things when her husband walked into the kitchen with the newspaper.

"Anything interesting in the news?"

"Nothing special. There's a lot about a film star's wedding."

"Millie Court. Press has been building it up for weeks. Just before she became famous, she was here in a musical comedy. Colin Forth was also in it. Do you remember? I took Heinrich with me."

"Will ye tek a look at this picture, Hilda. There's something verra familiar aboot t'other lassie in it."

"I can't believe it. That's the girl in Heinrich's photo. The one he kept looking at and crying. His lost love. The one who drowned on the night you saved him. Yes, it says her name's Lily. And look at that brooch she's wearing, just like in his photo. McFee, we have to get hold of him!"

In London, Heinrich walked heavily away from his return visit to the Red Cross offices. Mark was waiting for him outside.

"By the look of you, the news isn't good."

"My brother and his wife and the two younger boys perished in Auschwitz. They think the oldest boy, Erich, escaped and possibly reached Palestine. My niece, Tova, was sent away on the *Kindertransport*, but they haven't been able to locate her."

"I'm so sorry, Henry."

"Perhaps your Sarah's contact will come up with something about Tova," said Heinrich hopefully.

Mark put his arm around his friend's shoulders. "Let's go and get a drink."

They passed a boy hawking a pile of newspapers shouting, "Read all about it. Latest news. Millie Court weds. Read all about it."

Mark threw a few coins at the boy and took one.

Heinrich was deep in thought and didn't say much as they waited to be served. Mark set the newspaper aside and waited for his friend to break the silence.

"*Arbeit macht frei* – work sets you free. That was the wrought-iron slogan at the entrance to the Auschwitz concentration camp. You remember I was in the Pioneer Corps for a while? Their motto is *Labour omnia vincit* – work conquers all. Almost identical sentiments, but so very, very different in purpose. I feel sick thinking about it."

The waitress brought their coffee.

"How could this happen, Mark? Martin was a good man, a generous man. His only crime was being a Jew. And Golda and the children? Murdered just for being Jews. Six million slaughtered. It's unfathomable." He began to cry. The waitress looked embarrassed and hurried away.

"Did you find out anything about the girl who was also looking for your family?" Mark asked.

"No, she hasn't been back yet. But they will let me know if she does return."

"Are they going to try and trace Erich?"

"They said that the Jewish Relief Agency might have more luck, so I will speak to them."

They fell back into silence.

The waitress came back to take their empty cups.

"Can I get you anything else, gentlemen?"

"Just the bill, thank you."

As she took Mark's cup, she accidentally knocked the newspaper onto the floor. Mark bent down to retrieve it, but before he reached it, Heinrich scraped back his chair and got to his feet abruptly. "I have to get out of here, Mark. I need some fresh air and I prefer to be alone. No offence."

"None taken, my friend. I understand. Let's be in touch later when you've had a chance to clear your head."

Heinrich left the café. A bus was pulling into a nearby stop and he hopped on to it, not caring in which direction it was headed.

The waitress returned with the bill. She picked the newspaper up off the floor and put it back on the table.

"Doesn't that Millie Court look gorgeous?" she gushed, pointing to the large photograph on the front page.

"What? Oh yes," Mark replied halfheartedly, not wishing to appear rude. But then he took a closer look at the picture, unable to believe his eyes. Heinrich's Lily standing next to Millie Court. It was impossible. She looked a little older than the girl in his friend's photograph and the hairstyle was different. But there was no mistaking the face and the signature lily brooch.

He ran outside to catch his friend, but he was too late. He looked up and down the street, but Heinrich was nowhere to be seen. He went back inside to retrieve his paper and read the article about the wedding. It appeared that Lily was the couturiere who had designed Millie's dress. There were very few details about her, but he guessed it wouldn't be too difficult to track her down. He'd call Sarah, he decided. She would know how to find the address of Lily's business.

Heinrich sat on the bus deep in thought oblivious to everything around him. He felt adrift; every link to his past was now lost. He had mourned his father when he was almost too young to understand his loss. He had never completely recovered from the deaths of his two idolized brothers, followed shortly thereafter by the demise of his mother. Losing Lily was almost beyond bearable. And now his brother Martin, who for a time had been a surrogate father to him until they had fallen out when he decided to enlist in the army, and who had risked his own safety to help him escape from Breslau and certain death. The bus came to a sudden stop. Heinrich looked out of the window and saw that they had arrived at Liverpool Street Station. He followed the other passengers off the bus and made his way to the ticket office. He needed the warmth and comfort of the only family left to him. The train to Lowestoft was ready to depart. He bought a ticket, ran to the platform, and jumped aboard just as it began to pull away.

CHAPTER FORTY-SIX

Heinrich's landlady was getting fed up of running to the phone. Someone called McFee, whom she could barely understand, had phoned several times looking for her lodger. His friend Mark had also rung a couple of times. There seemed to be some sort of emergency, but Henry was not home, she had told them repeatedly, and she had no idea where he might be. "Please stop calling," she insisted eventually. "You're wearing out my feet and the carpet. As soon as he comes in, I'll be sure to let him know you're looking for him and that it's urgent."

The soporific swaying of the train lulled Heinrich into an emotionally exhausted sleep, punctuated by nightmarish images of skeletal bodies and heaps of bones. He was jogged awake when the train screeched to a halt in Norwich. As he got to his feet groggily, a discarded newspaper on the opposite seat caught his eye. Something looked familiar, but he had no time to look more closely, as he had to disembark quickly or else miss his connection to Lowestoft.

McFee had just got off the phone to Heinrich's landlady for the umpteenth time when he heard a knock at the front door. The woman had been a bit gruff with him, making it quite clear that he wasn't to phone again. He could only hope that Heinrich would get in touch with him. He opened the door and was surprised to see Colin Forth standing there brandishing the newspaper.

"Morning, McFee. Is Hilda in? I wanted to be sure she saw today's paper with the lovely picture of Millie Court."

"Aye, that we have." He called out to his wife. "Hilda, ye have a guest."

McFee left his wife and Colin gossiping over a cup of tea. Colin regaled her with stories from his theatrical days with Millie, basking in his short-lived closeness to the famous star.

"What can you tell me about her designer, Lily?"

"Well, we didn't know that much about her. The story went that she had come to England from Europe, Switzerland, I think it was, to visit a relative and then war broke out and she was stuck here."

"How did she know Millie?"

"They met and became friends when the company was touring. We often had return bookings in the same towns and some of them even began to feel like home with familiar faces."

Colin got up to leave. Mrs McFee saw him to the front door, where she found Heinrich standing fist raised in the air about to knock.

"Henry, lad, what a lovely surprise! Come in, come in. Colin was just leaving."

She didn't like the look of him. Had he seen the paper? Was he in shock?

"Are you all right, Henry? You look a wee bit off-colour."

"Oh, Mrs McFee, I've had the most terrible news. My brother and his family were murdered in the Auschwitz concentration camp."

"That's just awful. I'm so sorry." She wrapped her arms around him and hugged him into her ample body. "Sit yourself down, luv. McFee," she called out, "Henry's here."

"We've been trying to contact you all day. We have a bit of shocking news for you ourselves."

"What are you talking about, Mrs McFee? What else could possibly shock me today after the news I just received?"

She pushed the newspaper towards him, pointing at the photograph. Heinrich blanched and began to tremble. McFee poured a shot of whiskey and handed it to his stricken friend.

"I don't understand. It's not possible. McFee, you said there were no other survivors. I saw the ship go down with my own eyes."

He looked again at the picture, trying to make sense of what he saw.

"Do you know, twice I thought I saw her. Once was in a newsreel after Dunkirk and the second time when we went to see the Millie Court play. I was sure it was my imagination playing tricks on me."

"I remember that day. You looked like you'd seen a ghost."

Could it really be his Lily? The brooch! She still had the brooch he gave her. He stood up. "I have to get back to London to find her."

"Now then, laddie ..." McFee held his arm. "There's noo train back this evening. You'se best be getting a hot meal inside ye and a good night's rest, and we'll have a think as to how ye can find her."

"I must phone my friend Mark and let him know where I am. He'll be concerned after the way I left him today."

Mark picked up the phone on the first ring. "Thank God you're safe. I was worried about you," he said.

"Have you seen the newspaper? The picture of Lily?" asked Heinrich, still incredulous about the events of the day.

"I saw it just after you ran off. I tried to catch up to you. Where in Heaven's name are you?"

"Lowestoft. I can't get back to London tonight, but we have to find a way to find her."

"I already have Sarah working on it. She knows more about fashion than we do and I'm sure she will be able to get some information."

"I pray you are right. I will be on the first train back tomorrow."

The following afternoon, Heinrich and Mark arrived at the address Sarah had given them. It was Lily's salon. Heinrich's heart was racing. Had she forgotten him? Could she still love him after all this time? Surely she must have moved on by now? He read the name above the door. Perhaps the "G" in Lily G was her husband's initial? His hand trembled as he rang the bell.

Nothing.

He rang again.

"It's no good, Mark. There's no one here."

There was still no sound from behind the door, but Heinrich refused to give up. He rang the bell again and then knocked several times. Still nothing.

Deflated, he turned to leave, but was stopped by the faint patter of approaching footsteps. He held his breath.

The door opened.

"Sorry for keeping you waiting, gentlemen. May I help you?" It wasn't Lily.

"I'm looking for Lily. I'm an old friend," he added, seeing the suspicious look on the girl's face.

"She's gone away. Having a holiday after all the pressure and excitement of the past few weeks."

"Where has she gone?"

"I can't say."

"When will she be back?"

"In a week or so. Give me your name and I'll tell her you called."

As they walked away, Heinrich turned to his friend and said, "I can't wait a week, Mark. Not now that I know she's alive. I don't want to wait one more minute."

Going into the nearest red public telephone box, Heinrich dialed McFee's number. Mrs McFee answered.

"I've found Lily's business, but she's gone away. Her employee won't tell me where. I thought maybe your friend Colin might have some idea of where she might have gone."

"I'll see what I can find out. You go home and wait by the phone for my call."

In the end, it was Colin himself who phoned Heinrich.

"Lily joined the company when we were in Bournemouth. It was just after a terrible bombing raid when our wardrobe mistress was injured. She and Millie had been friends for some time and it was Millie who brought her on board. If I recall, she lived in a guesthouse. The Waves, I think."

So, it had definitely been her that he had seen on the newsreel about the French evacuees in Bournemouth. Why hadn't he tried to locate her then, and again after glimpsing her in Lowestoft? Had it been the hand of fate, or perhaps God, that had made their paths almost cross, beckoning him towards her all these years? He should not have lost faith so quickly, he berated himself, but how could he have denied the facts as presented to him, affirmed as they were by his own eyes and the image of the sinking ship?

Colin didn't have any other useful information to offer. "That's all I know, mate. Hope it helps. Good luck."

As the train chugged its way southwards the next day, Heinrich went over and over in his mind what he would say to Lily. Was she married? The newspaper article said very little about her. In fact, they called her Millie's *mysterious couturiere*. If by some happy chance she wasn't married, that didn't mean she was unattached. She must have had plenty of suitors over the past eight years. He hadn't exactly been celibate himself and he understood the need for physical closeness and comfort in time of war. What would he do if she wasn't at the guesthouse? He prayed that Colin's hunch was right and that she was indeed in Bournemouth. This could be a wild goose chase, but it seemed to be a reasonable guess that The Waves was where she had gone ...

CHAPTER FORTY-SEVEN

Sally met her friend at the station. Lily was delighted to see that Bournemouth was looking better than the last time she had seen it. It was hard to believe that she'd been away for over three years. They walked hand in hand through the Gardens and down to the promenade. Lily drew in a refreshing breath of sea air laced with the perfume of fragrant flowers.

"Let's pop into the Pavilion for tea, for old time's sake," suggested Sally.

"Has Beales been rebuilt?" asked Lily when they were seated at a table with a lovely sea view.

"Not yet. The basement where you used to work has been refurbished and is a sales floor. To get to it, you have to go down a flight of stairs from Old Christchurch Road. The Metropole was torn down." Sally noticed the shadow of unhappy memories that passed across her friend's face. "Work has started on reconstructing the pier. It's a bumper year for visitors and I have a good feeling about the future. Tell me about the House of Lily G. Now that you've been made famous by the newspapers, you will be flooded with clients."

"Actually, I'm thinking of changing direction."

"You are? What do you mean? Your dream has always been to own your own couturier house."

"But dreams don't always come true," said Lily, thinking more about Heinrich than about her fashion house. "To tell you the truth, I am getting a bit tired of the demands of my upper-class clients. They expect me to dance to the tune of their every whim and often give me unreasonable deadlines. I clearly recall Frau Schwartz having the same complaints."

Sally nodded. "I can't compare what you have to tolerate to how

I have to please my guests, but I do understand the pressure you must be under and the frustration that goes with it."

Lily continued: "I believe change is coming within the fashion industry. Rather than confining myself to dressing individuals, I would like to make haute couture-style pieces for a wider market of discerning customers."

"That sounds quite innovative and very exciting," agreed Sally.

"The fashion magazines are calling this idea *wholesale couture*. The designs would be mine, and the House of Lily G would be my brand, but I would adopt some of the inspirational manufacturing and promotion ideas coming out from America. Most of the work would be done on machines making it possible to produce a quantity of the same design, but quality hand finishing with special signature touches would create the effect of exclusive elegance and style."

"That sounds like a marvelous idea and I'm sure you'll make a roaring success of it."

"Well, I think I'll have a better chance if I stake my claim now while the idea is in its infancy. I'm certain it is going to take off and later it will be harder to secure a foothold amongst the competition."

"Do you remember that day we went to Beales and I tried on that dress I couldn't afford?"

Lily smiled at the recollection.

"Well, I can't wait to see an entire range of House of Lily G designs on their exclusive fashion floor when it eventually reopens."

Lily could feel herself unwinding. She had made the right decision to take a break after the madness of the past few weeks. It was a real treat to be sitting here with her friend making light conversation without having to consult the clock or rush away for an appointment or a fitting.

The relaxing atmosphere would help her refocus and give her plenty of quiet time to mull undisturbed over her plans for the future. She was convinced that a change in direction was the way forward. While she had made a name for herself through her connection to Millie she admitted to herself that she was never going to be Chanel or even Worth. But she could take a leading position in this new niche. She also needed a break from Steve. He seemed to be getting far too attached to her and she didn't really want to take things further. She wanted to channel all her energies into herself and her business. And anyway, he was heading back to America sometime soon.

After sleeping in late the following morning, Lily collected her sketchbook and pencils, threw a cardigan around her shoulders and, shouting goodbye to Sally, she left the guesthouse. The weather was perfect. She made her way down the chine, her spirits high, soothed by the familiarity and protection of the place she still considered home. When she reached the beach, she settled herself on a bench in a secluded spot and waited for inspiration to guide her pencil across the page.

After a while, the glare from the sea which sparkled in the sunlight tired her eyes and the warm sun and fresh air made her drowsy. She nodded off, her chin falling forward to rest on her chest and her sketchbook sliding to the floor. She had no idea how long she had been dozing when she awoke with the uneasy sensation of a presence hovering behind her. Her old fears surfaced and nervously she slowly turned her head around. She gave a startled jump.

"I'm so sorry if I disturbed you," Gracie apologised.

"It's okay. You just surprised me, that's all," said Lily, her pounding heart returning to its normal rhythm.

"I thought you might like some refreshments. I've brought a flask of coffee and some of Mum's buns warm from the oven."

"Thanks, that's really kind," said Lily, taking a bite of a bun. "These buns are delicious."

They chatted for a while before making their way back to the guesthouse.

"After lunch, Larry's going to take us on an outing," announced

Sally when they got back to The Waves. "It'd be a shame to waste such lovely weather."

They left Gracie in charge of the guesthouse and drove off in the direction of the New Forest. Now and then, Larry pointed out an interesting feature, sharing his knowledge of the flora and fauna of the area. At Burley, Lily was enchanted by the ponies that freely roamed the village, causing a traffic jam on the narrow country road.

"Since we seem to be stuck here, let's stop and get ourselves a cream tea," suggested Larry. "Perhaps by the time we're finished, the obstruction will have moved on," he joked. He parked the car and they maneuvered their way around the animals and into a small tearoom.

"Coming," shouted Gracie in response to the doorbell. "May I help you? I'm afraid we're all booked up at the moment." *What a gorgeous man*, she thought and blushed, hoping he couldn't read her mind. Heinrich removed his hat.

"Actually, I'm not looking for a room," the man said with a nervous cough. "I am looking for Lily. Is she staying here?"

He had the hint of an attractive foreign accent to match his appearance.

"Maybe ..." Gracie replied suspiciously. "Who's asking?"

"This is all a bit awkward. I don't wish to startle her."

Gracie frowned.

"My name is Heinrich Graber."

The name meant nothing to Gracie, who had never been told all the details of Lily's past.

"I'm afraid she's not here at the moment."

"So she is staying here. Can you tell me when will she be back?"

"I don't know. She went out with my mother and stepfather for the afternoon. I expect they'll come home when it starts to get dark." She could see the disappointment etched on his face.

"Is there somewhere I could wait until then?"

"Have you come a long way?"

"You have no idea how far. I won't be any trouble. I just want to make sure I don't miss her."

Gracie considered his request. Her mother might be furious with her for inviting a strange man into the house. On the other hand, they were always letting people they didn't know stay at The Waves. And she wasn't by herself. A couple of guests were in the lounge and others would be back soon for their tea. He seemed respectable and didn't look like a murderer.

"Why don't you come through to the garden."

"Thank you. I'm most grateful."

Gracie was busy serving the guests their high tea, when Larry, Sally and Lily arrived back at the guesthouse. Lily went upstairs to refresh herself and Gracie took her mother aside.

"Mum, there's a man outside in the garden looking for Lily. Good looking, foreign accent. Says his name is Heinrich Graber."

"What? But that's not possible."

Sally looked out of the kitchen window. He certainly fitted the description, but even so …

She went outside. "I'm Sally. I own the guesthouse."

The man got to his feet. "Heinrich Graber, Ma'am."

"You'd better come inside." She led him into the kitchen.

"How do I know that you are who you say? Lily is famous now. You could be anybody. An opportunist."

He hesitated, before saying, "I knew Lily before the war. For reasons I won't go into now, we were on a ship escaping Germany. The ship sank. I was rescued by a fisherman and believed I was the only survivor. I have mourned Lily for all these years believing her dead. And then I saw the picture in the newspaper. I gave her that lily-of-the-valley brooch on New Year's Eve, 1937, the one she is wearing in the wedding photos. I promised that one day I would be rich enough to have it remade in real gold with genuine gems."

Sally took his hands in hers, tears in her eyes. These were details that only the real Heinrich Graber could know.

"My brother was the ship's Captain. He threw her into a lifeboat with details of how to find me. He promised to bring you to her, but he went down with the ship. Lily believes you also drowned."

Just then, the kitchen door opened to reveal Lily.

Gracie caught her as she fell to the floor in a faint. As she slowly regained consciousness, hearing a distant voice from the past calling her name over and over, Lily wondered if she was waking from one of her familiar dreams or nightmares. No. She could feel the touch of his hand on hers. He was pulling her to her feet. This was real.

They stood looking at each other as if suspended in time. What should she do? Throw herself into his arms? If he had come all this way looking for her, he must still care for her. But she mustn't jump to conclusions and make a fool of herself.

Heinrich was feeling equally awkward. It was almost like their first date in Breslau. But Lily was no longer that innocent young girl. She was a woman he hadn't seen for eight years, who had matured into a self-sufficient businesswoman. He had no idea what her life had been or if she even thought about him anymore. And she was definitely holding herself back. He longed to embrace her, but he kept himself in check.

Why don't they just fall into each other's arms, thought Gracie? This was just like something from a romance novel or film. What were they waiting for?

"Let's sit down," said Sally, breaking the spell, "and Heinrich can tell us what happened to him."

Lily began to visibly recover from the shock of seeing Heinrich "back from the dead", as he put it, and she, Sally, and Gracie listened as he described all that had happened to him since the shipwreck. He only left out his job in the M room, about which he was sworn to secrecy, and his passionate affair with Celia.

When he reached the part about Dunkirk, Lily interrupted: "I thought I saw you on the Pathé News. But of course I knew it couldn't be you because you were dead."

"I also thought I'd seen you on a newsreel helping French evacuees, some of whom ironically, I may have brought back myself. And then again in the Lowestoft theatre."

"So it was *you* I glimpsed in the audience. I thought I must be imagining it."

Sally stood up. "Why don't you go for a walk and finish catching up while I make the dinner." She winked at her daughter. "Gracie, love, give me a hand."

Lily led the way out of the guesthouse and up the nearby cliff path to a bench overlooking the sea.

"I thought you were trapped in the ship when it sank," began Lily. "I didn't want to leave you, but Captain Jameson gave me no choice. He promised me he would save you and bring you to me. I was rescued by a lifeboat which took me to Margate. All the time I was in the water, I kept saying your name over and over. Chaim, Chaim, Life, Life. God must have heard my prayer."

"My Hebrew name? But how?"

"Your brother Martin told me. That was the night I discovered you were Jewish and understood why you hadn't asked me to marry you."

"Lily, was it you asking the Red Cross to trace my family?"

"Yes. But on the day of my appointment, I was too busy to go, so I sent Millie's young sister. Did you find out anything?"

"My brother, his wife, and two of their sons perished in Auschwitz. The oldest son, Erich, may have escaped Germany. I am trying to locate him. And their youngest, Tova, came to England with the *Kindertransport*, but I don't know where she is now."

"I'm so sorry. I remember Erich," said Lily. "A lovely young man. He accompanied me home on the night of your attack."

Lily continued to describe what had happened after she was rescued.

"I can't believe that we landed so close to each other," said Heinrich, "and yet no one knew we had both survived. Margate and Lowestoft are on the same coast; barely half a day's sailing separates them."

Lily explained how Sally had generously taken her under her wing and concocted her new biography so that no one would suspect she was German. As she related the details of how she had spent the years since they had last seen each other, Heinrich interrupted now and again with exclamations of sorrow and wonder at the different turns of her life. He was amazed at her courage and her determination to make a good life for herself.

"I didn't want to let you down, my only love."

Those three last words must have been the cue Heinrich had been waiting for. He took her in his arms and kissed her passionately, as ravenous as a starving man at a banquet. Her greed matched his and she pulled his body closer to hers.

"How I've longed for this moment which I believed would never come," he whispered in her ear as she nuzzled his neck.

An elderly couple passed by, tut-tutting at the public display before them. Embarrassed, they pulled apart.

"All this time no lucky fellow snapped you up?" Heinrich asked.

"There was someone briefly. But he wasn't you." She paused for a moment summoning up the courage to ask the question whose answer might not be what she hoped for. "What about you, Heinrich? You haven't found someone special in all this time?"

"I haven't stopped loving you and I never will, my darling. Please tell me you feel the same way." He dropped to his knees. "We aren't *Mischlinge* any more. Will you do me the honour of becoming my wife? We can go at once to the Registry Office and make it official."

Lily looked lovingly into his eyes. "I have always felt married to you even though Captain Jameson, may he rest in peace, never got to perform the ceremony. That's why I call myself 'Lily G'. But the answer to your question is 'No'."

He stared at her in shocked silence. "No? You can't mean it, Lily. You won't marry me?"

"Of course I will marry you, my dearest. Let me explain. I won't marry you at a Registry Office. After I found out that Millie was Jewish, I decided to begin the process of conversion with her family's help. When I complete it, I will happily marry you in a synagogue. Our union will avenge the lives of your brother's family and we will be helping to redeem and rebuild the Jewish people whom Hitler tried to exterminate."

CHAPTER FORTY-EIGHT

1947

Ten years since their first encounter and a year to the day after they had been reunited, Lily and Heinrich stood under the wedding canopy. The House of Lily G label was taking off, while Spencer and Grant Properties were also showing the first signs of success. Heinrich was now known to everyone, including Lily, as Henry. The future looked bright and they finally felt that they could leave the past behind.

The wedding was nothing like the one Lily had dreamed of as a young girl and was very different from the one she had pictured on the ship. But it was perfect. Her happily ever after.

The synagogue she chose for the intimate gathering was much smaller than the grand building where Millie's wedding had taken place. Even so, most of the pews were empty. All the people who mattered were there except, sadly, their immediate families, who they hoped were looking down on them from above and giving their blessing.

The guests included Sally and Larry with Gracie, and Rob with his new wife. Millie, fussed over by proud father-to-be Reggie, hugged her burgeoning stomach. Mark and Sarah, recently engaged, had helped with the arrangements and were making plans for their own nuptials.

Hilda and Alasdair McFee, dressed to the nines in his kilt and sporran, looked uncomfortably out of place. Doris and Fred had come from Margate, surprised and delighted to have received an invitation.

The reception was, of course, catered by Mr Graber, who was overjoyed that Lily had found his namesake.

Jewish Relief had finally located Tova, who was relishing her role as bridesmaid. They would officially adopt her once they were legally married. Millie's mother and father happily accepted the honour of escorting the bride down the aisle. Lily's radiance lit up the room and her cherished brooch sparkled, given pride of place on her dazzling ivory dress and jacket ensemble which cleverly camouflaged the small mound of her early pregnancy.

Standing under the *chuppah*, Heinrich turned to watch his bride make her way towards him. His heart swelled and tears of happiness pricked his eyes. Who would have believed this day would finally arrive?

The end of a nightmare and the beginning of a dream come true.

Acknowledgments

Heinrich's portrayal as a 'secret listener' was loosely inspired by Helen Fry's historical work *The Walls Have Ears*, Yale University Press, 2020.

Printed in Great Britain
by Amazon